SOMBRE

S.B. NORTON

More titles from S. B. Norton

The Otherworldly Operatives Series

Flames from the North
Southern Vexations
White Eyed Children of The East

SOMBRE

S.B. NORTON

Dedicated.

To the Norton–Wallace's

To Michelle for continuing to put up with this longwinded dream of mine.

To my kids, Spencer and Lucy, for their general good behavior.

Love you all.

CHAPTER 1
THE TROUBLED SLEEPER

"Sombre ...

Hope Kelley let the word hang in the air. She said it again - this time in a whisper, "Sombre." The whisper gave it shape, something tangible. It made it feel real.

Sombre deserved at least that.

Leaning on the bathroom vanity, Hope gazed at her reflection in the mirror. She sighed as she studied the pockmarked paddock across her cheeks and forehead. The pimple rash seemed to be getting worse. Frowning, she grabbed her toothbrush and stared as she cleaned her teeth. Her glasses sucked. Big thick, dorky lenses she was condemned to wear. Hope was born with woeful vision, ('Myopia' was the technical term) about as sharp as her grandmothers. Her sight had never gotten any worse, but it would never get any better. Toothbrush protruding from her pursed lips, she pulled her brown hair out of its ponytail and let it hang, framing her face. She didn't mind her hair; it had its own natural wave thing going on. But lately her complexion was zombified. Complimenting the pimple outbreak, she had dark rings forming under her eyes.

All of this had to do with her sleep.

Sleep was exhausting.

With a spit and rinse, she gave herself a final look in the mirror and left the bathroom. She pulled at her fingers as she crossed the hall; a nervous habit, with her left thumb and index finger she pulled and shook each digit of her right hand one at a time. She would do this often, until she thought she'd better stop, or someone pointed it out making her stop. She entered her room.

Bed awaited. Her mother believed in buying only the best bedroom linen, and her fluffy and expensive, violet coloured Parisienne quilt sat folded over on one edge, inviting her in.

Lately, she found the whole ensemble about as inviting as a coffin.

Resting her glasses on her side table, she slipped under the cover, and let her eyelids collapse. She hoped for a dreamless night tonight. No Sombre. A night of nothing. She *needed* nothing - just a restful sleep; a wonderful, dreamless sleep.

It wasn't to be.

∫

Pale pink roses and violets filled the room. Her cousin Sophie stood with her soon to be beau, Stuart. The straight-faced best man, Carmine, wearing an olive complexion and oiled black hair, stood two feet away. A smiling Jenny, the bridesmaid, was at Sophie's back. The elderly celebrant delivered his service in a gentle tone. This was Sophie's wedding. Hope loved Sophie. And she remembered this being a great day. Hope and her sister Kate had been flower girls.

It was happening in slow motion, and that was alright, this was a dream.

This was the rite of passage.

Hope scanned the church from her vantage point at the front - her mother and father, friends and relatives; all seated in their suits, their ties, their dresses. All were happy, dabbing tears and smiling proud. She turned and looked at Kate. Her sister rolled her eyes, smirked and then shrugged. Kate often thought that she was too cool for just about anything – she would have thought she was too cool for this as well. Kate was thirteen, two years younger than Hope, yet always tried to act at least two years older. Hope saw a trickle of something run from the corner of Kate's mouth. Her sister's smile had darkened. She wondered what she could be up to.

Rings were given and placed gently on fingers. The couple exchanged vows. Bridesmaid Jenny's eyes welled with tears. On both saying 'I-do', loud applause filled the room - the noise unreal and deafening. Hope's attention swung to the celebrant; he was doing poorly. He was staring in horror at her sister; sweat suddenly running down his cheeks, he began pulling at his face, as if needing to strip the skin from the bone. Like a possessed soprano, the old guy began screaming - high pitched and wet, sounding out like a kettle whistle. Face a furious hellish red, pressure building, his head seemed to be growing. The poor fellows scream changed to an impossible swine-like squeal, then cut off short as his skull combusted in final release. Broken bloody chunks sprayed Sophie's wedding gown, patterning her elegant white features in a stark, red spatter.

Hope watched on, horrified as her sister revealed a mouthful of blue liquid. Gasoline! Kate Kelley shut her gob. Puffing up her cheeks, she spat it at the newlyweds in an impossibly long hosing of blue. From under her flower girl skirts, she produced a box of matches, "Ha!" she giggled and feverishly slid the packet open - striking four at a time, she threw the matches at Sophie and Stuart. Mouths agape, clothes burning, the couple fell to the carpet and rolled in each other's arms. Hope looked to where her mother and father were sitting, they were gone. Her sister was on the move. Hope spotted her on the other side of the chapel, blonde hair out of its carefully coiffured Chignon. She was running, with one hand hitching her dress, the other holding a long knife. Where did she get a knife! Stabbing everyone in her path, screaming, swearing, "Come here, you dusty old fossils! Taste some of this shit! Time to put you all out of your misery!"

The whole chapel had risen, guests running this way and that way from her knife-wielding sister.

Hope wasn't running – she was too stunned to move. Why was her sister doing this? Appearing from nowhere, her mother and father faced her, both wearing the same murderous expression as her sister. "Don't think you're getting away Hope!" Her mother screamed. "All of this is your fault!" Eyes wild, she charged, blade held high.

Hope cried out loud, 'No! Why?' Her mother bared down, she swung the blade and although this was a dream, Hope felt it.

Laughing harder still, her mother slammed the knife into Hope's mouth.

For tonight, her rite of passage was complete.

Hope's vision went black as her sleeping self was taken on ... to Sombre.

CHAPTER 2
She Fights In Hell, Denivens Hell

Its tongue licked at the air. It spat blood at the toes of her boots.

"Oh, you're a disgusting thing, aren't you?" Halliday Knight said sizing up her latest obstacle. The devil-imp was a hideous cross of Neanderthal baby-human and shaven mangy street dog. Claw-like hands scratched at the dirt. A wasted, bony body and leathery, oily skin. Prowling on all fours it coughed and spat more blood.

Halliday took a smart step back.

The creature guarded her entry; the foot of a small rising knoll. Sombre had called her to Denivens Hell, a potentially very lethal part of Sombre, even for a Gatherer of her stature. Tying her long blond locks in a knot, she looked onward through the flames and smoke. The place was hot, unbearably so. Once past this disgusting first point of contact, she wondered how long she would be able to last without burning to cinder. Dark crawling shapes prowled in the distance, silhouetted by the rising fires. "More of you ugly filthies' no doubt," she said reminding the creature again of how vile she found it, "I shall enjoy killing you."

It stepped closer in response, its head twisting a full circle, eyes flickering from black to red, then a sickly yellow white.

Her feet were feeling rather hot in her black boots as she played with the trigger of her Remington. Would a bullet stop this damnable creature? Her sword was sheathed at her back. Maybe that was the go? Lop its head off. She took a step.

With a low growl the monster gnashed its teeth and lunged, maw wide, exposing its full set of fangs. She pumped the trigger. The bullets punctured the flesh, smashed the Beating Clock face at its chest. It kept coming and she wheeled backward on her hot heels.

"Oh, you bugger! Now I'll have to cut you!"

Spinning almost elegantly in a full 360' she pulled her sword. With one swift strike, the head went flying. The rest of the monster collapsed.

Halliday charged into Denivens Hell.

Trill, overly familiar voices filled her head,

"The Nightmarer, Halliday! You need to find the Nightmarer! You haven't forgotten, have you?"

"You know, I' would have done, by now. This has been quite the lackluster showing."

"I agree. She's having a go, though. She has a lot to live up to ... I was a wonderful Halliday."

"Oh, go away, this isn't helping me!" Halliday snapped at her antagonistic Other-selves. She had four Other-selves, and all four were a constant bane on her existence.

The devil imps of Denivens Hell were suddenly everywhere, charging in their ten's and twenties, hot sparks flying at their clawed hands, lunging through the smoke.

"My god! Are you all breeding?!" she shouted with disbelief. With quick thinking, Halliday used a combination of the butt of the gun to smash them sideways and the razor-edged blade of the sword to slice and stab. The imps smashed into her legs, in a bid to take her off her feet.

She held strong. Halliday was tough, with a body built to take most things. She had her limits though. Hamish the Mender had warned her of another stroke on her Beating Clock – quite simply, she couldn't afford one.

She kicked and sliced with her blade, cracked her gun across snouts. There was blood aplenty - the creatures seemed to have an endless supply in their gullets - most of which was spat at her face. She coughed and gagged and resisted the disturbing urge to lick the foul wet from her lips.

"Well this is just great isn't it!? The Nightmarer at the end of this better appreciate that I have suffered a face full of imp blood!" Her anger driving her on, she ramped up the violence and cleared the area. She ran.

The terrain dipped into a gully full of screaming, metamorphosizing (not to mention, quite naked) men and women, crawling over the fiery dirt.

"My word! It's the devil-imp making place!" Repulsed, she stood watching the shaking, growing bodies. This was always tricky. Who were the residents of Sombre and who weren't? There would only be one, it was rare that there was a second Nightmarer. Halliday looked for the Beating Clocks. Patting a flame out at her hem, licking her dry lips, she crouched down and hurriedly lifted heads so she could see the timepiece in each chest.

Apparently, it was time for more advice,

"You know these humans are ready to turn ... I'd be careful, Hope's Halliday!" an Other-self pointed out.

Another Other-self chimed in. *"If it was me, I wouldn't bother checking ... can't she see the eyes? No pupils, just yellows. They're all good to take down."* And then another Other', *"She moves like a snail, this one ... I wonder if her Hope is the same in the waking world. You have to hurry, Halliday Knight - I can see tails forming!"*

"So, what all of you are saying, in an extremely roundabout sort of way, is go quickly and be careful?" Halliday said through a tight mouth. She began flipping the quivering bodies onto their backs. She registered how helpless they all were – not that they would be for much longer. Skin was burning away rapidly, curling like the edges of lit paper, revealing the devil-imp under their bodies.

"If you do feel the need to comment ... ugh!" There was a sudden, complete metamorphosis from human to imp. Halliday felt a snap of jaws at her hand, she pulled her digits back just in time, "Oooh! Almost got me!" She swung her sword and decapitated the newly formed monster, then finished her train of thought, "Yes, if all of you *must* comment, don't just state the bleeding obvious!" Satisfied there was no Nightmarer in the gully, she left the soon-to-be monsters and continued on.

As she ran, a thought occurred to her. (As thoughts sometimes did when her mind wasn't being bombarded by her Other-selves) She supposed that the original Nightmarer of this hellhole was either named Deniven or surnamed Deniven, and he had dreamt of his own hell. Sombre thought his nightmare worthy of a spot in its nightmare world. In so many ways Sombre was quite a simple place, just not a nice place.

She spotted a clumpy shadow in the smoke – a body accompanied with at least three devil-imps. This was her Nightmarer, she was sure of it. He or she had definitely expired.

She sighed, a little defeated, "Anyway, I got you, I guess."

It would be just in the nick of time, as her whole body appeared to be cooking, her pale arms and legs glowing a worrying, heat flushed pink. She wondered, if she boiled, would her skin start to bubble?

There was movement from behind. She swung round.

The new imps had finished their disgusting metamorphosis and were prowling unsteadily, moaning and coughing up blood as they tested their new hands and feet.

"Brand new devil-babies," Halliday surmised.

They weren't babies. They would attack. She had to finish up. Turning her back on the next impending invasion, she approached the Nightmarer. Halliday stood over a young policeman lying face down in the fire swirls. Was he a real policeman? Or was he just dreaming of being a policeman? It didn't really matter.

She had arrived far too late for this one. Half the skull had been torn open exposing brain matter. The poor fellow's arms were twisted at wild angles. Three gurgling and giggling imps continued to work the carcass over, claws digging into the flesh, mouths tearing through the clothes and finding bare skin. Bits of snapped rib poked through the clothes. The team of Denivens' filthy beings had gotten to his insides.

"Well, I hope you're proud of yourselves, you scummy things! Look at the mess you've made," she said kicking a gorging imp away from the lower back of the man.

So very engrossed with feasting on their kill, the other two didn't even move. This made it quicker. With two sharp blows she severed the heads of the creatures and pushed them off the mauled Nightmarer. The other imp had recovered from Halliday's size 8 boot kick. Gore filled mouth squealing like a banshee, clawed hands out, it flew at her chest and caught on, fingers and nails tore through her dress, punctured her skin.

"Oh geez!" somewhat surprised at the ferocity of the imp she dropped her sword, lost her footing and fell backward onto the policeman's corpse – she was back to back - her back on his.

"Oh no! Yuck! Yuck! Yuck!" she cried, grabbing the imp's fat neck with both hands, "Get out of it you devil monkey!"

The policeman's corpse felt wet and hot. "Oh, this is beyond the call, surely!" She wrenched the imp's neck. Its body was heavy. The monster had her in its grip and wouldn't let go, clinging on, sharp hands and feet doing her all sorts of damage. She felt her dress catch on fire. This was no good at all - she had to do something fast. The imp's mouth searched for her face and pulled it close to its own. It spat hot blood at her mouth.

She thought of the gun digging into her hip - she couldn't reach for it - there was no way she could hold this thing back with one hand.

"You're not costing me a stroke, you ass!" she cried out.

This was always a last resort.

But it had to be.

She engaged her Morphia.

Halliday completely lost control.

She was no longer Halliday.

She was her Morphia.

Jaw breaking, her mouth transformed, her skin split and cracked open revealing a hideous inner. The Morphia's body convulsed and muscularized under the devil-imp. Laughing gutturally, her Morphia grabbed the head with both hands and pulled the imp in closer.

Her monster *wanted* it close.

Her now iron-like jaw snapped, biting the creatures face viciously. Her hands ripped its neck open, pulling out the innards. It searched lower, broke and tore the ribcage wide. It slung the abused corpse away like rubbish. Still laughing like a lunatic, it turned and watched the inhabitants of Denivens Hell scatter.

The Morphia vanished.

Halliday Knight was left lying on a corpse.

CHAPTER 3
The Menders

Her Other-selves were unsympathetic - plain nasty, really.

'Well, that was quite an ordinary showing.'

'You're being too kind – it was downright awful! Look at the poor fellow! Hope's Halliday certainly struggles, doesn't she?'

'Hamish will be most upset.'

'She had to resort to engaging The Morphia as well! Ha! Very pissy indeed!'

Dragging the policeman's corpse through the rest of Denivens Hell, Halliday couldn't help but agree with them. How could she argue? This mission was a monumental failure. Ahead, she saw a hilltop at the outskirts, with a signpost wrapped in barbed wire protruding from its peak. It looked flame and fire-free enough to call out to her place of employment.

Scaling the hill, she read the sign, 'Gavin Denivens Going to Hell'.

"Ah, Gavin, eh? You *were* a frightened one ..." she mused.

She let the Nightmarer's body slump on the safe spot. His arm flopped down heavy. She realized just how bad the poor gent was. "Ugh ... god, you're a wreck aren't you!" There was half of a head. The torso was very ripped up and raw. She shuddered. Just moments ago, she was laying on top of that mess.

She pulled down self-consciously at a flapping piece of her dress, it appeared she had around 50 per cent of it left. Most undignified. In fact, all that remained complete of her attire was made of leather - the sheath and holster belt at her waist and her trusty long black boots. Most of her hair was scorched at the ends.

"A definite low point for me ... oh well," she looked to her Nightmarer then back to where she had come from, "it will be best to get a wriggle on, murdered policeman, wouldn't it?" The devil imps hadn't followed her to this spot yet - her Morphia had scared them sufficiently enough - but she didn't trust that the monsters wouldn't find some pluck and come again.

Trying her utmost to not sound dejected, she called out to Sombre's skies, "Halliday Knight. I am done. I have the Nightmarer. Could I ask you to bring The Funneling directly to this spot as I am on foot!"

A few seconds passed. A rectangular shimmer formed in the air before her. Halliday grabbed the collar of the policeman and stepped in. Both were lifted and taken from Denivens Hell.

Singed hair blowing in the wind gusts of The Funneling's gaseous passage, Halliday walked with complete indifference of the overwhelming stench of human organics and exhaust-pipe burning smells, dragging the Nightmarer's corpse toward the double wooden doors to The Office of The Menders. With a sigh, she entered.

Sapped of energy, Halliday couldn't be bothered with the usual announcing of her arrival; she had brought nothing worth advertising. With the Nightmarer's gathered carcass slumped on the floor by her feet, she waited to be noticed. The Office of The Menders was its usual hive of endless activity.

The room was expansive and unfussy with a floorplan purely for fast service. A large gold clock face adorned the far wall. Wide surgical benches ran up and down the length of the room in a U-shape. Lying on the floor in the rooms centre were piles of silver and gold, Beating Clocks. The heady stench of a myriad of chemicals and ointments invaded the senses. Hardworking men and women, dressed in light blue, blood stained scrubs, attended to a whole host of Sombre's citizens and new Nightmarers, who were positioned head to foot on the benches. Procedures of every conceivable kind were being performed by the entrusted Menders: resewing of limbs, intricate reconfigurations of re-engineered inner workings; resetting of clocks, readjusting and replacing of all sorts of broken, sliced, chewed, ripped, decapitated and severed body bits. Blood repeatedly splashed onto the floor and was mopped away. Cogs, thread and wire were skillfully replaced and tightened. Flesh was sliced open, bone re-melded and fused with metal, strings and thread. Flatbed trolleys lined the far walls where yet more sheet covered bodies, awaited procedures.

Halliday was only looking for one Mender. She spotted Hamish, the chief, over near the far wall, hands deep in the chest cavity of a very large beast. She waved tiredly and caught his attention. Frowning, he called to a short girl Mender with black spiky hair. Halliday knew her as Llewellyn - a friendly and very capable sort - who left her own lower leg procedure to another Mender and took over Hamish's chest invasion with well-practiced aplomb.

Hamish walked toward Halliday wiping his hands on an alcohol-soaked cloth. His eyes dropped to the sad looking, well eaten, lump on the floor at her feet. Nodding he peered up at her with a look that said it all, "Well, I suppose I should say thanks, Halliday?"

She answered sheepishly, "yeah, er ... you really don't have to."

Hamish eyed the state of her. "Denivens Hell gave you a lot to chew on, didn't it?"

She fidgeted with what was left of the bottom of her dress. "The imps were quite a handful."

"Well I won't need to set your clock forward a stroke, that is a bonus I suppose." He knelt down and turned the deceased policeman over. He checked the Nightmarer. "I have a lot to rebuild here."

"It would have been easier and quicker if I could have taken Wilder, but the terrain wasn't so good for a horse. Flaming hot cookery of a place ..."

Halliday said trailing off. She wondered where Wilder might be, although, she wasn't overly concerned. The Machanihorse had a knack for finding her.

Hamish stood up, wiped his hands on the rag again and examined her wounds. "Yes, well, there are a few parts of Sombre you won't be able to take your horse, Halliday. You seem not too bad actually. Some gouges to your chest, a bit of burnt hair. Ointment, cosmetics and a new dress should do you. How were your Other-selves, this mission? Last we met you were being quite vocal about them?"

"As nasty as they always are. Were they really that much better than me?" She said rolling her eyes. She was sick to death of their judging.

Hamish gave a short laugh. "Let me see ... Cindy's Halliday, the third Halliday Knight, probably had the best record. She was the smartest. Judy's Halliday, number two, went through her twelve strokes at a record pace – far too reckless. Number four, Eloise. She was just before you ..." he rubbed his chin as he searched his thoughts. "Actually, she was quite good – she brought me some good, clean, not completely dead Nightmarers – but through bad luck, she went through her strokes too fast as well. Sometimes, it is just bad luck in Sombre."

"And the first Halliday?"

She had always wondered what the initial Halliday Knight had been like.

Hamish grinned, "Well, Liza was the first Halliday. It was all brand new. Lots of trial and error as we learnt about Halliday Knight's character. A brand-new Gatherer of any sort comes with a lot of weight and expectation. Liza's Halliday had to create a whole range of reactions, brain function and attitude. You have all shared and built on the personalities she helped establish. She went through her strokes quickly." He focused his attention back on her, "Sombre will always throw you many a challenge. We as Menders can only hope you'll be as efficient as possible. This goes for all our

14

Gatherers. This poor clod at our feet isn't your greatest catch, Halliday. You've done better."

Two Menders arrived and lifted the policeman onto a trolley, wheeling him to a vacant spot at the wall where he was left.

"I think we had better get you cleaned up and back into the field," Hamish guided her by the arm to a spot on the bench next to some awful ongoing procedures. She sat flanked by a decapitated female citizen, (Beating Clock, stroking at nine) and a great pile of butchered body parts, leaking bloody water. She held her nose.

Dropping the Remington and her sword to the floor, Halliday positioned herself uncomfortably. Desperate not to touch, she crossed her legs, and tried to make her body as small as possible. She eyed the two awaiting procedures with revulsion. "You couldn't find a girl a nicer seat? This isn't really my style, Hamish."

"Uh, yes ... no. We really are inundated at the moment. Take a look around, Halliday. We are beyond capacity. You all get your twelve strokes unfortunately and you all just keep coming back."

He sighed, "Anyway, for you, a new dress is in order – sorry, just the one colour."

"Oh, ha-ha," Halliday said of her tiresome garment.

"It never goes out of fashion, a classic," Hamish said grinning as he pulled out a large leather surgical roll from a shelf under the bench. Untying the straps, he revealed the varied implements of a Mender: spanners, screwdrivers, scalpels, hammers, rolls of surgical thread, needles, tubes and bottles, spoons, small saws, knives and scissors. Pulling out a tube of ointment, a needle and thread, he began work at the cuts and gouges in Halliday's chest. His skilled hands worked fast, and he kept Halliday covered, working under and around what was left of her dress. Hamish believed in privacy where it could be helped, which she was always grateful for.

"So, you stay at two strokes only, Halliday. Not bad, given you had to engage The Morphia on this mission."

"How can you tell?" Halliday said with more than a little shame. Engaging her monstrous self was meant to be her very last option. She had been warned from the outset of this. The Morphia meant she had lost control. It was a rabid killing machine, but no control really meant *no* control – no regard for self-preservation at all.

Hamish frowned as he studied her features, "Your jaw, you still have tightness where it extended, and your skin's dry from where The Morphia cracked it."

"I am sorry, Hamish. But you know, I had an imp on my chest! It wanted to bite my face, so I had to bite it first! A girl must do what a girl must do!"

"Your sword? You have it for a reason."

"I dropped it."

"The Remington?"

"I couldn't reach it!" She'd had enough. Her hands gripped the bench, hard. She shot him a look and gave him a mouthful. "Now listen here man! I gave you my best and that will do you! Are we finished? Where's my dress ... I need a bleeding drink!"

With well-practiced tolerance of her short fuse, Hamish tapped his finger on the glass of her Beating Clock. He kept his tone even, "Let me remind you, Halliday. You only have *twelve* strokes. You're on two. Ten left. They will go quick."

"I know! I have heard all of this before! Must you be as tiresome as my Other-selves, Hamish! What a burden all of this is sometimes!"

Hamish studied her face, "we are almost done. Please stand up and turn around." With a huff, she did as she was asked. He ran a solution through her golden hair, fingers light and confident, starting from the scalp combing through to the tips.

"Halliday, I just ask you to take care ..." he paused. With a sigh he continued on, "I have been holding onto this information. but I think it would be best to tell you this sooner rather than later. Hope's Halliday, you have a higher calling here in Sombre ... something unprecedented, something far greater than any Halliday Knight has ever had to exist for."

"What do you mean a higher calling?" More than a mite curious, she turned to face him.

"Turn back round, please Halliday."

Raising an eyebrow, she did as she was told and listened.

Hamish continued on as he slipped a comb through her revitalized locks, "keep still please."

"Now, no other Gatherer has ever had this type of calling ... I'm sure you'll be happy to know no other *Halliday* has ever had it either."

"What is it?"

He ignored her. "The importance of what's to come for you can't be understated, it will need to be taken seriously," he pulled down on her hair for the last time, "You're done."

He began spraying down his implements with cleaning solution.

She turned with an agitated flick of her hair and stood with hands on hips. He had ruffled her. Now he was showing her indifference. "Oh no you won't be leaving me hanging, man! So, what is it! Spill the bloody beans!"

Hamish shrugged, "I don't love clichés Halliday, but I will have to use one now." With a blank expression, he looked her straight in the eyes, "All will be revealed in good time, Halliday Knight. All in good time. Just try and stay safe. That is all I ask for now."

∫

Hope woke with a gasp.

Chapter 4
The Drudgery of the Waking World

Staring up at the ceiling, Hope rubbed at her chest through her nightie. She was so sore. Any normal person would have thought they were on the verge of some almighty chest infection. But the pain was straight from Sombre. Hope knew it. Halliday Knight had been clawed and gouged by devil imps and then mended by Hamish the Mender. And she, Hope Kelley, was to feel a version of it. Why? She had no idea. Was she meant to gain something from experiencing some of Halliday's pain in the nightmare world? Apparently so.

Incidences while dreaming were well documented. There were so many examples: manic thrashing around in sleep, near death experiences through lucid dreaming, of people actually dying from dreams of falling from great heights and inevitably hitting the bottom.

Sombre was something else again. To say every dream was a 'vivid' one, didn't do it justice at all. No one dreamt like this, she was sure of it. This was so very different than anything she had read about. When she slept, she was *in* Sombre. She *was* Halliday Knight – Hope's Halliday, version five – fifth in line.

Exhausted, chest still aching she stood on stiff legs and rode the sickly wave of dizziness. She felt like a fifteen-year-old going on fifty-five. Reaching for her water bottle, she flipped the lid and gulped it down. Feeling a little better, she took a deep breath and coughed.

"Hmm, best get to it, Hope," she sighed and grabbed her glasses from her desk. She changed for school: jeans, a white t-shirt and a peach coloured cardigan. Peach might just help the pale complexion. She looked at herself in the mirror on the wardrobe door; hair up or hair out? She held a makeshift ponytail and could have sworn the pimple paddock had harvested, bearing more fruit overnight, red splotchy things on a ghostly pale canvass. "Great look," she muttered and grabbed her compact. She dabbed concealer on the worst of the spots. Deciding hair out would be best; she ran a brush through it and gave it a shake and tousle.

Repetitious music came from Kate's room down the hall. She had no idea what or who the artist was and had no desire to find out. No doubt it would be the latest, clique-approved bilge Hope always found to be an assault on her eardrums, and intelligence. But that was Kate. Unlike Hope, she knew how to fit in. At a mere 13 years young, she had the smarmy attitude and the look. Kate Kelley was popular. She could talk it, walk it; and if she really had to, pat her head, rub her belly and quote the unwritten teen encyclopedia of accepted behaviours backward.

Hope never could – and didn't really want to.

Week four in a new suburb, the move to Pento so far had been a tough one. Sacramento had been tough as well, but at least she had gotten into her own sort of loner-groove back there. This was the third move for the Kelley's in a small handful of years. Her father's firm, Health&Co, was spreading its wings in a good natured, well-meaning bid to take over California. 'Fast Health - Fast Healthy Drinks/Fast Healthy Meals' was the company motto. It was working as well. Health&Co was turning over millions.

Hope didn't want to be a loner, yet it seemed the closer her family moved to Los Angeles, the more painful the kids her age became. Her mother once told her that she probably had an old-soul, a rare maturity for her age. 'It might just take a while for other kids to catch up to you, Hope,' she was assured by her mother; a so very positive bit of chirpiness that the socially popular Evelyn Kelley would bestow when in the mood. It was meant to be a compliment – but it just came off sounding like something she had read in a woman's magazine, storing it away for the appropriate time to use it on her 'troubled' first child.

Hope knew that her parents loved her. But it felt like a pitied love. Hope was always the worry. Hope was the pale one. Hope had the poor eyesight. Hope should find a *good* friend.

Sombre definitely wasn't aiding her cause. It would help if she wasn't living another life beside her actual life. Most days she felt like a wasteoid, enduring an existence of endless recovery from one disturbing night's sleep after another.

Jarring her from her thoughts, her mother called from the kitchen, "School, girls! We're now officially running late! Move your butts, grab a snack bar from the fridge, I'll be in the car."

Hope entered the hall and fell in behind her sister. She watched the back of Kate's perfectly shaped blonde head, noticed the cute twisted braid (that Hope always wondered how she managed to do without help) and took the steps by twos, calves and thighs aching like a bitch.

Grabbing a Health&Co Fruit, Nut and Carob bar from the fridge, Hope chased Kate through the front door, where her mother was already hitting the horn.

∫

"Have a good day, Hope. If I'm running late tonight, start walking and give me a call," Evelyn Kelley said pulling to the curb in front of Centurion High. "Have you got your phone?"

"No."

"Why?" her mother shook her head, incredulous.

"Forgot it."

"That was silly wasn't it."

"Anyway..." Hope said and got out. Slinging her bag over her shoulder, her muscles pulled, and she had to rub her chest with her palm.

20

It was still sore – *Halliday* sore.

Her mother noticed this. In a bid to be heard over the Jeep's car radio, she yelled, "do you need a new bra Hope? We can go shopping if you do."

Mortified, Hope rolled her eyes and dropped her hand straight away, "No! Geez! Really, mum?" she looked round at the droves of kids walking the pavement.

"Just wondering, dear, you girls are growing so quickly," Evelyn grinned.

Scrolling through her new followers on Instagram, her sister didn't even look up at the exchange.

"Yep, goodbye, see you tonight," Hope said shortly and shut the door. The Jeep flew down the road, took a right and was gone.

Pushing her glasses up on her nose, she laboured into the school grounds. Why she was worried about being embarrassed by her mother's tactless observation of the fit of her bra was anyone's guess. To say the kids of Centurion High couldn't have given a shit, was an understatement of the highest order. Most days she was either a ghost, or just the newest strange thing to be sniggered at.

Next year, her sister would arrive at Centurion' with her ready-band of followers riding her tail.

'Herding her sheep,' Hope thought nastily, jealously.

The morning air broiled, So-Cal in July - humid, without a breath of wind. The heat seemed to drain her of more energy, she took her steps slowly. Kids walked alongside, crossed her path, fist-bumped, chest-bumped, spoke on phones, tapped on phones, waxed lyrically about upcoming parties, why 'he's a dick' and 'who's she seeing now?' The usual fare. She was meant to find it interesting – she just didn't. How could she?

It all paled in comparison to Sombre.

This thinking was not going to help her with her leper status, and she knew it; but it couldn't be helped. Sombre was all encompassing, a greedy beast - swallowing her consciousness and subconsciousness, piece by piece.

Maybe she would disappear entirely one night.

Just a crumpled imprint left on her bedsheets.

Hope Kelley - gone.

"Oh, how she'll be missed!" she said under her breath and laughed to herself derisively.

Looking straight ahead, her exhaustion escalated, she did her best to keep her legs functioning.

Sombre had chosen her for this. She had been *chosen* to be Halliday Knight. It wasn't make-believe – how could it be? It was actually happening to her, night after night. The fact that Sombre was a nightmare world, a place she only went to in her sleep, didn't make it any less real. Not for her, no sir! She had the exhausted body and mind to prove it.

Sombre left her feeling odd, looking odd. Looking *old*. She was a wreck.

Making her way through a turnstile into the main foyer, she bumped into a tall girl, blond with an athletic build and short skirt. "Sorry," she mumbled as she peered up.

"Watch it, freak-zone. Oh Jesus, I've been touched!" Her two friends turned and giggled; savage looks in their eyes.

Hope stood still and waited for them to go. She didn't have to wait long. There would be no further altercation. They were gone. Girls like that didn't waste time on someone like Hope Kelley.

ʃ

Last period felt like penance. Stuck in a classroom with a flagging air conditioner in the old T building, Hope struggled to stay awake. She sat up front; pole position for the vision impaired - chin resting on her palm, blinking incessantly behind her bullet proof lenses. Her English teacher, Miss Sparrows, read a lengthy trial passage aloud from 'To Kill a Mockingbird'. As Hope drifted, the words slurred around in her ears, each sentence a lethargic jumble.

Miss Sparrows finished up and closed the paperback. "So, what was the basis of Atticus's argument? This was just one of the many thought provoking and era-challenging arguments of that time. Can I have a showing of hands please? Don't tell me you *all* nodded off." Miss Sparrows had a well-practiced, teacher-to-student coolness and she was well respected.

A few hands went up. Hope's wasn't one of them.

The teacher counted them, "Okay, 1, 2, 3 - 4 ... I can see Layne's hand at the back. Layne, please, share your thoughts."

"Well, you know, the man was black, and the colour of his skin shouldn't have made any difference?" Layne took a shot.

"Uh, yeah," Miss Sparrows wrinkled her nose, "not quite what I was after. Good to hear you at least know the basics of 'To Kill a Mockingbird' – *the very basics, Layne* – although, I appreciate the participation."

Someone made a fizzing sound.

"Misty, please tell me your thoughts," she continued on.

"That Atticus had to have faith that the system would work, and justice would be done?"

Miss Sparrows turned and strolled back toward the front of the class. "Ah, thank you Misty – that's a very good point." The teacher changed tact, "Hope Kelley, would you like to elaborate on Misty's point? You would have read this book before no doubt?"

Put on the spot, Hope froze. She sat up straight and cleared her throat.

"Um, no I *haven't.*"

Hope surprised herself with how sharp her response actually sounded.

"Okay."

The teacher left it.

Hope instantly felt bad. But why did every teacher think that just because you had the nerd glasses, and had the nerd look, that you would have read every book in the whole friggin library?

"Sensing a bit of attitude there, Miss," said the designated class football jock, Joel Frazer from the back. There was some sniggering and a slap of Joel's hand.

The bell rang to end the period and the students rose as one.

"Can I please see you for a moment Hope?" Miss Sparrows said through the thud of footsteps, the sliding of chairs and chatter of the students.

Hope left her bag half packed and stayed seated as the last of the students disappeared through the door and her teacher pulled a chair over to speak to her.

"So, hi Hope. I won't keep you long," she began, her tone soothing. She frowned, "I'm not used to my students dozing in my classes."

"Sorry," Hope said not realizing she had been so obvious.

"It's okay, I forgive, I forget," she smiled warmly. "Everything okay at home? How are you finding Pento? Big change from where you're from, I'll bet. Remind me again where that was?"

"Sacramento," Hope answered and pulled on each of her fingers – Miss Sparrows noticed it. "Everything is good at home as well ... I've been watching too much T.V. that's all," she apologized again, "Sorry."

"And your friendship status, how are you going there? It can be hard to find your way at a new school."

Hope thought Miss Sparrows already knew the answer to that. She lowered her eyes, "it's okay."

Miss Sparrows got up and put her hands on her hips. "Hmm ... anyway, I told you I wouldn't keep you long. If you ever have a need to talk, come and see me. I know how hard a new school can be. I moved a half dozen times myself when I was growing up."

Hope looked her teacher in the eye as she finished gathering her things, "I will, thank you, Miss Sparrows."

The teacher smiled. "All good, get to bed early and try and stay awake in class. You are going to give me a complex, my girl!"

Hope left.

ʃ

Sitting on her bed in her pajamas, with half of a badly written science essay on her laptop, Hope yawned while her eyes watered. She couldn't fight it; she had to sleep. She looked at the time, 11:30. Prolonging it any longer would only make her more zonked tomorrow. She felt a stabbing bolt of anxiety in her gut, as her thoughts went somewhere rather murky.

What if on this sleep her body and mind couldn't cope with being Halliday? What if she died tonight? Would Sombre do that to her? It might. It was a pretty bad place.

The troubling thing was that there was a major part of her that liked being Halliday Knight. Halliday Knight's existence bettered her own by a long way. Existing as some sort of character from a nightmare world was far more appealing than her own real life. She knew, that psychologically, that wasn't a good thing. She was probably suffering depression. Was that the reason Sombre had chosen her to be Halliday Knight? A pathetically easy target? A weak and half blind, fifteen-year-old girl with no friends?

Well and truly pent-up, she shut her eyes and took a long deep breath, then let it seep out slowly, like a leaky valve.

"Shit ... you need some sleep, Hope," she said miserably and pulled her glasses off.

Snapping her laptop closed, she slipped it into her school bag.

Feeling just about as alone as she had ever felt, Hope eased her head onto the pillow and curled up into a ball.

Lights out ...

Chapter 5
Drinking at The Ruptured Spleen

Aunt Sophie's wedding nightmare, Hope's rite of passage into Sombre, continued on.

Her mother, wild eyed, screaming like a savage, stabbed the knife into Hope's body. It was all very real. Hope could feel everything. Could hear every sickeningly dull strike as the blade plunged and punctured her flesh.

"How dare you, Hope! You always ruin everything! This is what happens when you don't stay clean!"

'What? Why? - No! What do you mean?" Hope heard herself shriek as she fought back.

Her mother laughed at her daughter's audacity. "You dirty wretch, Hope! That's right! Fight me!" She stabbed with more fury.

Hope slapped her mother's bloody face with more force. Suddenly overcome with the need to maim her, she hit with one open heavy palmed slap after the other. Evelyn laughed harder, even as Hope overpowered her and she fell to the carpet. Hope stood on the arm holding the knife with one foot; and trod on her mother's face with the other - a white high heel from her fancy flower girl shoes, sinking into Evelyn Kelley's eyeball - moosh! With her wailing mother-turned-wild-daughter-killer pinned underfoot, a profusely bleeding Hope stood and watched the rest of the room.

Relatives continued to run around the chapel in surreal slow motion. Hope counted eight slumped and lifeless bodies along the blood smeared pews. She watched as her sister jumped over them like a psychotic hurdler and dove at her great aunt Louise, slamming her knife into her gaping mouth.

Finally succumbing to her own wounds, Hope felt herself fall sideways off her mother and land on the burning corpses of the bride and groom. She rolled down and nestled in ghoulishly between the two. Lying on her side, through watery eyes she gazed at Aunt Sophie's burning hair, at her face, melting and popping away like wax. She was so sorry for it all.

Her listless, dreaming self knew none of this made sense. It was all just a nightmare, a bad one. Hope's rite of passage went black.

∫

"She is such a faithful nag."

Halliday Knight mused with signature drink in hand – a strong Scotch and Dry. Both she and Dave Bi-Plane, a fellow Gatherer, stood leaning on the balcony of Sombre's one and only drinking spot; The Ruptured Spleen. Blandly shoe-box shaped with a façade of tinted windows on each side; the bar sat precariously on the peak of The Unexplained Mountain.

The two Gatherers' peered down, a long way down, to Halliday's machanihorse, Wilder. The mare wandered around vehicles, haphazardly parked at the dusty parking lot at the foot of the mountain. For the land Gatherers – Sombre's expeditiously irregular cars, tension ratioed speed cycles and high-powered speed trucks: for the Gatherers by air - jet stream-receptor air balloons and airships. And Dave's tan coloured Sopwith Camel - his beloved Bi-Plane.

Every Halliday always liked every Dave Bi-Plane. The original Dave Bi-Plane came to Sombre without a surname, so the motley conglomerate that was the Gatherer's, affectionately surnamed him after his transportation. He was a burly fellow, with a kind smile and demeanour to match.

"A mechanical horse," Dave pondered scratching his stubbly chin. "Does she ever breakdown? What does she eat?"

"A Machanihorse, Dave," Halliday corrected him as she stirred the balance of her drink with a straw, she nodded, "And not a lot, really. Pecks the grasses, drinks from The River occasionally. She is quite chock full of her mechanisms, you know. She needs a tweak from The Menders here and there."

Dave raised his thick eyebrows, "Hang on, back up a bit! You are kidding, Halliday Knight! Corpse water from The River! Are you having a lend of me? Why would you let her?"

Halliday shrugged, "Well, I don't go out of my way to take her there! But at the times when we have to cross, she stops and has a swig. She is wetting her whistle, I suppose."

"Oh, I feel quite ill," Dave grimaced. He looked down at his empty mug, "And there is nothing better for that than another ale." He made for the open double balcony doors of The Ruptured Spleen.

"Would you like another, Miss Halliday?"

She grinned and crunched on a block of ice. "Yes, I would. Ensure to tell Orty, two *decent* shots please. That was a little too gingery for me. I need it sharper."

Halliday heard an unmistakable roar from below, she looked down and spotted her horse scamper away under a clump of trees. Lucretia St Aimes rode into the clearing on her massive, twin piped eyesore of a motorcycle.

"And there goes the serenity," Halliday muttered to herself. Frowning, she turned away and listened as Lucretia revved her metallic beast a few more times in her quite stupid, obligatory bombastic way, before parking.

Dave returned with the drinks, rolling his eyes, "and the nasty arse cometh, eh? That will ruin a nice evening." He handed Halliday her glass. "Think I'll have this and take off early. No point hanging around now." Dave Bi-Plane was a tolerant man, but he had never been able to suffer through the company of Lucretia St Aimes. He peered down at the parquetry flooring.

Halliday tried to keep him talking, she too had been enjoying this down time with Dave Bi-Plane - such an agreeable fellow. "Well, you'll never guess what?"

He sighed and sipped his lager, "what?"

She was losing him. He was now eyeing the elevator door of the bar, dreading Lucretia's entrance.

Licking her lips, she paused for dramatic effect. "I wasn't going to mention it, but I, Halliday Knight, have been given a calling. Hamish has said this is so."

Dave raised an eyebrow, "Oh? And what do you mean by a 'calling,' Halliday? We all have one, don't we?" He scoffed, "to serve bloody Sombre."

"Ah, *that* is not really a calling, is it. *That* is a job. And that would be far too pedestrian to be considered a calling, wouldn't it?"

She took another sip of her scotch. She thought that the bar-keep, Orty, was a little off his game this evening – the drink definitely needed another shot of one or the other. She continued, "Hamish wouldn't tell me what it was, though. He can be such a painful clog' at times. Although, I did wonder if *he* actually knew what it was himself."

Dave shrugged, "He might not have. He receives his orders the same way we all do. He may have been drip-fed a piece of information about you, that's all ... Sounds like it could be interesting though." Dave chugged the rest of his beer. He placed the mug on a nearby metal tabletop.

"Anyway, that will give us something to talk about when next we meet, Halliday Knight." Dave pulled his leather aviator helmet from his bag and slipped it on. Next came the brown tinted goggles.

Halliday always thought his protective wear made him look like a stubbly faced frog. She smiled and told him as much, "You look like a frogman, Dave."

"Yes, I know, Halliday. Thank you. And as usual, I have no comeback." He waved his gloved hands at her lazily. "Farewell. Do not say hello to Lucretia St. Aimes for me."

Without any further ceremony, he turned and left.

Leaning on the bannister, Halliday took a deep breath - in through the nose, out through the mouth – 'this was a nice night,' she thought to herself. Gazing down at the parking lot, she toyed with the idea of awaiting her next job aboard Wilder, let the machanihorse meander around for a bit. Dave Bi-Plane would await his next job from the skies. A Gatherer never had to wait long. The waking world nightmared at such an alarming rate.

A new job would come to her as an intruding thought. And she would know where instantly. Whether she had been there before or not didn't matter. Sombre would always guide the way.

With a misfire and piston stutter from the rotary motor, Dave Bi-Plane's Bi-Plane started and took off from the parking lot in its unconventional way – straight up like a helicopter. Halliday gave a little wave as it flew past the façade of The Ruptured Spleen. She smiled, she really liked Dave. She didn't think she loved him, but she *did* like him. She wondered if Sombre would even allow such a thing as love. It wouldn't be a very lasting love, she thought to herself; twelve strokes on your Beating Clock and you were gutted, de-clocked and floating in The River. But she did wonder. Maybe it was the drinks, but she felt a little whimsy, a little light and gentle. And dare she admit it, a skerrick of longing.

Then she heard the laughter coming from within the bar. Savage and confident laughter. Lucretia St Aimes. She sighed and muttered, "That might just ruin it all."

She knew she would have to at least acknowledge the incorrigible Gatherer's presence.

Lucretia was a similar build to Halliday, tall and strong. They both shared similar skill-sets, handy with weapons and fists – yet, the comparisons ended there. For reasons unbeknownst, Sombre gave Halliday a lightness and Lucretia an obvious darkness.

Halliday wandered inside the Spleen' and assessed the room. It had filled out quite a bit from when she had arrived. Smoke filled the air; cigarettes, cigars and old codger tobacco pipes. Truckers, aviators of the ballooning and shipping variety, speed cyclers and drivers intermingled between tables. All drank up and wound down while they could, awaiting the inevitable call – the next job.

Lucretia's black leather jacket was hard to miss, emblazoned with silver leather lettering reading 'Death Witch'. As was the long black hair, black leather pants and boots. She stood at the bar, having demanded the attention of the spiky jet black haired, Recalcitrance Bexley and Captain Andrew Feister, both ballooners.

Tall glass of a black spirit in hand, she stood with her back to Halliday, and talked at both of the Gatherer's, who to Halliday, seemed to be part frightened and part obligated. Both nodded with what appeared to be convincing surface interest,

"They whinge and complain about what we give them ... what *I* give them! If a Nightmarer comes in in bits, then it's bleeding bits they'll get! You know what I mean? They're Mender's, aren't they? That's their job! Fix them! Make them right again! ... You hear me, don't you? Do they want the job done? ... You got a smoke for me?"

For a moment Halliday thought she might be able to slip out unnoticed. It wasn't to happen.

"Halliday Knight! Come here and chat with us, you pretty thing!"

"Nuts," Halliday muttered under her breath as she feigned a smile Lucretia's way. It was probably just her slightly tipsy state, but Lucretia looked quite striking this evening. The woman's dark purple eyes seemed almost bejeweled; her tattooed black lips fuller than the last time they met. Halliday peered down at her Beating Clock and noticed her stroke rate was quite high – she was at eight.

Lucretia caught her stare and raised her eyebrows, "I see you looking at my chest there Halliday. Yes, I've been mended recently. I look wonderful, yes? Of course, not as pretty as you ... never as pretty as you." She snorted and took a long swig of her spirit and swilled it around in her mouth for a while, not taking her eyes from Halliday. For an alarming second or two, Halliday actually thought Lucretia might spit it at her. The woman finally swallowed, "Are you drinking?"

Captain Andrew Feister was already calling to the barkeep, he turned to Halliday, eyes alight, twisting his barber shop mustachio with his thumb and index finger. "Your poison is hoppity scotchity and dry-dry if I remember correctly, ha-ha!? Am I right?"

"Yes, but just one," Halliday said forcing half a smile, "I have to get down to Wilder, she'll be missing me."

Andrew Feister was quite the obnoxious fellow. He laughed at his own terrible jokes and considered himself a sort of suave and debonair airman, when he really wasn't. He was just odd. He was balding, but didn't wear it proudly, combing it over in wet, oily strands across his scalp. In the company of women, his poor sense of humour really came to the fore. He was now surrounded by three women. Puffing out his chest, he handed Halliday her drink.

"There you go, have a swill at that. Mixed it myself ... ha-ha! No, I didn't ... ha-ha! But enjoy that won't you." He finished, nodding to himself.

Knowing him far too well, the spiky haired Recalcitrance Bexley shook her head and gave it to him straight, "It's just a drink Andrew. It's not like she's in some sort of debt to you. You haven't done her some massive favour.

You have only made her feel like she has to stand here and listen to you waffle on while you tell your shitty jokes!"

Halliday hid a smile behind her glass and said nothing.

Lucretia laughed out loud. "Ha! She's got you pegged, hasn't she? Oh, how you ballooners struggle to be nice with mixes' in you!"

Snorting, Lucretia eyed Halliday's chest as she drained the rest of her glass. "So, Halliday how's your kill rate? Are you getting some flesh under those pretty nails? I notice your clock hasn't advanced much. Are you actually doing what you're supposed to do here in Sombre? You and that silly little horse you have down there ..."

"I quite like Wilder," Recalcitrance countered, "she's clever and her machinations have to be admired, if you must travel Sombre on land, she would be quite the companion."

Halliday smiled at the ballooner, "she is good and fast through The Byways as well. Never flinches."

"Never flinches?" Lucretia smiled darkly, "Oh, that's rich! She's a skittish thing, Halliday Knight! That would drive me batty. I see her run like a rabbit when I come anywhere near her." Lucretia sneered and clicked her fingers at Orty, "another, barkeep!" She burped. The ever-quiet barman slung a towel over his shoulder and fished out a tall glass.

Halliday sipped from her glass and watched Orty. To her, he always seemed sad. His big bald scone shone in the down lights, the ever-present white t-shirt hugging his soft and pudgy frame – his silver Beating Clock set to three. She wondered how he'd even managed the few strokes that he had? What possible trouble could a barkeeper get into that would cause a Mender re-build?

"You're low, Halliday, another one?"

"What?" Recalcitrance's offer caused her to look away.

"Oh, yes please." Halliday said without thinking, realizing she had been in a bit of a stupor just then. This was going to take her well beyond her standard five drinks, but that last one had tasted better than the ones before. She knew Orty wasn't suddenly doing a better job; her taste buds were just a little less fussy now. She accepted the drink and listened as the wildly annoying Lucretia St Aimes waxed on about her latest exploits. It was all getting hazy; all guns and revving motorcycles and kills, chopped up bodies, visits to the unappreciative Menders. Halliday hadn't needed to say anything, she just smiled and nodded while the Death-Witch leered at her and sipped her scotch. She was quite full of them. Too full.

She really needed to go to the toilet.

§

Hope woke up with a full bladder and a god-awful pain in the stomach. With blurry vision she looked over at her bedside clock - 3:20 - hideously early a.m. Still another 4 hours of sleep to go.

Swinging her legs out of bed she touched down on the carpet and stood up – feeling very giddy. "Damn!" she whispered. This had happened the other time Halliday had drunk herself under the table at The Ruptured Spleen. She stumbled to the door and switched on her light. Things were getting urgent, swinging the door open she ran for the bathroom across the hall.

Halliday Knight loved a drink way too much.

Chapter 6
A Disgruntled Horse and Girl on a Mission

Hope's stomach settled somewhat after peeing and she fell back asleep. And as always, her rite of passage picked up where she had left it.

Aunt Sophie's wedding nightmare had taken an unexpected turn.

The chapel had cleared. Everyone had left – or been removed. Hope was sitting cross-legged on the floor. Dark red bloody stains covered her dress. Her mother had done a thorough job on her.

She surveyed the state of the room. A bride and groom shaped singe-mark stained the carpet next to her, a horrible, coagulated black. Slippery looking blood covered the pews. Crumpled burnt flowers were scattered everywhere. The fires were petering.

Hope was all that was left.

She felt guilty, as if the whole massacre was her fault somehow. How was that fair? Kate was the cause of all this! Her damn sister had a mouthful of gasoline, for god sake! Spat it at the bride and groom! She was the first to start stabbing everyone!

Feeling incredibly sorry for herself, she peered down at her dress again and cleared her throat. Her mother had told her that this was what happened when you didn't stay clean. Right now, she felt very unclean. Is that what she had meant by that? And why did it even matter? This was a nightmare, just a nightmare. Like some discarded, larger than life flower-girl horror doll, she sat alone in a burnt-out wedding chapel soaked in blood. None of this was real. It was a bad dream. Yet the guilt still gnawed at her.

At the front of the chapel a door slammed. There was whispering in the foyer - maniacal. *"She's unclean. Unclean! Unclean that one ... What to do with the unclean? What to do with the unclean? Unclean! Cleanse the unclean!"*

Hope began sobbing uncontrollably.

Someone was coming.

∫

"Wilder, come here! You willful, cow!"

Halliday stood at the bottom of The Unexplained Mountain and called for her generally faithful Machanihorse. She was more than a little bit drunk and Wilder knew it.

"Oh, how we judge though, don't we!"

There was a snort from somewhere behind the parked balloons and speed trucks. The machanihorse wasn't coming. Halliday could picture her standing there, judging her - so could her Other-selves apparently,

"You need to not drink so much, Hope's Halliday! I could hold my scotch!"

"Wilder always loved me, drunk or sober!"

"Tell her you'll have Hamish give her an oil-bath. She hates those."

"They are good for her though. She can be such a stubborn thing."

"Whatever ... she'll bloody well come when I call her," Halliday said mostly to herself. She sucked in air through her teeth and strutted with purpose through a shadowy laneway of Gatherer vehicles.

She found her aggravated horse standing under the sole tree.

Wilder was tall - 19 hands. Her machinations were impressive, gear and cog-work at each shoulder and knee-joint. Her long face was part-metal armour, part equine. Three glass gauges sat just beneath the Beating Clock at her chest – measuring her oil, her steam and her petroleum levels. Her coat was shiny Buckskin, black legs and silvery black mane. She was all horse, yet she was all machine as well. She snorted and stomped her left hoof at the ground on seeing her master.

Halliday couldn't stifle a smile, "Ah, Wilder, be nice please. I have only had a few drinks – I will ride you well, I promise." Tying her blond locks in a make-do ponytail, she approached and the machanihorse stood still for her, with stubborn obedience. She mounted the mare and sheathed her sword in the saddle's holder. She kept her Remington on her hip.

"So where are we to wander while we wait? Maybe Sombre has forgotten us, eh?" Halliday mused giving Wilder a small kick in the side.

The two were only metres from the parking lot when Halliday's thoughts were invaded. "My nag, I spoke too soon ..." Her body went rigid in the saddle as she held her head. Wilder stopped and waited while her master received her orders.

Halliday spoke aloud, "Hmm ... there is a Nightmarer in The Hills, girl. Not our favorite part of Sombre by a long way, I know, but we shall make the best of it, yes?"

Wilder leapt into action. Halliday held tight to the reins as the machanihorse turned in a gallop and charged from the clearing, steam blowing from her nostrils, shoulder gears whizzing and spinning from her intricate inner piston-work.

"Faster you lagger!" Halliday shouted with drunken thrill.

Reaching The Unexplained Mountain's dusty outskirts, the atmosphere warped and the two slipped into The Byway.

ʃ

The Byway was Sombre with its volume set at its loudest. It screamed. It invaded the senses.

Infinite and immense; The Byway was a Gatherer's greatest tool – an ethereal path through Sombre's great nightmare machine. Solid road at its surface and an ever-altering sky above. Every city and town - and the miscreants and killers that filled them - flashed by, hundreds at a time, with a strobe light flicker. The Byway could be ran through, flown through and driven through, and in Halliday and Wilder's case, *ridden* through ... at a ridiculously high speed.

Halliday had regretted calling her machanihorse a lagger. The mare seemed to want to go faster. She felt every drink she'd just had at The Ruptured Spleen threaten to make way to the surface in a very undignified way. The constant barrage of imagery and white noise made her head spin. She shut her eyes, "Uggghhh!"

The Byway vanished suddenly and gave way to darkness. Wilder slid to an abrupt stop, and Halliday was thrown forward, grappling for her mare's mane.

Feeling giddy and extremely ill, she sat upright in the saddle and breathed deeply, "Good god." She eased herself off and touched down on a muddy slope near the foot of The Hills. "Well, I definitely received my come-uppance then, didn't I."

With her hands on her hips, she swallowed down another wave of nausea. She walked around the machanihorse a few times in a bid to recover.

An indignant Wilder stood perfectly still.

"Bleeding judgy thing, you are ..."

She puffed the cold air and peered up at The Hills. Not that she could see a great deal of anything. Night was only going to make this mission harder. She knew she had to move. Time was running out for her Nightmarer.

"A couple more burps and I shall be good to go."

She wondered what poor unfortunate had landed here this time. She had found all kinds in the past: postmen, cashiers, makeup artists, good for nothing lay-a-bouts, drug addicts, town drunks – she had just found a policeman. Whether they were these people in their waking lives or not was anyone's guess. That was who they were in Sombre.

She was ready. "Okay, my nag. Let's go find our troubled dreamer, eh?"

Picking a way up through the trees, Halliday and Wilder set off. The 'phwssh, phwssh, click - phwssh, phwssh click,' of Wilder's shoulder and knee mechanisms, along with the cracking of twigs under her hooves, held a lone clarity.

The Hills were ominously quiet.

"Has our target already perished, I wonder?" she thought aloud.

Halliday's machanihorse just snorted, shook and nodded her head.

"Negative nag, aren't you? Ha! Check your mood! I had to take time to settle myself down back there, Wilder, or I may have been sick all over your neck! I did you a good turn!" Halliday said pulling her Remington from the saddle holster, "it is quiet though."

There was a howl in the distance. Followed by an ugly chorus of pitchy barking. "Ah, a pack, signs of life. That is encouraging."

With a steam-filled cough, Wilder ploughed through scrub and bramble, crossing makeshift paths. Halliday blindly ducked and weaved in the saddle, doing her utmost to avoid getting caught in the branches.

Human voices had joined the hunt above, guttural, with a mangy pitch – lots of 'wahoo's!' and yelping, cracking branches and general untidiness filled the air.

"Ah, the Whitely's, vile little gnomes! We shall have to be at our best, my Wilder."

One hand tightened on the rein, the other squeezed the gun resting across her hip and saddle. Suddenly, the echo from the Whitely's and their dogs seemed to be everywhere. The hunt was close.

"Whoever dreamt up these odd little strangers in the first place was a deeply disturbed individual, Wilder. You must agree?" Halliday said not expecting any sort of answer. She spoke to herself a lot in these situations. She felt in control. The alcohol in her system finally wearing off.

The machanihorse took a left turn with purpose and mounted a rough path. With another shot of nostril steam, Wilder went into a trot as new screaming pierced the air, unmistakably female.

"That would be our Nightmarer, Wilder. We might still have time! Quick, now – we can bring her in in one piece!" Halliday thrilled. For once, maybe she wasn't too late!

With another turn of speed, the two kept on in the direction of the discordance ahead; hungry shouts and barking canines - and screams from a nightmaring female.

The path elevated and the wood darkened. Loose powdery dirt caused Wilder to fall into a jaunty trot. Eyes peeled; gun at the ready for the first sign of action, Halliday tasted the night's chill and licked her lips.

"Nothing, yet," she narrowed her eyes, "They will come, and we'll be bloody ready, my nag!"

Introducing themselves with phlegm coated barking and hacking, a pack of five dogs, sprinted around the corner. Even in the darkness, the black oily coats of the beasts shone. Ears were pinned back, snarling mouths housed yellowed fangs. There wasn't an eyeball between them; just empty cavities where their eyes should have been. Nightmare dogs.

"Stop!"

Wilder obeyed and Halliday jumped from the saddle, and instantly recoiled.

The smell of excrement was overwhelming,

"Oh, good lord, Wilder!"

She could handle blood and burning flesh – but poo she always had a terrible time with. "Oh, that's dreadful!" She covered her mouth and nose with one hand. The other had already drawn her sword. Learning from the devil imp's at Denivens Hell, she thought a sword would be more effective on creatures like these.

Yet she was losing her mettle, she actually felt faint.

She cough-cried, "Ugh! Why did it have to be poo? Bloody animals! You're all such ... such ... bloody animals!" The dogs circled, ready to pounce.

"Get a grip, Halliday!" She yelled at herself as she backed away. "But they've been rolling in poo! Probably their own!"

An Other-self chimed in with some helpful advice, *"Oh, good god, Hope's Halliday! Get on with it! Yes, we don't like poo. Just try not to get your hands on them, or your clothes. Don't let them touch your skin at all. If you miss with the blade, just kick them with your boots."*

Wilder had scampered up the hillside to clear the way.

The five mangy creatures lunged.

Gritting her teeth, sword strong in her hands, Halliday slashed with sharp short strokes, taking the heads of two. Almost dancing in her bid for avoidance, she kicked another away with her size 8 boot and rammed her sword through the gaping jaw of its friend.

"Wilder, I haven't been touched! Not yet! Faeces free!" Halliday chimed loudly, as the last dog bolted straight for her legs. She jumped just in time. Changing tack, she ran straight for the creature as it kicked up the dirt and came at her. She lunged and lopped the head off and skillfully side stepped to avoid any touching on the follow-thru.

Wilder was already at her side and she mounted the mare in a second. Charging around the bend, the terrain descended and dipped into a small gulch. "Whoa, girl!" Halliday pulled on the rein.

The scene was almost comical in its simplicity.

The Nightmarer was up a tree. A few dozen Whitely's and their eyeless dogs were at the foot of the tree. They wanted her down. She didn't want to come down. They weren't the greatest climbers. Podgy little bodies with stumpy legs and arms, on the surface the Whitely's wouldn't have qualified as the most intimidating of Sombre's citizen's. Men and women alike, their clothing and bodies were impossibly dirty. Mucky faces wore crooked, mostly toothless scowls.

But Halliday knew them as dangerous trash of the highest order. Hungry types – hungry for a kill. All carried an array of hunting knives. She was fairly sure cannibalism would be frowned upon by The Menders – and equally sure the Whitely's couldn't have given a flying toss about such things. This girl in the tree was in trouble and destined for a stewing pot in some Whitely hollow in these very hills.

Feet on shoulders, the Whitely's were forming an awkward looking ladder. The tree was a high one. Without a protruding branch to be seen as any way up, Halliday couldn't help but wonder how the girl had managed to get up there in the first place? "She climbed that tree like a monkey, Wilder!" she stated with awe.

She could make out a white and red striped skirt, matching socks and white trainers – for some completely inexplicable reason, the colours the girl wore looked familiar. "Hmm, we need a plan, my nag," she rubbed her chin. "The only way I think I'll be able to get up there is by standing on your back ... she will be untrusting for sure ... I will need to introduce us properly."

Her attention went to the Whitely ladder. "And I am sure I will need to shoot some of the dirty little things. Make a statement they will understand."

"Don't belittle the Whitely's. If you shoot even one, Hope's Halliday, the rest will come at you so fast, you won't have time to pull the trigger," said one Other-self.

"Protect your horse, Halliday. I would have always thought of Wilder," another chimed in.

"The dirty little urchins you have here will chop each of Wilder's legs off at the knees."

"I know all of this! I *have* dealt with them before!" she said shaking her head. Although they were all valid points. She was running out of time. The Whitely ladder was working. Blades were being stabbed into the trunk for a better a hold.

Curiously, the girl didn't seem overly frightened.

"Ha! Good for her ..." Halliday muttered.

Opting to not shoot until she absolutely had to, Halliday made her way with Wilder, down into the gulch.

Chapter 7
Badly Spoken Negotiations

The eyeless dogs bolted toward Halliday and Wilder as if possessed; snarling, teeth gnashing, flicking gulch mud. Halliday leapt out of the saddle splashing putrid water up her dress. 'Halt!" She bellowed and fired a warning shot into the air - which didn't stop the dogs whatsoever.

She pulled her sword and decapitated the first of the dirty creatures. Lunging protectively in front of her machanihorse she rammed the blade in through the mouth of another, skewering it.

"Here!" She shoved the sword further through the canine, slammed it down, piercing it into the mud. It sat upright on its protrusion, a putrid piece of hairy butchery. She hoped this would make a statement, a showing of strength. A Gatherer had come to call!

The rest of the dogs stopped and sniffed the fallen member of their pack. It seemed to have worked.

"Hello!" Halliday said almost brightly, smacking her hands together.

Every Whitely in the gulch turned, the tree-ladder toppled, the little men and women fell confidently to their feet, with extremely well-practiced mud awareness. They walked toward her, some snarling, some grinning hungrily. Halliday noticed the Beating Clock faces at their chests were so covered in mud they were unreadable.

"I've come for the Nightmarer," she announced with a tone full of business. The gulch fell quiet. Halliday noticed the girl in the tree had pulled herself on to an outer branch for a better look. Again, the red and white of her skirt looked so familiar.

A woman-Whitely spoke first, her throat impossibly phlegm-filled.

"Aw, 'ave ya, garl? Dat's nass, dat as'." She licked her lips.

"Oh, dear, what did you just say?" Halliday had forgotten how woeful their speech was. There was more to come, a grinning man-Whitely spoke next.

"Aw, di' ya thunk ya'd juss' cawm'n un ere' and stub us awl wiv yaw' blaad! Gaw'an wit ya'!"

Laughter was had all round as every one of The Hill's native's lifted their dirty half blades. Halliday stood on the dog's carcass and pulled her sword from its impaling. The other dogs continued to sniff the dead one as it slumped to the mud.

Eyeing the large group warily, she cleared her throat,

"I am Gatherer, Halliday Knight," she announced officiously, "I will be taking the Nightmarer whether you like it or not, of course you all know this. I would like her unscathed. I would also like to avoid any of *your* bloodshed." She twisted the sword in her hands and added, "This can be easy, or this can be hard." She looked into the tree and added forthrightly, "You haven't been able to reach her, have you? This has a lot to do with your stature – you are all very little. You are all little, tiny people."

With that last observation, she realized she'd probably said too much. An offended sounding murmur went through the group and they all walked toward her.

"Nowt we git er'!" said one.

"Froogin smar wun ont cha!" said another Whitely.

"Er nug'll cuck naass et' wull!" one grinned hungrily.

She thought that last threat was directed at her horse. "I haven't understood much of what any of you have said as your speech is quite poor," Halliday announced eyeing the bloodthirsty throng with caution. She wasn't feeling particularly brave - she was hopelessly outnumbered. Some of the dogs had returned to their masters with renewed pluck and begun snarling at her.

Another gluttonous few peeled away from the action, mouths full of dog-coat, dragging their slain companion off to feast.

Halliday backed away protectively covering her machanihorse, she feared for Wilder's legs – that's where they would hit first. Wilder wasn't all machinations, there was still plenty of flesh and bone to cut or chew through. Reaching over her shoulder, she grabbed her Remington from the saddle. She now held her sword in her left hand, gun in her right. Her gun would auto-load for her – she had bullets for all of them, and she was a good shot with one arm. Resting it on her hip, she was as ready as she could be.

'Hope's Halliday, you have to avoid bringing The Morphia into this. Keep your resolve for once,' reminded an Other-self.

'Wilder will bolt, you know she will!' said another Other-self.

"I bloody well know that!" she snapped. "You all obviously think I'm stupid!"

At the sight of the gun there were a few apprehensive expressions among the Whitely's. A woman with a reasonably clean clock face (that Halliday noticed stroked at seven) piped up, "She canna showt' ows ull! Arsays' we git er'!"

A dog snapped at Wilder's shin and her mare whinnied.

"Don't let them get your horse!" the girl Nightmarer in the tree yelled unhelpfully.

The Whitely's pressed, all slapping the short blades in their palms, all agreeing with what the woman Whitely had just said. They were about to try and jump her.

There was no way to avoid bloodshed – she would be in massive trouble with The Menders for this. Nerves on edge, she shot the Remington and blew a Whitely head clean off from the shoulders. A dog ran for Wilder, and with a fast sword strike she lopped the head off the creature before it had a chance to sink its teeth in to her mare's leg.

"UUUUAAARRRGGGHHHH!!!" the unified war-cry filled the gulch and she was set upon. She and Wilder backed away as she fired. Heads exploded and holes were torn into guts with the close fire from the Remington. The Whitely's had just one fighting technique - hack and slash with their blades – and Halliday felt a few stabs at her middle and legs. "Nothing a decent mending won't fix, Wilder! Take a few paces back, horse! Give me some firing room!" she said relishing the task at hand. Wilder obeyed her master and scuttled backward up the gulch's slope. A dog tried to follow.

"Ah, no you don't you dreadful poo-soaked stinker!" Copping a few extra flesh wounds because of it, Halliday turned her back on the battle and swung her sword. Lopping its head off cleanly, the dog dropped. Spinning on one foot, she kicked an attacker, then kneed a bunch of Whitely's off her person, firing in quick succession, decimating the pack. She'd cut the Whitely's down by two thirds. Bodies carpeted the dirt. She was hurting; she felt at least a dozen stab wounds. But she was standing.

"Relent and call off your dogs! Or the rest of you will fall the same way!"

"Ruhn! Git ower ere! She's froogin' maah!"

Grabbing their eyeless dogs by their filthy scruffs the Whitely's did relent – scurrying away like scared rabbits.

She had dazzled herself. This was a relatively clean mission! Sure, there were copious amounts of bodies scattered all around her, both canine and Whitely alike, bloodstains on her dress aplenty ... but the Nightmarer was in one piece.

"Come Wilder. Let's see who we have here."

Halliday and her machanihorse stepped across the carnage and made their way to the trunk. Wide eyed, the girl glared down at her. Halliday couldn't tell if those eyes read scared or incredibly peeved. Again, the white and red of her skirt and socks seemed so familiar to her. The girls face was wet with sweat and her mouth was dirty. Long strawberry blond hair was in tangles. Halliday was sure the uniform was that of a cheerleader's. A real cheerleader or a dreamt cheerleader, she couldn't tell, and it didn't really matter in Sombre.

"You there," Halliday hollered, "I am your Gatherer, your rescuer."

"Are you? Where in the hell am I? What's going on? I'm asleep. This is all some bullshit dream, isn't it?" The girl said with a mouthful of attitude.

"Hmm. So, you're not scared, you're angry. Interesting ..." Halliday said a mite curious. The girl seemed quite an awful type.

"I *was* scared. Now I'm pissed off! I want out of here. Where in the hell am I anyway?"

"You're in Sombre. I'm a Gatherer, and I'm taking you to The Menders. I'll probably not see you again after that, well, maybe I will, but only by chance ... but not as you are now, I'm rambling ... I must apologize." She laughed the giddy laugh of success. "It's just not very often I find my target in one piece!" Halliday rubbed her hands together, "anyway, do you think you can jump?"

The girl looked at her incredulous, "Are you kidding?"

"Well, you did get up there."

"I was being chased. I just sort of ... just got up here somehow. I'm not sure I should even go anywhere with you."

Quite taken aback at the girls attitude; Halliday had heard enough, she turned around and Wilder stepped to her. "Yes, well you ruddy well have to! I'm coming up now. Stay where you are."

She climbed Wilder and stood on her back like a circus performer, with her left hand on the trunk for balance, she'd reached high enough to touch the girl's white trainers. The girl moved them.

Halliday held out her free hand, she blew a wisp of fringe from her face, "Okay. Here I am. Please make this easy. Come now. What is your name, girl?"

"Parker," she said and added, "This doesn't look very safe."

Halliday raised her brow, "You know, Parker, I must tell you that you were going to be sliced open and cooked by the Whitely's - those little ferrety men and women that trapped you up here - that's what they do to every Nightmarer. Just let yourself go, Wilder and I will break your fall."

Parker shifted forward in the crook of the tree. "Okay, but where am I again? Why do I feel like all this is real? Jesus! You've been stabbed a lot! And what's with all the clocks in your chests?"

"Let's just do this first ... give me your hand, come on now, before you fall and break your neck – it would just be my luck." Halliday grabbed her wrist and pulled. Parker fell headfirst. Halliday dropped to the saddle and slapped a bracing hand on the girl's back as she landed on Wilder.

"Grab her mane. She can take it!" Halliday let out a spirited, "Woo-Hoo!"

Parker was draped across Wilder's shoulders on her front like a sack of wheat. Halliday planted her free hand at the girls back.

"This is a wonder, Parker! You are my first unscathed Nightmarer!" She gave Wilder a spirited kick in the sides, "Come on my nag. Let's get this one to the Office'!" With a snort and a rush of steam from her nostrils, Wilder trotted with spirit, up and out of the gulch.

Parker began to wriggle around. "Jesus, bitch! You still haven't answered any of my questions! What's with you?"

"I shall ignore your poor attitude, Parker – I am in too good a mood." Halliday looked down at the girls cheerleading uniform; the colours were still so familiar to her. "So, are you a cheerleader in your waking life, Parker? I am curious. This outfit of yours, I feel like I have seen it before."

50

Parker tried lifting her head. "Yeah, I cheer' so ...? God, can I at least sit up in the saddle? This is so uncomfortable!"

"Oh, woops! I do apologize!" Halliday pulled on the rein, "Whoa, Wilder. Yes, of course! I am so used to dead ones; I forgot that live ones get uncomfortable!" She hopped down and helped Parker get seated.

She stood peering up at the cheerleader. She was a very pretty thing this girl. A good pouty mouth of full lips, high and strong cheek bones – striking eyes with fat lashes.

"What?"

"There is something about you ... I'm quite sure I haven't seen you before – there is no way I could have," Halliday tapped her lip. "Oh well, it may come to me, it may not." Halliday mounted Wilder again, and they were off.

"So, am I dead?" Parker said from behind as she held onto Halliday's waist. "Did I die in my sleep?"

"No, I don't think so. I really don't think that happens very often. This is a world for troubled sleepers. You would've had to have had quite a nightmare to get here, though. You will now be a citizen of Sombre. To what degree, and who you will ultimately become here, will be completely up to the absolute power that is Sombre." This was a spiel Halliday hadn't used often, but she had prepared, nevertheless.

Parker fell quiet, she seemed to have nothing else to say for the moment.

With much puffing and snorting, Wilder steered them off the path and down into the dark bramble. They made their descent. With satisfaction, Halliday called out to Sombre.

"Halliday Knight. I am done. I have the Nightmarer. Please bring The Funneling."

The shimmering silver light of The Funneling appeared at the bottom of the hill. Bursting out from within; an eight door, eight wheeled, carrier-truck started its climb up the mountain, crunching through the terrain. A Mender clean-up crew in full bodied protective clothing sat in the vehicle's few seats, wearing grim expressions. The driver veered the flatbed vehicle out of Halliday's path as they passed.

"Oh, they look unhappy," Halliday said stating the obvious. She felt Parker grip her waist tighter as Wilder suddenly went into a gallop; dodging and jumping the rough terrain like an expert mountain equine, snorting and puffing steam, gear-work clicking with precision.

"This isn't a normal horse is it?" Parker yelled out at her back.

Halliday thought the girl sounded quite thrilled. "No, Wilder is an amazing mixed bag of bolts and body bits, aren't you girl? Hold on, Parker. The Funneling is quite the rush!"

"YAH!" A very pleased Halliday yelled as the three hit the brilliant light at speed and left The Hills.

CHAPTER 8
Seen Her Before

Hope stood in the shower, yawning.

Halliday's victorious capturing of an unscathed Nightmarer had taken its toll. The hot water felt good, but not really good enough. As she gently washed her skin, she could feel every point where the Whitely's had stabbed their knives into Halliday's body, like a form of internal bruising. Her neck felt like it had been wrenched.

All of Halliday's fast twists and turns had messed with her muscles – she just wasn't that fit.

Taking in a mouthful of water and swishing it round, she thought of the cheerleading uniform that Nightmarer, Parker, had worn. Centurion High colours. The Centurion Sparks – rich, fit and pretty elitists, standing on the top rung of the school's social ladder, looking down at everyone with pretty sneers.

"Coincidence," she said as she spat out the water. She tried to recall Nightmarer-Parker's face and found she couldn't. She remembered the hair; tangled, strawberry blond. The chance that Parker the cheerleader would be someone at all was a longshot. Sombre was a nightmare world, very vivid, but imaginary. More than a fair chance Parker didn't exist anywhere at all.

Hope shut off the taps and reached for a towel. Stepping out she dried her face, then saw her reflection in the mirror. Was the left side of her face yellow? She wrapped the towel around her and got closer for another look. It looked like a bruise! A bruise that covered half her face – "Shit!" She rubbed her hands down her cheek. She looked sick! Was she getting sick? The yellow then crept over her whole face. She cried out. "No! No! No!" She shut her eyes and breathed, "Calm, Hope. Keep calm. You're just tired."

She opened her eyes again.

The yellow was gone.

∫

Hope sat on Centurion sports field's plastic seating, up high in the back row, and ate her lunch alone. The cafeteria wasn't a great place for her generally, and it was a nice day anyway. The sun felt good on her skin. She looked out over the field and watched the coach of the football team set up for practice. Her first two periods hadn't been very successful. Both Social Studies and Economics had papers due, which she had completely forgotten to get started on. Sombre was messing with her life majorly.

Pento was at the core of the problem, she was sure of it. She had only begun dreaming of Sombre since the Kelley's had moved here. Was this her minds way of coping with change? Coping with loneliness? Escape to a freaky fantasy land every night? Beat herself up in her sleep? It wasn't like she had ever had many friends anywhere else she had lived. Maybe she needed to see a shrink? Seeing yourself as some yellow ghoul in the mirror couldn't be good.

She knew she had to combat the tiredness somehow. She took another bite of her chicken and lettuce sandwich – it tasted as papery as the paper it was wrapped in. Should she hit the energy drinks? They were meant to give you a kick in the ass. Her father hated them (didn't really fit the Health&Co ethos). Her mother snuck them occasionally. Hope might have to do the same. Nicotine was meant to help you keep alert as well – cigarettes probably weren't the way to go, though. Not really the image and life choice she wanted for herself. Her Aunt Josie in Wisconsin, her father's younger sister, had just been diagnosed with emphysema – her breathing 'rattled like a bitch, and she coughed like a backfiring Oldsmobile' (her father's analogy, not hers).

54

Thinking a few cans of Rockstar might be the go, she put her sandwich down and rested her chin on her palms. Her attention was drawn to the left side gate of the arena. The cheer team entered for some lunch time practice. Hope's heart rate elevated, she wasn't about to miss this opportunity. She was looking for a cheerleader called Parker. It was a long shot - *the longest.* Worth a look though.

Leaving her bag and lunch, spy-like, she ducked and covertly made her way down to the front for a better view. She sat on the second row of seating, bent over she made herself as small as she could.

The Centurion Sparks walked across the field in signature training tops, full of purpose, chatting and giggling. Their voices carried. Hope could hear a little of what they were saying – which wasn't much of anything. Ponytails high, the fourteen girls spread out into formation and the team's captain put a portable stereo on the ground. Echoic music sounded tinny in the arena, and Hope watched on as the Spark's hip swiveled and clapped and chanted 'team!'. It was all the usual cheerleader fare. Hope always failed to understand the point.

Her sister was destined to be a part of this vivacious bilge. Hope sighed.

Squinting she eyed each of the girl's faces. She counted five blondes, six brunettes, a red head - girl thirteen had dark braids and the other Hope couldn't really tell the colour of from this distance – it looked like lots of rinses of colour. "Like seaweed?" she muttered to herself. Trying to stay as inconspicuous as possible, she bent down further, peering over the front row. Her attention settled on the blondes - the captain and the other four in the row behind her. Throwing her arms in the air in frustration; and spouting an overly dramatic "STOP!" the captain killed the music mid cheer. "Well that was crap! What are we doing? We know this! We've got this! Let's do it again! I need to see hips!"

The music started and the team went through the routine again. They finished. "Okay, two minutes, take a break," she said. She looked to one of her blonde girls, "Parker, come here a minute, we need a cheer-chat."

Hope froze.

Parker.

The captain led her away from the group by the arm. The two began speaking in hushed tones. Parker looked down at the ground. The captain was angry. Parker was being served. Hope studied Parker's face. She did recognize her. She'd had an altercation with her just yesterday. 'Freak-zone' was the word used. Hope darkened at the memory.

Was it Parker from Sombre, though? There might be a resemblance? It *was* very dark in The Hills, and Halliday had been in a rush.

The two girls turned suddenly.

Cover blown - she had been spotted.

"Hey! Pervert! What're you looking at?" Hands on hips the captain paced toward Hope, with Parker following behind.

Hope got up to leave.

Hands on her hips, the captain scowled at her, she spoke quickly, her tone venomous. "Please, don't get up. You've come out to get some sun, you poor pale thing! Nothing like getting out in the daylight is there! I haven't seen you around. You're an import - you must be. What's your name?"

"She is an import," Parker confirmed studying Hope's face.

"Uh, sorry ... ah, I need to go," Hope said clearing her throat. Her stomach tight, she felt sick, she burped chicken sandwich.

"She's a rude little ghost, isn't she Parker," the captain said smiling.

Parker didn't answer. Her expression had changed to consternation; face rigid with anger, and if Hope didn't know better - fear?

"We are not used to strange imports like you leering at us. Can you please refrain from doing so? It is unnerving. Piss off! Get out of here! Or you'll get my cheer-foot in your ass!" the captain's eyes widened.

She meant it. Hope didn't know where to look. Parker kept watching her. What was she looking at?

The captain turned and left, "Parker, come on! You've been awful at best today. We need to practice."

Then Hope saw it.

A yellow shadow crept over Parker's face.

The same yellow she had seen in the mirror just this morning.

Had it been on her own again as well?

She couldn't breathe.

Suddenly, Parker the cheerleader looked like she was about to cry, "Uh!" she gasped.

Drawing her eyes away from Hope, she turned and paced toward her captain - rubbing her face and shaking her head. The rest of the Sparks were waiting, standing ready in formation.

Hope ran back up the steps, she grabbed her bag and dropped her lunch – she left it for the birds. Her body felt like it was made of ice. What just happened?

Chapter 9

Brave Hope

The rest of the day had been a write off for Hope.

English, her last period, was turning into a self-induced farce. She still hadn't read 'To Kill a Mockingbird.' Every class was going to be about the damned book as well. She was sure Miss Sparrows knew she hadn't read it. Each time she would ask the class a question about the text, she would look to Hope threateningly for the answer, then move on to someone else.

Hope hadn't even been able to get past the first chapter without the words sliding sideways and her dozing off. She would have to bring herself to read it somehow. She'd watched the film – but the questions related to the prose and word usage.

Although, the looming book report paled in comparison to what happened at lunch.

A clash of worlds.

Parker existed.

Now something had to happen.

But how would she approach her? The girl was a year older, and at least six tiers above her on the social scale. She recalled how haunted the cheerleader looked at the field. It was the sickly yellow. Parker had seen it on Hope's face too, she was sure of it. How could it have been anything else?

The night before, Parker had been rescued by Halliday Knight. It's not like Hope looked anything like Halliday. She snorted to herself at this,' ha!' Whatever the yellow was, what it meant, it seemed to just be for Hope, and now, Parker.

Mercifully the bell rang. As always, Hope waited for everyone to shuffle past her. Her teacher didn't seem to want to talk to her today. As early as it was in her first year at Centurion, maybe Miss Sparrows had given her new, partially blind student up for a lost cause? Hope gathered her books and left.

Entering the hall, she was mostly alone. No one hung around on Friday. Friday was like a prison break.

Shuffling along, she was in no rush. Her body was still Sombre-sore. "Halliday's a painful bitch," she said under her breath and laughed.

Afternoon light splayed through the windows that ran the length of the hall. She gazed toward her locker in the far corner and faltered. Parker the cheerleader was leaning on it. Bag draped over her shoulder; arms folded, the older girl was dressed in a short skirt and loose-fitting top, her long, strawberry blond locks were out, ensconcing her front - like a teenage lioness.

Hope looked down at the ground and walked toward the girl. The tapping sound of her footsteps seemed to be everywhere in the empty hall – just her, Parker the cheerleader and an echo.

"So? What is it? I woke up with it." Parker said.

What's what?" Hope answered with her head down, struggling to meet the girl's eyes. "How did you find my locker?" She was genuinely curious.

Parker wasn't about to indulge her. "Don't play fucking dumb with me, ghost! Your face has a yellow shadow thing. So's mine!" The taller girl took a step toward Hope. "What is it? Tell me! Is it a disease?"

Meeting the older girls tense glare with a meek one of her own, Hope answered, "No. I don't think so." She then blurted, "I saw you in Sombre!"

There.

She said it. It was brave, probably a bit stupid as well. How on earth could she know how Parker would react? She regretted it instantly. Fidgeting with her glasses, she looked down at the ground again.

Pushing off from the locker door, Parker took a step toward her, "Stop looking at the ground! You-you cagey thing! What did you just call it?"

"Sombre," Hope said looking straight into Parker's eyes.

Parker's hands made fists. She gave Hope a look filled with venom. "This shit better stop! That's all I know! I'm not like you, ghost!"

"Hope," Hope said her voice breaking.

"Yeah, whatever," she said and walked away. Holding her breath, Hope faced her locker and waited until she heard Parker force the exit door open, swear something terrible, and leave.

ſ

"Profits are up but can still be improved on. I think we'll be in Pento for the foreseeable future," Devan Kelley announced at dinner as if he were addressing a table full of shareholders. Hope's father had a handsome face, a strong square jaw. A Californian fit guy – embodying the Health&Co brand and ethos to a tee.

"That's nice dear," Evelyn Kelley said swallowing a mouthful of beef curry, "profits are always good." She took a sip of her wine. "So, how were your day's girls? Are we both on top of our homework?"

"Haven't got any," Kate said picking at her bowl of curry with disinterest. "When are we going to have something nice for dinner?"

"Whatever do you mean my child? This is from our 'Elite Eat' range," Devan said wiping his mouth on a napkin.

"She means fries and greasy chicken," Hope said. She wasn't particularly enjoying hers either. She swore she could taste the plastic packaging the meal came in.

Evelyn shook her head and shrugged. "None of that type of food until your sisters face clears up, Kate."

Hope shut her eyes and swallowed. She didn't love having it pointed out, but there was nothing she could say in her defence, really. Her face *was* bad at the moment. She opened her eyes and took another mouthful of the plastic tasting curry.

"Wonder if we can get some hormone drugs from the doctors?" Evelyn thought aloud and added, "I think I might have been on them for a time when I was mid-teen and a hormonal mess."

"Is Hope a hormonal mess?" Kate snorted, "Ha!"

"It's nothing to be laughed at, Kate. Your sister is going through all sorts of changes – and she's at the peak of that hill at the moment. It helps if she eats right," Devan said, "drinks a lot of water. It might help with her obvious tiredness and energy levels as well."

"Is everyone done talking about me?!" Hope said throwing her fork down. "I feel like a test subject! None of you guys know what I'm going through!"

"We do, Hope. Well, I do," her mother said smugly, sipping her wine. "Breathe, dear... I think maybe we look into some strong contact lenses for you. Pretty you up a bit. You look puffier than you need to in those glasses. You were such a beautiful toddler."

"She needs to meet a boy. Everyone her age has a boyfriend. She needs to wear makeup and cover up the pimples. That's what Angie's sister does – she has a boyfriend, he plays basketball," Kate said pushing her fork around in her meal, scowling at the curry as if the meal held the answer to everything that was wrong with the world.

"Heavy makeup's no good for the complexion, blocks the pores. That will just cause more – she definitely doesn't need *more*," Hope's mother frowned and added, "and let's not worry about a boyfriend at the moment. Just a friend or two would be a good start."

"I think we should all stop talking about my first born now," said Devan scrolling through endless emails on his phone. "This is only a stage for her."

"What, dad? My ugly stage? Have you all had enough of a go at me now! Jesus!" Hope said and pushed herself out from the table. "I don't sleep well! I'm tired all the time! Don't you think that has something to do with my *obvious* ugliness?"

"Hormones," her mother said calmly, "can affect your sleep."

"Do we take her to see someone?" said her father.

"Yes, the optometrist for some contacts. A psychologist for everything else," said her mother. "Please don't call yourself ugly, Hope. You are not. We are only concerned for you."

"The glasses suck sister."

Hope had heard enough. "Can I be excused please? ... I'm just going to be excused."

"I'll book some appointments in the morning. We'll make it all better, darling," Evelyn Kelly said taking another mouthful of wine.

"Love you, beautiful," her father called out after her as she left the dining room.

"Don't call me that, dad. You don't mean it."

∫

It was a typically dead Friday night for Hope Kelley ... a shower, a bar of Toblerone and a movie. 'Christine,' from her beloved Stephen King collection played on her little flat screen. She had worshipped every book and movie the horror god had made since she was eight. No one else in the family liked scary films, which delighted her to no end. She watched on intently as Arnie the bespectacled skinny geek, creepily caressed and whispered to the duco of the '58 Plymouth.

The nastily pretty face of Parker the cheerleader appeared in her thoughts. They would never be friends. She was fairly sure that Sombre's new strange, joint-gift of a yellow facial shadow, wouldn't make a bit of difference. And Parker seemed truly awful anyway. If Hope had an actual 'type' of friend, Parker the stuck-up cheerleader wouldn't be it. Why was Sombre giving them both this link to each other? Did she really want to share Sombre? She had wished it would leave her so many times. Sombre was messed up. It was a bad place. It hurt. For all she knew, it could kill her in her sleep!

But it was hers. For some, probably perversely dark, self-hating reason, she wanted the nightmare world just for herself. Being Hope's Halliday gave her some sort of identity. She didn't have a whole lot of anything else. Why should she share it? She knew she wasn't meant to, but she felt real sympathy for Arnie – Christine was *his* Sombre – she was no good for him, but she was his.

Yawning, blinking her heavy eyelids, Hope watched until the credits rolled.

She switched the TV off and fell asleep.

CHAPTER 10
COLONEL. EM CONTUSION

Like always, sleep brought everything flooding back, playing on like a serial.

The nightmare, Hope's rite of passage into Sombre, picked up right where it had left off. Now she was crawling commando-style on her front across the carpet of the empty wedding chapel. She sobbed uncontrollably. Her pain was excruciating. The knife cuts in her gut; the cuts her own mother had dealt her, pulled and ripped with each movement. She was making her way to the foyer, toward the voices. They were getting louder.

"She's unclean, unclean! We cleanse the unclean! Hope, the unclean!"

The dark foyer beckoned. She had to see who they were. *Why* was she so unclean? This infuriated her - even in her current abhorrent state.

She stopped. Suddenly there were hands at her back; she felt spidery fingers run up and down, searching underneath the material of her dress, nails clawing her flesh. She shuddered bodily and rolled over and over, smashing into the pews to her left and right. The fingers stopped. The pain was unbearable. She couldn't move – could only lay there with her nose pressing the carpet. Her back felt wet, really wet. With horror she realized she was soaking the carpet with her own blood. Her back had been torn apart.

"You're so unclean." It was her mother's voice, hate filled. Close. She looked up.

The pointy toe of a white stiletto kicked her in the eye.

Ş

Halliday sat aboard Wilder, Parker the cheerleader at her back, clutching her waist. The great machanihorse walked them toward the double wooden doors of The Office of The Menders. "The Funneling has taken you down a peg or two, hasn't it." Halliday said with a knowing smirk.

"Huh!" Parker let go of Halliday straight away and sat up. "You suck, woman. I want out of here ... and off this smelly nag, now!"

"Ah, again with the attitude, you are an affected one, aren't you, Parker the cheerleader. I think they'll mend you very darkly, child. In just a few seconds you will have precisely half of what you are asking for."

Wilder pushed through the doors and the trio entered.

Sombre's one and only mending station was in a state of citizen overflow. Every bit of bench space taken. Bodies lined the walls, some on trolleys, others were slumped on the hard-wooden floor, bleeding under white sheets.

"The Office' is quite the raw meat market at the moment," Halliday observed and jumped down from Wilder.

An awestruck Parker followed, "My god! What is this place? This is a horror movie!"

"A horror movie? Oh, no, that is where you are wrong! This is a place of healing. It is a little unsavoury at first glance, I'll grant you that," Halliday said, "and busier than usual." She spotted the chief Mender with his hands wrist deep in the chest cavity of a scarlet coloured beast, "You-Hoo there, Hamish! Look what I have for you!" She grabbed Parker's wrist and pulled her arm up in the air.

"Ow! Let go of me, bitch!" Parker pulled her hand away. "Touch me again and you'll get a slap!"

"She's a foul-mouthed creature, Hamish! But in one piece!" Halliday announced and added triumphantly, "Job done!"

Wiping his bare hands on a wet towel, Hamish walked toward Halliday and Parker. Halliday recoiled. "Don't you wear gloves, Hamish?"

"No," was the short reply. He was smiling. "The work is too intricate. Gloves slip."

"Oh, right," Halliday said staring at the Mender's hands, "that's quite unpleasant."

"It can be ..." he agreed. His attention went straight to Parker. "So, Parker Wright, welcome to Sombre. Halliday has brought you to me in one piece. Good."

"W-What are you going to do with me?" the tall cheerleader said. "How do you know my name?"

"I was told."

"By who? This is all a nightmare isn't it? A fucking bad one..." she said looking around the Office.

"She's a terrible swearer, Hamish," Halliday interjected shaking her head.

Hamish smiled, "It is *sort* of a nightmare. You'll see soon enough, Parker."

He turned to Halliday. "Guess what, Halliday?"

"What?"

"You're going to watch Parker's transformation."

Halliday had no interest in this.

"Ungrateful swine-child, no-" she looked Parker up and down, then turned to Hamish. "Actually, no, I'm off to have a drink at The Ruptured Spleen, Hamish ... not to mention a bit of a brag. I brought you a whole one, after all." She peered down at her front, "I could do with a new dress and a dab on the stabs ... I will be off after that, though. Thanking you for the very unappealing offer all the same."

Hamish gave her a look she had never seen from him before. Was it dread?

"Sorry to do this to you, Halliday, but no, you are to stay. I'll clean you up and give Wilder an oil bath ... she likes those."

"What's this transformation you're all talking about?" Parker asked, eyes darting between the two, "What's going on? When am I going to wake up from this crazy shit?"

Hamish ignored her and continued to stare at his Gatherer. "Hope's Halliday, this is Parker Wright. You're about to become quite a big part of Parker's existence here in Sombre."

Halliday lowered her eyes and her tone, "Whatever do you mean, Hamish. I'm not a damned babysitter!"

"If you recall, the last time we met, we spoke of a higher calling for you. Parker here is where it starts."

He placed a hand at the middle of Parker's back, "come with me please."

"Get your hands off me, leech!" the cheerleader threw an elbow out. Hamish caught it and held it tight – Parker's face paled. A business-like Hamish turned to Halliday. "Follow me, please."

With a gulp, Halliday followed the Mender.

ʃ

Eyes wild, Parker was swearing like a petulant foul-mouthed child as Hamish jabbed a needle into the enlarged vein in her jugular. The girl shut her eyes and fell limp.

"Thank Sombre for that!" Halliday said as she watched on. "So, what is this all about, Hamish? Why do I need to watch?"

Hamish rifled under the bench for implements. "You are Hope Kelley's Halliday Knight. You know this much. You have probably never thought about what it truly means, though ... I'm sure this girl has appeared familiar to you?"

"Yes, this cheerleader uniform – the red and white. I had wondered if it had something to do with Hope of the waking world."

"Well, you wondered correctly," Hamish concurred.

Laying his leather tool pouch out along the bench, he pulled a four-inch blade. What followed could only be described as professional surgical sadism. Halliday looked on in horrified wonder as skin was stripped from the chest, peeled away like a jacket. Parker's ribcage was incised, the Mender cut skillfully through vital ventricles and arteries and the perfectly healthy heart was dropped into a 'wet' bag. Her ribcage was then cut open wider still. A Beating Clock was slid across the bench by a fellow Mender.

"Thank you, Iris."

Hamish placed the gold timepiece in the centre of Parker's chest with practiced precision. The Beating Clock emanated light and the cavity was suddenly glowing.

"The witchery!" Halliday exclaimed as valves and arteries to the left and right began to fuse with the device, crawling like electrically animated worms - the lightest of beating could be heard. Hamish leant down and put his ear on the face of the glass. "That's working well."

"This is quite appalling to watch, Hamish. Again, why is it that I need to see this?"

"Sombre would like you to understand the significance of the work that goes into a citizen - particularly this citizen. This is Parker from Centurion High – Hope Kelley's school in the waking world. You are to be her guardian here in Sombre."

"What? You are kidding me! I told you before, I am not a babysitter!" Halliday backed away from the table. "No, no sir! I'm a bloody Gatherer, Hamish! This is an injustice of the highest order!"

"No one said you would have to stop gathering, Halliday," Hamish said evenly as he dealt with the lightshow going on in Parker's chest. "Now please come here and watch. This is what you really need to see. I have to close this chest up."

Halliday peered over Hamish's shoulder. She gasped. Wet miniature bodies inside the cavity were shaking like gelatine, creepily looking around – all clutching the rim of The Beating Clock.

One was Parker.

She saw herself.

She saw Hope.

Halliday had never seen Hope before, but she knew it was her. The facial features were that of her own. She seemed pitiful, blinking meekly behind her glasses.

Halliday turned to the Mender and looked at him accusingly, "What is all this voodoo, Hamish?! I had no idea!"

"Nor would you, Halliday, this is knowledge only a Mender knows. Sombre wants you to see this."

"Why, Hamish? Why *this* nasty girl?"

"I was only given this as a directive, Halliday. You know this is how Sombre works. The instructions just come to you. They come to me in the same way. This citizen has *you* inside of her, has Hope Kelley as well."

Halliday stood leaning on the bench, feeling very heavy all of a sudden. "So, what does this mean? How involved am I to be with this person? I work alone, well, with Wilder of course. Who is the bleeding child even to be in Sombre?"

The Mender gave her a quick glance, "Halliday, you know I don't have all the answers. You will still be a Gatherer, but your Hope Kelley needs you in some way. Parker the cheerleader is a direct link to her. Sombre wants this. And what Sombre wants Sombre gets, as you know." Hamish covered the cavity and face of The Beating Clock with a blood-soaked flap of chest flesh. "Anyway, you are about to get the answer to your last question, at least. This is why we prefer our Gatherer's bring us whole Nightmarers. This part will be quick."

Hamish took a step back as Parker's body began a transformation. Invisible fingers knitted the skin together from where Hamish had opened Parker's frame. As if succumbing to a creeping flesh disease, the girl's face and body lost all muscular definition; skin tightly compressed against skull and bone. Impossibly scrawny legs were covered in brown leather, torso dressed in a heavy aviator jacket over a thick navy coloured jumper. Hands were skeletal, chapped and weather beaten. Parker's hair grew even longer, stayed blond and fell the length of her body. Her skull contorted, an unmistakably gaunt, tight, grisliness came over her face. Bloody pink skin, like freshly butchered meat, became her new complexion. Lips disappeared, thin skin around her gums forming a permanent monstrous smile. Eyeballs were set deep down in her eye sockets.

Halliday threw her hands in the air in exasperation. She knew what this was. "Oh no, Hamish! Why a Hell Flyer?! They bleeding well crash their planes all the time!"

The Mender gave her a doubtful shrug, "what do you want me to do about it, Halliday?"

"Well, I won't be able to keep her alive very often, if that's what I'm supposed to do! She will fly through her strokes ... so to speak," Halliday continued to watch the transformation.

A cursively embroidered, 'Col. Em Contusion,' appeared on her top right-hand pocket. Breaking through her flesh and the wool of her under jumper was The Beating Clock. It twisted and moved into place, dead centre, wet with blood. Hamish stepped to and gave the glass face a spray with a bottle of cleaner and a wipe. He rubbed her grisly forehead, ran his fingers over her permanently bared teeth.

"Colonel Em Contusion, wake up please, you are ready for transportation."

Blinking her lash-less eyes, the girl who was once Parker Wright, woke up. In a voice full of gravel, Em Contusion peered up at Hamish and Halliday and spoke her first words. "In the air! Now! Fly! Fast!?"

Halliday rolled her eyes, "Oh' spare me!"

§

Halliday bent down and peered straight into the sunken eyes of Colonel Em Contusion, then recoiled, "Uh!" as the new Hell Flyer sat up straight on the bench and used her body for the first time. She swayed and almost toppled – Hamish caught her shoulder.

Halliday wasn't happy about this situation, not one bit, and she let her new cross to bear know it. She chastised the long-haired monster, "I told you Sombre would mend you darkly. Ugly people get an ugly transformation. You got what was coming to you! Ha! I said you would and here you have it!"

Em Contusion just stared back at her and said blankly, "Me in the air! Fly up in the sky?"

"My goodness what a dolt you are!" Halliday said scowling.

Hamish put a gentle hand on Halliday's shoulder, "Come on Halliday. She has no idea what you're talking about. Em won't be much for conversation for a while. Imagine a fully grown, newborn adult. This is what you will be dealing with for at least the next few hours."

They left Em to gaze around ghoul-eyed at The Office of The Menders. Hamish garnered the attention of a fellow Mender and a new dress was brought over.

"For the next few hours?" Halliday repeated the Mender's statement from before.

"Until you get her in the air," Hamish smiled mischievously. "I best get you on your way. Your cuts are fairly superficial, this shouldn't take long."

Hamish, with cloth and ointment in hand, dabbed and sealed Halliday's wounds while she leered over at Colonel Em Contusion in silence. What did this mean now? Why now? What was Sombre playing at? She knew where she had to take her at least - to the 45th Hell Squadron's base at the Terminal Air Strip. She sighed, "How am I to keep a hell-bent kamikaze pilot from using all of her strokes? What an implausible idea Sombre has with this."

"That's quite a defeated tone you have there, Halliday. I have never seen a union for any Gatherer or citizen before. It will be interesting to see how it will work, but in the end, you are doing it for Hope. You will have to do your best." Hamish finished up, giving her a wipe on her mouth. He looked her face over once more. "Okay, that will do, the wounds will smart for a bit, but they'll heal nicely. Get changed, I'll give you your privacy."

ʃ

Dressed and clean, Halliday managed something that resembled a confident swagger as she walked toward Colonel Em Contusion. Parker the cheerleader's new Sombre-citizen sat staring straight ahead at the wall. Had she moved at all? Halliday wondered. She didn't think so. She waved her hand in front of her face. "Em Contusion, we need to get you out of here."

The Hell Flyer turned her head slightly and registered Halliday. "In the air?" She pointed a knobbly looking index finger skyward.

Halliday took a deep breath; this was going to call for all sorts of patience. "Yes. Can you please move now? I require you to move. The catatonic bit you have going on will wear very thin with me, I'm warning you. Now get up."

Em continued to sit.

"Do you not know how to move?" Halliday said and poked at her arm. She turned and pleaded to Hamish who was now attending to another patient nearby. "Oh, she's pathetic, Hamish! How long will this go on for?"

The chief Mender was smiling, clearly enjoying her new misfortune; he called over, "Just use a bit of force. You'll have to guide her along for a bit. She'll get a sense of herself as time goes on."

Halliday huffed, grabbed Em by the arm and pulled her off the bench. Thankfully she didn't just fall in a heap, her legs were strong. The new Hell Flyer was ready for travel. Holding her by the arm, she guided Em through the office.

"Think happy thoughts, Halliday!" Hamish said unable to stifle a laugh.

"I feel like I'm walking my geriatric aunt!" Halliday snapped back.

Wilder awaited her at the doorway. Looking every bit majestic, the machanihorse appeared brand new. Her coat shone. The saddle was well oiled. Halliday checked for her sword and Remington – both where they should be.

Invading her head, Halliday heard the laughter from her Other-selves as she pushed the doors open.

She sighed, "Wilder, we will not be our usual effective persons for some time I'm afraid. Meet Colonel Em Contusion. Don't expect her to speak often. She seems quite dim. She just wants to fly her planes. Isn't that right Em?"

Em Contusion didn't answer.

Chapter 11

Daylight Voyeurism

Hope wasn't really one for parties.

Lately, the Kelley's seemed to be getting invited to them all the time. Saturday afternoon in Terra Vista, at one of her father's customers. The Wachinsky's house was stark white and monstrous. Three storied balconies and tinted windows. To Hope, it looked like a very unimaginative, larger than life Lego model. The garden was nice, she supposed, lots of green grass and old shady trees that gave much needed relief from the early afternoon sun. Caterers walked around with trays of drinks and finger food. There was an outdoor bar with champagne on ice and a fridge full of Becks and Heineken.

The Kelley offspring stood side by side under one of the shady trees.

Hope played with the light fabric of her pale floral shirt. Her outfit for the day was completed with denim shorts and trainers. This was her mother's choice. The shorts rode up her backside a bit, but she felt she looked presentable overall.

Kate wore a denim skirt and lemon singlet, looking every bit the California poster-child, mirrored sunglasses glinting in the sunlight.

"Plenty of rich bitches at this place aren't there?" Kate stated too loudly, as she balanced a plastic plate in her hand, a half-eaten Vietnamese roll lying in a pool of sauce in the centre. "I saw a cute guy before, but I think he was working."

"Ha! If he was working, he'd be too old for you anyway," Hope said realizing she sounded at least forty.

She held real fear for her sister. She was so reactive, wanted to try *everything*, needed to jump on every trend. They were sisters, yet so completely opposite to one another. It wasn't just a stage she was going through; Kate had always been this way. Hope was probably being a doom merchant, but she couldn't see anything but drink, drugs and bad guys in Kate's future.

The Kelley's had been at the party now for about twenty minutes. Their strained conversation inevitably lulled, and Kate placed a hand on her sister's lower arm.

"Well, you're boring. I'm off to get another soda from that cute guy at the bar," she announced and walked off.

Hope pulled at her shirt fabric; a bit of sweat-stick creeping in. She wondered what the temperature was. She had been left tired as usual from her Halliday Knight experience, although not as sore, just heavy in the legs.

Her sleep had been like a Sombre information night.

Parker the cheerleader was now Colonel Em Contusion. Did Parker know this? Did she know who she now was in Sombre? And what's more, did she know that Hope was Halliday Knight? School could get interesting. If Sombre wanted them to somehow come together as friends – 'it', if she could call Sombre an 'it' - was really barking up the wrong tree. To someone like Parker, Hope was like wet mud on her shoe, something to be wiped off on the grass and forgotten about. She gave a hard laugh under her breath. Sometimes she longed to be just like Halliday. A story book, cavalier type of personality that took no shit, had strength and smarm.

"And no acne," she muttered absently tracing her bumpy cheeks with her fingers. The acne was unnecessarily cruel. Other girls her age had it, sure, but not to the same degree. If it was just a hormonal thing, hopefully her mother's idea of tablets would work. She caught sight of her in the crowd, wine in hand and dressed to the nines, laughing away like some sort of heiress to the kingdom of good health and great wealth. Hope wondered if Evelyn Kelley actually thought it was *her* party – she seemed to be jumping from one social group to the next as if she was the host. Hope spotted her father with a small group of men. All bigwigs, rich suppliers of the food and distribution industry. She grinned. Ludicrously, they all seemed to be wearing almost identical, collared sports shirts and knee length shorts – looking for all the world as if the local Lacoste outlet just had a 30% off sale. Men were much more guarded than women as a rule. In a group, chat didn't flow as freely. The main topic was sport. Once sport was exhausted, it generally went to work. If it all got too forced and awkward a member of said group would 'down' the rest of his drink, usually beer, announce he needed another, and wander off. Hope observed others well - she just didn't mix well.

Gazing down at her near empty bottle of seltzer, she decided to go and get another from the bar. Crossing the garden, carefully dodging around each herd, she was aware of glances from a few kids around her age. She knew none of them. Didn't think they went to Centurion', although there was always a chance they could have, the school had around a thousand students. Avoiding any eye contact, she stood at the bar.

"Hello, what can I get you?" said the broad chested bartender with a well-intended smile. He was a good-looking guy, blond, around twenty, with a nicely chiseled jaw - a look that wasn't lost on Hope. Was this who her sister was talking about? She shook her head gently and snorted to herself. She cleared her throat. "Ah, just a seltzer please. Could I have a slice of lemon in it? Do you have any?"

"No, sorry – I hear you though - fizzy water can be a bit dull on its own. Would you prefer soda? We've got Coke and Mountain Dew."

He was a nice bartender, thought Hope. They were usually pricks at these functions. She didn't need the sugar, "No, seltzer will be fine, thanks."

He smiled and twisted the lid for her, "Have fun."

"Th-Thank ... you," she muttered, turned and walked away. That was way too much good-looking, nice bartender for her.

Deciding to make toward the back of the yard, Hope sipped her drink and headed to the trees for some shade. The Wachinsky's had so many of them! The swanky new house out front was obviously a result of a knockdown and rebuild, had to be - these trees were old - oaks and gums and full, leafy elms.

Drifting into the foliage, the party seemed to slip away. This suited her. She shut her eyes gently and just felt her way – a blind girl shuffle. She did this sometimes. Tried to imagine what it would be like if she lost her sight completely. She probably wouldn't, but there was always a chance.

She stopped. Everything fell oddly quiet. There was a stillness here. Opening her eyes, she shivered as the sweat on her back turned cold. The temperature had dropped unnaturally.

"Uh!" Hope staggered sideways as her head went into a spin. She held her brow and rode the giddiness. Of course, this wasn't the first time she'd had a head spin - they were almost a common occurrence these days - but this one felt different. There was a metronomic tapping in her head – no, a ticking – it was a ticking.

The pain and the tick were followed by a stabbing pain in her left temple. Her vision blurred. "Ow! Geez!" She lifted her glasses and rubbed her eyes with shaky hands. None of this felt right. It was time to leave. Heart racing, she turned then stopped dead.

Only ten feet away, partially obscured among the trees, someone stood watching. A male. Dark shoulder length hair; a pale face. Well overdressed in a long black raincoat and black pants. A dirty creep in the trees, lecherous, his presence an invasion. Whoever he was, he was fixated on her. His attention was unwavering.

A chill crept from her throat down through her chest. Her vision had cleared a little, she squinted, took a step and choked out a, "Hello ... What do you want?" She took another step.

He left. Or vanished, it happened so fast she couldn't tell.

Despite her head, she paced outward to the edge of the trees. She searched the party. No trace. "Like a ghost," she said under her breath and coughed.

Had he been real?

The ticking stopped, but the pain didn't. It left her temple and travelled; on tour around her cranium. Her whole forehead burned now.

Haunted, Hope stood staring. Sombre, her dream world, was messing with her reality. Was she losing her mind? A tear trickled down her cheek. The pain pulsed and her vision blurred again.

She shut her eyes.

She collapsed.

∫

"Hope! Wake up! Jesus! What in the hell are you doing?"

The voice seemed to come from miles away. A girl's voice – Kate's. She felt her sisters hand pushing at her shoulder trying to rouse her. "Shit! Get up! Mom and dad told me to come look for you! Are you sick? You're covered in sweat! Yuck!"

Hope blinked, willing herself to wake. Glasses pulled up high over her fringe; she saw her sister's blurry concerned face peering down at her hers.

"You didn't have any alcohol, did you? If you did, I'm telling!"

Hope cleared her throat and licked her lips. "No. Where's my drink?" Gingerly, she propped herself up on one elbow. Her sister looked round and found the bottle. She handed it to her. It was warm.

Kate frowned, "Can you get up? Mum will make you go to the doctors. Your hormones must be *so* out of whack! You're a friggin mess."

"Don't tell mum. I'm fine. I just haven't been sleeping well, that's all. I drifted off ... this party is so boring." It was a feeble lie. Hope got to her feet.

Kate put her sunglasses back in place. "You're so weird, Hope. I love you, but sometimes I wonder how we are related at all."

"I wonder that as well ... please don't tell mum. She's already at me enough, okay?"

"Yeah, whatever I guess ... come on, they want to get out of here." Kate walked coolly across the lawn.

Her neck was stiff, but her head was clear. Running her hands through her sweaty hair, Hope adjusted her glasses and did her best to freshen up. Pinching her shirt fabric, she shook some air onto her clammy skin and took off after her sister.

She peered back at the trees. "He was there," she whispered to herself. "Someone was there." She wasn't sure of it at all. But it was best to believe it. She didn't need to be going mad.

CHAPTER 12

THE TRANSPORTER

That night, after a quick shower, (wondering if she was indeed getting sick) an exhausted Hope fell onto her mattress. Sleep came like a crushing weight.

The nightmare continued.

∫

'Dirty, filthy ... You've ruined everything, Hope!' Her mother hissed at her from somewhere in the chapel's foyer - definitely her mother's voice.

The foyer was trapped in an impossible darkness. Impossible because she could see through the tinted windows it was still afternoon on the street outside. She was alone. Just her on all fours; making a valiant attempt to get to her feet - and her mother, and possibly her father, although, if Evan Kelley *was* there, he wasn't taking part in any of the daughter-taunting.

'You filthy troll of a girl! See what you've done! This is what you do you dirty creature!'

"Mum?" Hope said her voice brittle.

'Don't you speak to me!? You've ruined everything! You don't deserve it, don't deserve anything!'

With horror, Hope saw the wedding guests suddenly appear at the windows, all bleeding and burnt, eyes wide with hate. Her sister stood at the front of the grisly looking horde. Grinning, Kate began to slap her hand heavily on the glass in a rhythmic way. Terrified, Hope watched as the guests joined her. The slapping got heavier, pounding. The glass shook. It was going to give way ... and then it did. Stomping through the shards, Kate led the charge into the foyer. Light from the street suddenly filled the room. Hope

80

screamed as she was yanked and pulled to her feet by what felt like fifty hands. She was lifted, body uncomfortably cradled and squeezed. Fingers dug into her skin, gripped her throat, her chin was lifted savagely to be in line her mother's hate-filled face. Evelyn Kelly laughed evilly, *'You're a pathetic wretch, Hope! A disgrace to everyone and everybody!'* Her eyes were wild, *'You need to feel this.'*

A knife blade protruded from the middle of her mother's right fist. *'You need to feel this,'* she repeated.

She proceeded to knife-punch Hope in the face.

∫

Halliday, Wilder and Colonel Em Contusion walked The Outer. Halliday had given up trying to ride with Em as a passenger, as the newly made Hell-Flyer kept forgetting to hold Halliday's waist. After falling off Wilder twice, Halliday thought that was quite enough. They were on foot.

Rubbish was a problem in Sombre - what to do with it all? The Outer was really just the nightmare world's dumping area; a strip of sandy land a couple of hundred feet wide that went on and on. To The Outer's right lay an energy fog – a buzzing obscure representation of Sombre's massive engine of nightmare cities and boroughs. To the left, The River ran.

Halliday felt itchy as she walked, this was always the case when she used The Outer. White plastic bags, full of lord knows what, indiscriminately discarded by The Office of The Menders, sat piled one on the other. Halliday knew that going this way was the fastest to get Em to the Terminal Air Strip. Stay away from The Byways. Avoid getting a job. That would be a lost cause with Em as baggage.

The worst part of travelling The Outer was that a citizen of Sombre was reminded of their ever-approaching end. Halliday tried to avoid looking at the fast flowing, carcass-filled water of The River, but couldn't help herself. She was compelled to look. Chest cavities, robbed forever of their Beating

Clocks, gaped open. Ghost-white and puffy, waterlogged faces with Mender-sewn up mouths and white milky eyes seemed to watch her as they drifted in the rot.

"Hmm ... I do apologize for bringing you this way, Em. But I need to get you out of my hair. I need to get back to work," Halliday said doing her best to look away from the rushing gore.

Em Contusion didn't answer just looked blankly ahead.

"Did you hear me I wonder?" Halliday said looking into Em's newly-skulled face. "You really are a bit of a hollow potato-head aren't you, a blank thing that needs filling up. It's okay, *I'll* talk, or I'll be bored witless."

Halliday patted her mare on the neck, "There's a good Wilder." She filled the silence, "So you were Parker Wright the cheerleader, did you know? Before you were turned into the rather ghoulish specimen you are now. We all are someone else. That someone else doesn't exist in Sombre though, well, they do for a short while, until a Gatherer catches you, and you are changed. A buggery of a system it is, I know." She found herself gazing at The River again, and snapped her head away, "Ugh! Nasty business that ... can-not-stop-looking though."

She went on, "So I am Hope Kelley's, Halliday Knight. I am a fairly big deal here in Sombre if I may say so myself. Ha!"

"The fifth best Halliday," reminded an Other-self.

She ignored the jibe. "I am a Gatherer; you are a Hell-Flyer. I and my willful mare here, Wilder, collect lots of troubled sleepers who have had the horrible misfortune of landing in Sombre."

Wilder snorted upon hearing her name.

"Clever nag," Halliday said with affection and continued, "I am very useful, but sadly Em, you are not. You fly planes and get shot out of the sky – or just fly them very badly – not at all sure which happens more often there. A Hell-Flyer's stroke rate is a high one. You'll be at the Mender's all the time.

82

Why you ended up a Hell-Flyer is anyone's guess! Ha! I can only think that it might have something to do with who you are in the waking world. To be frank, your 'Parker' is a bleeding snooty upstart! I can't imagine that my Hope and your Parker get along very well at all!"

Em turned to Halliday. "When am I going to fly, up in the sky?"

Halliday stifled a laugh, "Ho! You just rhymed, you funny thing ... soon Em, very soon. And ultimately, I am not at all sure what I am supposed to be doing with you yet. But do try and look after yourself won't you. I would imagine I am to take you to The Menders when you crash your plane. I have not one clue how that will work ... I will do my best to get to you. It might all depend on how busy I am. My calling as a Gatherer is to rescue Nightmarers, that's what I do. Being at your beck and call, particularly when your whole existence revolves around flying and dangerously crashing planes, will be very disruptive to my more important work. I am trying to be good humored about this situation, Em, but I can't lie, this is all a bit of a pain in my backside."

A large flushing out of dirty water came in a wave from Sombre's energy fog, filling the path momentarily. Halliday stopped and halted her companion. "We won't walk in that Em. That will be unwanted guts and fleshy things. The Menders can be quite thoughtless when they clear the floors and waste bins. They wouldn't expect anyone to be walking The Outer."

The filthy water thinned and seeped into The River. Halliday readied to set off again. A large mischief of rats, sniffing the fresh fetidness, exploded onto the path and Wilder whinnied, rearing up on her hinds, steam rushing from her nostrils. "Whoa, Wilder! You are a lot bigger than they are! Steady on girl!"

Em Contusion took off suddenly, surprising Halliday. "What are you doing?"

The Hell-Flyer began stomping and kicking at the vermin like a mad thing, her long thin, booted legs flying this way and that, missing just about every one of them in the process. The very random and erratic display shocked Halliday into laughter. "Ha! My god what has possessed you girl! You go Em!"

The pathway cleared and Em stopped dead - as if she was a coin operated attraction and the money's worth had just run out.

A grinning Halliday clapped her on the shoulder, "So, now we know you don't like rats! That's alright, we all have our things. Let's move, wild girl." Halliday pointed upward and cocked her ear like a curious spaniel. "Do you hear? We are close."

"Flying?" Em's mouth couldn't really smile, but Halliday assumed that she was.

"Yes. Let's hop-to' and go catch your plane."

Halliday studied the mist as they walked. She wasn't lying to Em, they *were* close, but to enter Sombre's great engine at the wrong junction meant that they could slip into The Byway and end up anywhere. She couldn't afford to make a mistake. She needed to get this done. "Wait here."

Em Contusion and Wilder halted and Halliday tentatively moved forward. She squinted at the edges. She spoke over her shoulder, "You have to be careful you see. Once you touch, you enter - you can't just step back out. Luckily I have done this a time or two."

She was well practiced.

"This is it, follow me please."

$\int$

Halliday led her machanihorse and Colonel Em Contusion across the tarmac with purpose. She peered up at the occasional passing plane. Although they appeared to be in daylight time, the weather was forever overcast at The

Terminal Airstrip; black and grey clouds threatening to break open and release the wildest of storms at any moment.

"You'll be flying absolute junkers' Em," Halliday pointed at the old tin flyers above, "Whoever the original Nightmarer was that dreamt this place up, had a love affair with world war two and the worst aviation has to offer. I hear the Gatherers talk and joke about it all the time at The Ruptured Spleen."

Even from the ground, she could make out the brown rust on the rivets and the dented shells. Halliday mused, "I will say that the 45th Hell-Flyer Squadron is very passionate about it all though." She smiled at Em knowingly, "You're excited, I can tell."

There was a sudden rush of spitfire guns. A plane fell from above in a wild, spiraling nosedive. Halliday stopped and scowled and waited for the sickening crush. It came and the three stood and watched the subsequent fire. A crackling air siren sounded, and a fire engine dashed out from the garage of a tower with 45th emblazoned above the exit.

Sighing, Halliday continued on, "so this is where things are for you now. You fly, you crash, and you get a stroke. We probably won't know each other very long."

Excited, Em paced ahead, "I'm gonna fly."

"Yes ... and crash, Em! You're going to crash!" Halliday ran to catch up to her as they approached the 45th Hell-Flyer control tower. She was going to make sure she dropped the girl off properly. This had to be done right. With excitement that bordered on feverish, Em charged into the tower garage.

Tools lined the walls and very flammable looking red barrels of fuel stood in rows in the garage. The oil stained floor was empty. Em's shoulders slumped. She turned to Halliday, eyes wide, looking pitifully confused – it was as if she expected to see a plane waiting with her name on it.

"Oh, Em." As dim as she found her, Halliday had grown a little fond of Em Contusion. She was about to tell her not to worry, that someone would be along soon, when from a stairwell to the left, there was a shuffle of heavy boot steps. The voice was a booming echo, "Colonel Em Contusion! Welcome to the 45th!" A massive man kicked the scuffed white wooden door open and came at his new Hell-Flyer, hand extended in greeting.

Halliday recoiled. He was frightening to look at; as bald as a misshapen cue ball, a barely fleshed, pink skull-face; like Em's, the oaf's mouth was set in that permanently lipless, Hell-Flyer – grimace/smile. Yet, *his* eye cavities were inset with melded goggles; the scratched and dirty glass of which looked like it needed a good wipe with petroleum. Stinking of sweat, he was wet around the mouth with white bits of spit. The man's arms were as fat as breakfast-sausages under his leather flight jacket. Halliday took another step back. She thought him everything she disliked in a man. Despite being a Hell-Flyer ghoul, (she could deal with that) he was every bit an unkempt boor that reminded her of a clumsy bloated toddler.

"The epitome of letting oneself go ..." she said under her breath, this last thought escaping her lips.

The bungler tripped on approach. Halliday noticed that his Beating Clock hand was set at four. "We have our latest recruit! Major Commander Acker at your service!" He looked Em up and down and shoved hard at her shoulders – she didn't flinch, "Ah, Hell-Flyer through and through! Let's get you enlisted and in the air!" Halliday noticed spittle leave the major's mouth and spray Em in the face. "Woeful man," she muttered to herself. Major Commander Acker hadn't even registered her presence. Em had seemed to forgotten she was still there as well.

"I'm going to fly," Em said with wonder as she allowed herself to be guided toward the stairs.

Halliday piped up, "By Em! Look after yourself!" Halliday felt a strange wrenching at her chest as Em left the garage area. The blighter didn't even look back at her!

The commander did. Completely changing tact, in a tone low and full of hate, he stopped on the stairwell and spat his words. "Piss off, Gatherer. Or I'll tie you to a wing! You've done your job, now get out!"

"You disgusting ass," Halliday retaliated, "Best be quick with your next Nightmarer. I'll be coming. I might have bullet for you as well!"

He stood glaring a moment longer, looking like he had something else to say, elongated drool dripping from his terrible mouth. Halliday smiled, he seemed smart enough to know a threat from a Gatherer was not to be taken lightly. Her Other-selves wanted more.

"Get your Remington, Hope's Halliday!" said one.

"Agreed, I would have had a bullet in that blight, by now," said another.

She backed away slowly as Commander Acker climbed the stairs and disappeared.

"Come on, Wilder. We are done here my nag."

Halliday hopped in the saddle and Wilder trotted them out into the airfield.

Her hand went straight to her clock's face. "What is this?" she felt more strange pulling from deep in her chest. She felt something in her head as well – she couldn't picture Em, but there was a sense of her there. She thought of how she watched the new Hell-Flyer's transformation at The Mender's; the miniature bodies of Hope, herself and Parker Wright. Of how she reacted just then on leaving her behind with her commander. Having a longing to protect her? Missing a piece of herself? Is this what it meant to be Em's guardian?

She sulked to her mare. "Oh, bugger it all, Wilder! My existence is over."

Her Other-selves laughed.

CHAPTER 13
THE BEATING

Hope's Sunday had been an uneventful one. Slow. She read a few pages of 'To Kill a Mockingbird' then toyed with the idea of riding her bike somewhere and found she couldn't be bothered. The morning crawled on toward lunch, she finished some homework in the afternoon in very unconvincing fashion.

That night in Sombre turned out to be quiet for Halliday as well. The Gatherer had pretty well holed herself up at The Ruptured Spleen, drinking herself into a sorrowful state. Wilder had run off on her drunken ass as well. 'Served Halliday right,' Hope thought when she woke up, feeling sickly hungover. There was never much to appreciate from Halliday's sessions at the Spleen'.

Her sister had called Monday morning shotgun – with a satisfied grin and exaggerated bottom wiggle she slipped into the front seat as if the leather held magical properties within its padding. Hope noticed her mother's latest look as she clipped herself into the back seat; Evelyn Kelley had just had a fresh grooming at the salon. Her classy blond was now a little shorter; wispy bangs fell like brushstrokes to her shoulders. She pulled down the vanity mirror, gave Hope a blank gaze and flipped it back up.

Did she think her mother actually disliked her? No. Her mother and sister had lots more in common with each other, sure, but Hope knew her mother loved her - just didn't fully understand who she was. It felt a little distant. Rightly or wrongly, it was the opinion that Hope was more work than Kate. Either her mother didn't have the time - or couldn't make the time – one or the other.

School was only a minute away. Hope pulled at her fingers, one by one. Rubbed her hands up and down her legs, then proceeded to pull at them again.

How was she going to approach Parker? Hope as Halliday was every bit the superior to Colonel Em Contusion in Sombre. Hope was a friendless nobody in school. There was a big part of her that almost preferred it as well. She hated real life drama. Friends brought drama by the bucket load. Flying under the radar at a place like Centurion, and Pento for that matter, until she graduated, could be good.

Her mother pulled to the curb and killed the volume on the radio. She turned and lowered her sunglasses, "I've made an appointment for you with a sleep guy, Hope. Tonight, after school - I'll be picking you up before last period."

"What? Why!?" Hope said stunned. This was the last thing she expected.

"What do you mean? I thought it was pretty obvious. I do listen to you, Hope. I'm your mother and I am concerned about your lack of sleep! You are a teenager. You are growing and you need good sleep – this is the logical next step."

Evelyn flipped the vanity mirror down and checked her lips with a pout. "His name is Doctor Marin. He's bitchingly expensive. But after having you fall asleep at the party on Sat-"

"Jesus, Kate! I told you not to tell her!"

"Sorry, what?" Kate pulled a headphone out of her left ear.

"On Saturday! I told you not to tell mum!" Hope fumed.

"Oh yeah ... well, I did," she shrugged, stuffed the earpiece back in again and went back to her music.

"Anyway, Hope, be ready to come to the office, around 2 o'clock. This guy is also a psychologist. He'll be able to tell us if it's the hormones or nerves with you. Regardless, you're having a bad time at this stage of your life. I was having a ball at fifteen. I'm not saying you need to be me ..."

"I'll never be you," Hope said folding her arms petulantly. This sort of thing really pissed her off. This is how her mother did things – no discussion, just action, like it or not. "You didn't think to ask me?"

"Well, no. I thought you'd be happy about it actually!" Evelyn snapped. She took a breath and shut her eyes. "He's the best, Hope. Your father and I think you need it. Anyway, no more discussion, just be ready. Out you get." The indicator was already on.

Without another word, Hope got out. Her mother drove off.

Then came the chaos.

∫

Head full of what going to a sleep specialist might possibly mean for her other existence as Halliday Knight, Hope dragged her heels toward the front gate.

The kid came from nowhere.

"Ow! Whatchhhh!" Hope squealed. Bent over, in a stumbling run, the boy ploughed into her stomach headfirst and they both fell to the ground. Hope would have hit her head on the concrete had it not been for her bag at her back. She rolled awkwardly onto her side.

The kid was screaming - no, *howling* in pain. Laid out flat, his chest heaving, white shirt bloodstained. Hope saw his mouth straight away. He was howling through a bloody mess of sliced up lips. His cheeks were purple and black with bruises, eyes rolling to the back of his head. Was he going to die?

A crowd formed, shouts of 'Help!' 'Someone! Get someone!' 'Is *she* alright?' ''What's wrong with him? He came out of – god! Shit!' 'Isn't that Jerry?' 'Jesus, its Jerry Cowle! What happened?' 'Quick! Here's a teacher!' 'Call 911!'

Hope was pulled to her feet by two senior girls. "God, are you alright? Why did he hit into you girl? Do you know him?"

"No," was all Hope could say, shaking, rubbing her elbow. She gaped down at the guy wailing through his bleeding, mutilated mouth - everyone did. "Jerry Cowle! Hang in there son, help's on the way!"

Teachers and security swooped on the area.

Still in shock, Hope could only stare at the boy. His sweaty hair was the same shade as her own, he had a strong brow and stronger cheek bones - although the cheekbones could just have been elongated from all the yelling.

Then she saw it.

Beyond the bleeding, Jerry's face was the sickly yellow.

∫

Still in shock, Hope sat on a bench in the schools infirmary. The only thing keeping her from having a complete meltdown was the erratic presence of another.

A very out of sorts' art teacher, Ms. Copeland, slung open cupboards and slammed them shut. Hope had never had her for any of her classes. She was a small woman but seemed very fiery. "Not a great day for the schools nurse to be off is it! Shit! Where does she keep anything in here?"

Hope went to get off the bench, "Seriously, the elbow's just a scratch. W-We could leave it. I'll just dab it with a tissue."

On her knees, head deep in another cupboard, Ms. Copeland shot the idea down quick. "No, school policy is that any wound gets dressed properly, Hope. That's your name isn't it? I'll have to fill out a damn report as well. Ah! Here it is - the Povidone!" She stood and held the small bottle up like a trophy, "God that was hard work. What a mess this place is. Show me your arm."

Hope lifted her elbow and the teacher dabbed the cut with a cotton ball drenched in the brown solution. She looked Hope in the eyes. "Are you a friend of Jerry Cowle?"

"No, not at all," Hope said shutting her eyes as a vision of Jerry's yellow bleeding face and mangled mouth invaded her headspace again.

"You're new and he's a senior. I wouldn't have thought so," the teacher agreed, "he ran straight for you?"

"Just unlucky I guess."

"Ha! You're telling me! Someone's done a number on that kid. I wonder what trouble he's got himself into," she said with a tremor in her tone as she smoothed a small plastic bandage over the elbow. "This will be fine. That's waterproof."

"Will he be okay?" Hope said grabbing her bag from the floor.

"I suppose he will. It looks like he's copped a beating from a gang or something. Best not to speculate, the police have been called - and his parents. Scary ..." the teacher's expression said it all. This wasn't normal. Not for a high school.

"I got to get to class. Thank you for the bandage."

Hope left. In minutes she was pushing the door open to her classroom.

All eyes were on her as she made her way to a desk toward the front.

"Hello Hope, are you alright?" said Mr. Daley, her Math teacher. "That was nasty. Are you sure you'll be alright?" He repeated.

There were plenty of whispers and curious looks. She nodded, feeling every bit the leper on parade. She sat down quick and pulled her math book out. Someone coughed a "Freak!" from the back.

"Right! Who said that!" Mr. Daley almost spat.

The room was silent. The burley teacher walked toward the back of the room. "Do you have something else to say, Burrows!"

"It wasn't me!" Came the typical reply. Hope wasn't watching the exchange.

"Grow up, all of you," he addressed the whole back row of desks. "A student is in hospital with serious injuries and a member of your own class has had a terrifying time. Show some sympathy! Next smart-mouthed comment gets two hours with me tonight."

The class settled and Mr. Daley restarted the lesson.

Hope shrank in her seat.

∫

It was a nice day, regardless of how it started out. A light warm breeze brushed Hope's cheeks as she sat with her back against a tree and ate her lunch - egg and lettuce on rye and one of her father's Health &Co apple and pecan muesli bars. She sipped from her bottled water and watched the school from her vantage point - an unpopulated area of Centurion's grounds, not far from the teacher's parking lot.

Now this Jerry Cowle person had somehow been touched by Sombre, she was certain of it. The notion was ridiculous - Sombre was *her* nightmare world – nothing more than that. She pictured his butchered mouth and the yellow in his face. Had anyone else seen the yellow? Why had he come crashing into *her*? Too coincidental to say the least.

"Oh, geez," Hope cleared her throat and sat bolt upright as the tall, strawberry blond headed figure of Parker Wright suddenly came round the corner - looking far worse than last she saw her, it had to be said. She seemed to be limping, dressed down in black jeans and a white t-shirt, long hair hanging, as if she hadn't bothered touching it after her shower. The yellow was in her face. From this distance, it looked like the remnants of an almighty bruise.

"What in the hell is going on?" Parker seethed as she got closer. "I'm injured? I went to sleep and now I'm injured!"

Hope peered up as Parker stood over her. She fidgeted with her glasses and shifted her weight on the ground.

Nerves hit her stomach – lunch was over – she bagged the rest of her sandwich.

"That happens in Sombre ... a lot." She looked at Parker's purple trainers – she realized the cheerleader could kick her in the face from this vantage point. She moved to one side just in case.

Seconds passed and nothing was said.

The older girl sat down and crossed her legs. Hope couldn't meet Parker's eyes.

"Look at me ghost. Look at my face. I look like shit!"

Hope swallowed and nodded. "That's what happens. I'm always tired, and depending on what Halliday does-"

Parker cut her off. "What? You get to be Halliday - that cute warrior girl with the horse? Ho! Oh shit, isn't that a switch!" She shook her head, and raised her eyes, "and I'm that ugly thing with the dead looking face."

Hope fidgeted with her glasses. "Ah, yeah. In Sombre, you're Colonel Em Contusion, a Hell-Flyer. I'm Halliday Knight – a Gatherer." Finally saying this out loud to someone in real life felt more than a little surreal. She was finally talking about her nightmare world with another human; a human who went there as well.

Parker rubbed her shin. "I'll have to miss cheer practice for this, ghost." She gave Hope an accusing look. "In some fucked up round-about sort of way, I think this has to be your fault. I'm nothing to you, and you're nothing to me. I can't work it out?"

Biting her bottom lip, Hope spoke to this scary girl, "Something is happening. I thought I was the only person who went to Sombre ... ah, dreamt of it." She shut her eyes, "I don't know how I've ended up there either."

Parker got to her feet gingerly. "We can't start hanging out. That's not going to happen, ghost."

Hope gave a nervous cough at the mere mention of such a thing. "I-It's okay, we don't have to." Clearing her throat, she stated, "But my name is Hope. Can you please stop calling me ghost?"

"Fair enough," the cheerleader said raising her eyebrows. "What was with Jerry Cowle this morning? I heard he ploughed into you and he'd been beat up?"

"His mouth was cut up pretty bad, he had blood all over his shirt," Hope confirmed.

"I heard that too."

Hope wasn't going to bring up the Sombre-yellow in Jerry's face just yet. Everything was still too fresh. It was as if they had both just lifted the corner of a bandage on a massive wound, they both shared – the wound was Sombre – an unreal place they went to in their sleep and somehow existed in. Both only wanted to take a peak, just to see how big and bad it all might be. There was so much to say. Now wasn't the right time to say it.

She began pulling her fingers.

Parker eyed her compulsion but said nothing.

"He's a bit of a smart ass. I went to grade school with him. He's obviously pissed off the wrong person – never heard of anything like that happening in Pento - *Upper or Lower.*"

"Hmm," Hope said and nodded.

"So, I'm flying planes in my sleep?"

"Yes. You're a Hell-Flyer." Hope picked her rubbish up off the ground. "I think you crash a lot."

"Already have ... didn't kill me though," Parker said as she turned and scanned the school ground. "See you ghost, oh sorry - Hope. Don't follow me. Give me a minute to leave. Remember, we're not hanging out."

Hope looked down at the ground. "Right, okay ..."

The first bell rang to end lunch. She screwed her rubbish from her half-eaten sandwich up in her hands and cracked open the wrapper on her muesli bar. She took a bite and watched as Parker hobbled around the corner of the school building.

She smiled.

CHAPTER 14
The Sleep Guy

Hope's mother had opted to wait outside in the lounge of the Marin Sleep Centre.

This was something that made Evelyn Kelley uncomfortable. The unknown. She could talk boys, pimples, clothes and gloss over Hope's schoolwork. But not this.

File this under a purchase of a 'something' - a 'something' that needed to be fixed - she had to pay *someone* to get *that* fix to happen. As Hope shut the door to the office, she had the distinct impression her mother thought she would just go in and come back out, walking and talking like a completely other person.

"So, Hope. Please explain to me what happens to us when we go to sleep, eh?" Doctor Marin sat cross legged in a high-backed, brown leather armchair; he sipped a powerfully red-looking herbal tea. He owned a full head of blond-greying hair, unsettling sideburns. Hope noticed he pursed his lips a lot. She thought him a Southern Californian, a-typical, professional idiot. There seemed to be quite a lot of them; her dad dealt with a lot of them – she wondered if Evan Kelley would become one.

"Well I go to sleep like everyone does. I just wake up super tired," she answered cagily.

"And do we remember our dreams, Hope?" He jotted something down on the pad on his lap.

"No. I never can. I'm sure I have them." (This wasn't completely untrue – she rarely remembered her rite of passage nightmare.) "I'm a bit of a lost-cause I'm afraid. I know my mother is paying you well for this ..." She re-crossed her legs the other way and eyed the diploma on the wall. He went to Berkeley, she observed. That was impressive at least.

"Yes, well, the important thing is that we get to the core of our problem, Hope, is it not?"

"Ok."

"So, what kind of sleep disorder do we actually have? We don't sleep well. All sorts of things can affect our sleep. We are fifteen, aren't we?" He pursed his lips together again, and for a moment Hope thought he actually kissed the air. She tried desperately to not giggle. Dr Marin's affectation was getting quite over the top.

"Ah... yeah, fifteen."

"How *is* life for Hope Kelley? Our friends, our school, have we any worries? We haven't been in Pento very long, have we?" He sipped his tea and made an even wetter kissing sound than before.

The laugh was almost out of her mouth. She managed to stifle it with a clearing of her throat. This guy was too much! She looked away at the door of the office. Her mother was wasting her money. "Yeah, well, I'm a teenager. I have the usual worries I suppose. I don't have heaps of friends."

He nodded. "That can be hard, Hope. But I feel we are being overly general here. That is fine, we have only just met. But I would like to think that we will learn to trust each other over these sessions."

"How often do I need to come here?" Hope darkened and swore under her breath. She didn't need this in her life at all.

"We need to establish which way to tackle the issue. We *need* to sleep well, everyone does. We may need to monitor our sleeping patterns. I would like to try and avoid medication at this point. Cognitive therapy will be best in a girl your age. Your mother tells me we have been exhausted, we're falling asleep at parties? We can't have that can we?"

She looked Doctor Marin in his enquiring eyes and searched for something to say. There wasn't much she *could* say. It wasn't like she *hadn't* been found passed out on the grass like a sad, drunken minor. That happened. From now on she would have to find a way to not let Sombre affect her waking life. As big a pompous twit as she found this guy, he was getting paid and he meant business. Having sleep therapy could be very confronting. She had no idea what her body did as she slept and ventured in Sombre - but the aftermath would generally allude to something pretty wild. She'd woken upside down, on the floor, no covers, buried way under the covers, on her feet facing her bedroom door.

Doctor Marin filled the silence. "Anyway, we have met. I have a small sense of who we are." He took another sip of his tea, and kiss-wiped his mouth. "So, to finish up, I'll run through a check list."

$$\int$$

"Can I not go there again please?" Hope sat in the passenger side staring hard at the glove compartment. She had just endured an exhaustive and somewhat embarrassing final checklist that queried everything from whether she had wet the bed to whether her menstruation cycle had recently changed. All of these things could affect sleep, apparently. None of this had anything to do with *her* sleep, though.

"Well I've made another appointment. I thought this would help you!" her mother said shrilly. Tapping her fingers on the steering wheel, she took a deep breath, "God, I'd love a cigarette." She faced her daughter, "I'd still love one, Hope, just occasionally, you know."

"Dad would divorce you," Hope said and smiled. She liked it when her mother showed her vulnerable side. The over the top, trying too hard to be a socialite bravado that Hope found so painful, was peeled away every so often. In Hope's eyes, this was the more likable Evelyn Kelly. She thought she would have liked to have known *this* Evelyn Kelly back when she was Hope's age. Real. Why couldn't everyone in her life just be real? They all seemed to be trying *so* hard.

"I had a message from your school, Hope. You were involved in an incident of some sort?" Evelyn said as she took a corner. They were almost home.

Hope lifted her elbow and revealed the sore. She'd taken the small bandage off just after lunch; the redness of the dry Povidone made it look worse than it was. "It's not much ... doesn't even hurt."

Evelyn gave it a quick look. "I'm surprised I didn't notice it before. What happened? The school was fairly vague."

"A senior ploughed into me before I got to the front gate. He was injured pretty bad. He had to go to hospital. I just happened to be in the way - wrong place, wrong time."

"What? Just after I dropped you off?"

"Yeah."

Evelyn shook her head, "That was bad luck. But you know, you need to make a bigger deal of things sometimes, Hope. I need to know about your life. I'm never that busy that I haven't got time for you, you know."

"Thanks mum. I know." Hope didn't think she really knew this at all. But they were sharing a lovely and rare moment. She was making the most of it.

They pulled into the drive. And her mother killed the engine. "Will you give Doctor Marin another go?" Evelyn gave her a rub on the shoulder and Hope met her eyes.

As fruitless as it probably was, Hope realized that this was something her mother was doing for her daughter. Hope had to play along.

"Yeah, okay. I'll give it another go."

"Good," she said and squeezed Hope's arm. She looked at herself in the mirror and ran her hands through her hair. She cracked her door open. "Burger's for dinner, then? I'll go to Denny's. I feel like eating crap tonight."

Chapter 15
Dead and In Bits in Tempestuous

With a belly full of burgers and chips, Hope turned in around nine and her hate-filled, rite of passage continued …

∫

Bloodstained white roses covered her disemboweled body. The wedding guests had done quite a number on her. Rose stems were stuffed in the open cavity of her stomach; stems protruded out from her open mouth, stabbed into her empty eyeholes. She looked every bit the gore monument, put to rest in the entry foyer of the church.

Her mother walked a figure eight around her, whispering, "Unclean Hope, pathetic wretch. How could it be any other way? They hated you. Needed you gone, you ruined everything."

It all felt so final, so empty and so real.

∫

Hope woke up.

"Jesus!" Gasping for air she started coughing, then retching. Was she going to bring up her meal? Heart pounding, she fought to bring herself under control. With shaky hands she reached for her water bottle on the floor.

That was her rite of passage dream? "Shit, Hope? What's with you?" she whispered and sucked in another mouthful of water. What in the hell did that all mean? Her relationship wasn't that bad with her mother, was it? Maybe she did need sleep therapy?

Once the urge to be sick had passed, she was left with a sadness. Should she try and be more like her sister? Is that what her mother wanted? She realized she could be a bit pathetic at times. But she wasn't worthless. She shouldn't be dead or anything. "Get a grip, Hope! Thinking like that ... you tragic asshole!" Angry with herself, she clutched her quilt in her hands, kicked her legs and shut her eyes tight.

Sleep didn't come for another hour.

∫

The church foyer was sunlit and empty. A wet, bloodstained, mark was left on the carpet. Her corpse had been moved. The feel in the empty chapel was overwhelming loneliness. She had been here. Her life had ended here.

∫

Halliday Knight's Morphia was a weapon.

The Morphia was the Jekyll to her Hyde, her monstrous alter-form. It was as strong as it was random. She could only engage it in the direst of circumstances. Things would have to get way out of control.

Things *were* about to get way out of control.

Ruing the call out to the Tempestuous Ganglands, Halliday and machanihorse, had flown through The Byway knowing the Nightmarer didn't stand a chance. Keeping her own self in one piece would be hard enough. She acclimatized to her hostile surroundings. "This place hasn't changed, my Wilder."

Tempestuous was a hellish version of roaring twenties Manhattan. Steam filled the streets. Locomotives ran on an archaic rickety system elevated above the city. Infernos in hi-rises were on continual slow-burn, pumping soot into the overcast early morning. Loitering the streets and thoroughfares, were sharply dressed skinny men in tuxedos and shiny shoes; just as skinny women wore tight cocktail dresses under long evening coats. Each citizen; man and woman alike, were unified in style, each had their hair slicked, every face sported black fat lips and black piercing eyes. They were hideous 'Lizzy's' and nightmarish 'Squizzy's', 'Bugsy's' and 'Baby's' - vicious killers, opposing street gangs in a never-ending nonsensical war with each other.

Ash filled the air and Halliday spit it from her lips as Wilder galloped down a main road. Dodging oncoming vintage Studebaker's and Ford's, evil inhabitants hung out through the windows and shot Tommy Guns and larger than life hand cannons, the never-ending, gangland riot of Tempestuous roared and roared.

Above her she heard the familiar stuttering, farting motor of Dave Bi-Planes aircraft and smiled in spite of her danger. This happened often, Tempestuous was a big city, and Nightmarer's sometimes ended up here in 6's and 7's.

"With luck we might see Dave," Halliday called out loud to Wilder. The horse snorted a puff of steam and whinnied. She liked Dave as well.

She kept her eyes peeled for something or someone out of place amongst the bedlam. It would be only a skerrick, a wisp of luck that would lead her to he or she. So often the Nightmarer was snaffled away in the backseat of an auto – taken for a final ride with a gangster. If she had no luck out here, she would have to search one of the many speakeasies or jumpin' nightspots.

From an alleyway ahead a figure came running, laughing like an unhinged hyena and spraying a Thomson machine gun. "A skinny Squizzy, Wilder, to our right!" Halliday yelled. Bullets flew off Wilder's armour; Halliday felt the staccato pellets puncture her right thigh.

"Blast it all to hell! I've been hit!"

"I would have been armed with my Remington at least, Hope's Halliday!" said an Other-self. *"You've come crashing into this hellish town armed only with utter stupidity and bombast!"*

"She's not an overly strong thinker at times, is she?" said another.

"And Wilder, woman! Think of your mare!" Another Other-self screamed shrilly, clearly upset at her audacity to use her machanihorse in such a situation.

"She hasn't a hope of finding the Nightmarer this time. What a monumental failure this is!"

"You nasty bloody trolls!" Halliday yelled back, pulling her rifle.

"Ugh!" They were right of course. Pain rushed up her thigh to her hip.

With a roar of motors, the road was suddenly full of oncoming vehicles, a vehicular ambush of sorts, and Wilder careered left to the sidewalk. Three blazing Molotov cocktails were thrown from the passenger windows; two flew past Halliday's head and smashed through the shop windows. The other cracked her in the skull - hard.

"Ow! Damn!" The glass smashed, petroleum invaded her nostrils, and she was sent flying from the saddle. A panicked Wilder continued to gallop onward.

Halliday's hair was on fire, her dress had caught alight and burned her torso. She was in trouble. She rolled over and over on the path until she hit a shop wall. "Oh! No! No! No!" Scalding her hands, she wrenched the dress off down to her undergarments, she smacked at her smoldering hair and head.

Her body began to shake - a force invaded her senses. She felt her face contort, her skin crack, her jaw stretch, "COME ON! COME ON!" Monstrously transformed, Halliday's Morphia growled as it got to its feet.

Tyres screeched, car doors slammed, boot steps pounded the pavement.

"The broad's turned freaky, boys! Bump her!"

Halliday's Morphia charged through a hail of bullets. "I'LL KILL YOU! CRUSH YOU, YOU LITTLE!" She grabbed necks and squeezed, crushing windpipes, whipping and throwing bodies around, rag dolling gangsters as they continued to shoot into her body. "FEEL THE HAND,

FEEL THE TEETH!" She was as vicious as her speech was woeful. Yellow eyes wild with fury, her iron jaw opened wide, snapped and ripped a face clean off from the skull.

Tempestuous had come to a halt; suddenly unified with a brand-new focus, gang wars momentarily forgotten, every man and woman came running and firing at The Morphia. Bullets opened her flesh to the bone. Switchblades sliced her monstrous face - and in turn - the arms doing the slicing were ripped from their sockets by The Morphia. Halliday's monster wouldn't quit – it didn't know how to.

"UGGGHHHHHH!" in a sickeningly animalistic display, she wrenched a gangsters doll' to the path and began biting her open from the neck down, ravenous, working quickly, spitting the woman's flesh at the gangsters. The bullets kept coming as she leapt to her feet.

"Make way, you lag-abouts! We got it!" a Bugsy hollered.

The crowd backed away, a bell rang as a fire truck entered and rammed her, pinning her into a wall. The wheels span and battered her further. More and more bullets shot The Morphia's skull apart.

"Yeah!!! Do her in!!!" The crowd of Tempestuous gangsters watched on as Halliday's monster finally went limp.

The Morphia vanished.

The fire truck backed away, turned and drove off.

With a loud "Hoorah!!!" the jubilant throng disbanded from their rare act of teamwork. Doors were slammed, motors were cranked into action.

Back to the war.

Tempestuous continued on.

Halliday Knight slid down the wall, then tipped over sideways, an unrecognizable, bullet riddled corpse.

∫

Halliday woke slowly from her rebuild.

She heard the voices – like tuning in through bad transmission; Hamish the Mender, some others - male and female. The chief Mender did most of the talking though.

"This isn't off to a great start is it? How can you tell a Halliday Knight that she has to try and stop this sort of thing from happening?" He tutted, "they are always brave, but insanely dopey when it comes to self-preservation."

"I don't think I've ever seen a more shot up face," said a female Mender.

"Tempestuous is Tempestuous. You have to play it smart. At least Wilder is in one piece. I didn't fancy full equination at the moment. This stunt of hers has flooded the room." He sighed, "Halliday, wake up. I can tell that you can hear us."

She opened her eyes and peered up at Hamish. He looked extremely annoyed. A fresh faced, girl Mender, with brown chin length hair looked down at her as well. She knew her as Veronica. It was probably just her new state of rebirth, but Halliday thought she looked like an angel. She considered that she must have been on a fair amount of substance for the pain. Her mouth was extremely numb.

"Yeth, but I am thtill thery groggy, Hamith," she said. "O! I can't eethen thpeak!"

"That will pass shortly," Hamish said grimacing. "We haven't had to totally rebuild your skull. The Morphia's version of your skull is dense, like a bone helmet; it left your regular face and cranium full of bullets. Had it been your Halliday skull, your head would have been shot off into hundreds of pieces - we might have had to go on a particle search of the grounds. For that much, I suppose we are thankful you engaged The Morphia."

"I help where I can, Hamith!" she grinned and dribbled saliva down her chin.

He wasn't in the mood. "My god! No, Halliday! Having to *engage* The Morphia at all was so bloody stupid! Putting yourself in that situation was stupid!"

"Itf not like I had a choith! Thombre called and I had to go!" she slapped her lips together; she was beginning to feel them properly again. "You know that, you foolith man!"

"Well this has cost you a stroke. You're now on three." He rubbed his forehead wearily. "I'm sure I told you that you now exist for two people? Hope needs you to stay in one piece. Exercise a bit of caution for god sake!" He looked to his assistant, "Ver, can you straighten the chin a bit."

Veronica had remained all but emotionless through Halliday's berating. Now she raised her eyebrows, "Okay, Halliday. This might hurt you a bit."

She felt the Mender's small hands search underneath her chin. With a skilled, two handed press on her jaw bones, she made the correction.

"Ow! Blast you to hell and back, Veronica! That hurt, you bungler!" Halliday said and sat bolt upright.

Veronica shrugged, "stopped your lisp though, and the drooling." She wiped Halliday's chin and turned to Hamish, "I'll go fix one of her victims now, shall I?"

Hamish scanned the room, "Yes, thanks, Ver. Take your pick."

Halliday hadn't totally recovered; shutting her eyes she waited for a bout of mild spinning to stop. When she opened them again, she noticed all the bloody bullets lying on the bench around her. Mauled mobster bodies lay to her left and right, mobster bodies lay all over the floor. A collection of sharply dressed grisliness; arms torn from clavicles, faces ripped away from skulls, chests had been stripped of flesh.

"So many Bugsy's! Did I do all that?"

"Well, your Morphia did, Halliday," Hamish answered her curtly and gestured to the surface of the bench. "As I mentioned before, these bullets were in you. Mostly in your face and head. In fact, your face was so full of bullets, we've had to retrieve your original mould and reshape your features." Hamish said as he wiped his implements with alcohol, returning each of them methodically to his leather pouch. Sighing he continued. "So, we've already had Colonel Em Contusion in here. You do remember who she is, yes?"

Halliday had to admit that she hadn't thought too much of her just recently. "The Hell-Flyer ghoul, yes, was she badly damaged?"

"Yes, she was. She had ceased, burnt beyond recognition in a fiery crash! It cost her a stroke on her Beating Clock."

"Well, that is the Hell Flyer's burden," she rolled her eyes and shrugged, "they crash and burn as if it were a fashionable thing to do."

Hamish bit into his bottom lip and looked at her with what could only be described as disbelief. In an exercise of strained patience, he blinked a dozen times and inhaled. "You are who you are, Halliday, I guess. I have to keep reminding myself of this. I wish Sombre had chosen another Gatherer, but it didn't."

She nodded and smoothed her hands down her dress, "Hm ... That's not the nicest thing you've ever said, Hamish. But I have to agree, it is a ridiculous burden I have been given. I am very valuable after all."

"You will have to find some way to get over yourself, Halliday Knight!' he said cutting her off. "Finding your crushed, shot up and near naked corpse in Tempestuous, was not what I consider in any way acceptable. Have you even tried to channel into Em Contusion?"

Halliday gave him a look, "Oh really! So, is that what I am supposed to do? She is a bleeding invader, man! I *have* seen her in my head, and I do my best to ignore her! How else am I meant to do my work?!"

"DON'T IGNORE HER!" he yelled causing the whole of The Office of The Menders to stop for a moment. Halliday Knight was being properly scolded - it didn't happen often. The chief rubbed his eyes, turned and faced the wall in an open bid for calm. Eventually he turned back around. Face red, looking more than a little ashamed for the outburst, he continued in a more civil tone. "You exist for two now, Halliday. My god, I thought I had made that pretty clear!"

"Oh, yes the little puppet folk inside Em. I had forgotten about those as well," Halliday said patting her mouth with a mock yawn.

"You can choose to ignore this calling Halliday, smash your way through your strokes, but what a waste! This is the first time being a Gatherer has meant something other than a mere servant of Sombre."

"We are more than mere servants, Hamish," she scoffed as she looked down at the mass of spent bullets on the bench around her person, she shook her head and laughed to herself, "goodness, there must be a few hundred bullets here ..."

"441," Hamish said, "We counted ... and really Halliday? You really think so? You honestly think a Gatherer is anything more than a servant of Sombre? You are serving a penance. Just like all of us. You are a bit-player within a nightmare existence. When you go, another Halliday takes over. When I go, another Hamish will take over this bloody blood-soaked office!"

"How dare you cheapen my existence, you blowhard!" she shot back and got to her feet. "I best leave now before I punch you in the gob, man!" Picking up a vanity mirror, she began smoothing the lines of her newly moulded face with an immediate fondness. She softened, "You do such good work, though ... you have your uses."

Hamish smiled in spite of himself. "Halliday, trust me. You need to keep Em safe. It will benefit both of you. Don't ignore her when you see her."

She walked toward the door with a confident, brand new swagger. She looked gorgeous and she knew it. "I shall do my best," she said and gave him an offhanded salute. "I need to go find my nag."

She left.

Chapter 16

An Existence of Failed Flight and Broken Sleep

The dark sky was filled with lightning, wind and rain - hardly the conditions for flight.

'Liberty Taken' emblazoned on its tin paneling, the old navy dive bomber's motor skipped, belched, threatened to blow a gasket and stall. Dipping involuntarily, it lost altitude. A nervous sounding set of pistons valiantly fought on – and the bomber rose up again. Its pilot, Colonel Ramiskus Terra-Firma, smiled the dead-maw smile of a 45th Hell-Flyer and adjusted the fuel mixture. Pulling on the yoke, the Junker soared higher still.

Colonel Em Contusion sat in the back of the twin seater Junker and whispered to herself the speak of the Hell-Flyer. "Vim-Vigor! Alpha! Bandicoot! Ca-ching! Woeful dove! Touch and Go! Tonevereturn! Crash and Burn Baby!"

She was learning so many new words! It was rare that she used them in a proper sentence. It was all about the terms. The terms of a Hell-Flyer. "Crash and Burn Baby," she whispered again. That was another term. That's what she did. A Hell-Flyer existed to fly. To Crash and Burn, Baby.

As more thunder clapped, a round of high-powered gunfire came at the *'Liberty Taken'* and Colonel Ramiskus rolled them left. Gliding haphazardly like a hiccupping eagle, the Junker once again threatened to stall mid-air.

"Enemy wings at our rudder!" Em thrilled in the back.

"It'll be Touch and Go! Set our guns! I'm about to lead us into a Chandelle, Em!" Colonel Ramiskus wailed in the front.

The *'Liberty Taken'* clambered for more air in the spirited, but gasping, 180 degree, left side-aerobatic move.

Em felt the rush and screamed with delight.

She loved to fly!

Now, she had to fight. Turning the small Browning gun around on its mount she used the scope and aimed as they pulled level with the enemy – she fired a rapid round of bullets. The newer and shinier nightmare craft went into a well-executed barrel roll and dropped from view. "We lost em', Ramiskus!" Em broadened her scope.

"We're in trouble, Em! That new black wing will have us! Nightmarer's in their dreamt-up craft! This old Junker can't compete!" Colonel Ramiskus punched the window and actually cracked it.

Silence filled the cabin after the pilot's outburst.

Em had learnt about her place in Sombre from Commander Acker. A Hell-Flyer flew, a Hell-Flyer fought, a Hell-Flyer had to bring down the Nightmarer's in their nightmare aircraft.

The black craft sped past them in the blur and drone of jet-propelled engines. Like a cantankerous old man, the *'Liberty Taken'* took exception to the newer plane's presence. It's worn out motor made a pinging noise and stalled mid-air.

"This blasted bird's shat itself again!" Ramiskus said and went about firing the ancient rotary motor up. One hand holding the yoke; the other manically flicking switches, the experienced flyer pulled the throttle and fuel. They were gliding on momentum alone.

Like an evil air shark, the black plane circled, taking advantage of their predicament, it flew straight at them. There were no guns firing from the nightmaring aircraft now - just a dreaming, deadly kamikaze at the controls.

"Em! That blasted Bandicoot has us!" Ramiskus screamed and began wildly thrashing about in the front. She cried, "I'm at eleven, Em! This is it for me... Come in Commander Acker! It's been an honour to serve you!"

No reply from the tower.

The black jet was almost nose to nose.

"Crash and Burn Baby!" Em bellowed stupidly from the back.

With a hopelessly late rumble from the engine, the Liberty Taken came to life. Em grabbed her own yoke and pulled - the nose of the craft tilted laconically, and the nightmaring enemy ploughed into the underside. "Tonevereturn, Woeful Dove!" Em yelled from her seat as the nose of the black wing crashed through and Ramiskus shouted something in return as she disappeared through the roof. The Liberty Taken was ripped in two - fuel tanks exploding at the wings as they tore free; the black plane passed through then vanished. The still seated Colonel Em Contusion was falling. Falling and grinning the unwavering grin of the Hell-Flyer. As she plummeted in what was left of the burning cabin, she whispered, "Crash and Burn Baby!" over and over. An empty whirring filled her senses, darkness was coming, along with her demise. Spinning around and around as she fell through the teaming sky, Em awaited the impact.

"Unfasten your seat belt, you silly wretch!"

Em heard the voice invading her head space. Far away but getting closer.

"Have you done it?!"

She did it ... just as she felt the lead-weight crush of impact. Her body taking the paralyzing hit, starting from the base of her spindly spine, rushing up through her neck. Death was next, coming in its final, inestimable gasp.

In a split second, one strong hand grabbed her by her pulverized shoulder - another by her limp, broken arm, wrenching her free.

∫

"You'll bleedin' well hang on, Em!" Halliday growled as she rode Wilder hard across The Terminal Airstrip. It seemed to be rush hour for crashing planes as another three Hell-Flyer junkers' came tumbling from the sky like mechanical carrion.

"What a waste of resources this place is!" Halliday steadied a limp Em Contusion, a dead weight across Wilder's back.

"This is our first try Em! I'm doing this for Hope! You need to hold on! Give me a grunt, girl!"

Reaching the outskirts, Halliday spotted the shimmering light of The Funneling ahead and charged. She let out an involuntary cry of frustration. How on earth was this going to work? Was she too late?

§

Hope rolled and rolled across the mattress and then hit the floor.

"Ow!" She'd fallen on her front. She coughed as she breathed in a throat-full of carpet dust. Rolling on her back she peered up at the clock, the blurry digits were somewhere in the 3 a.m.'s. Head still full of sleep, she asked the question of her bladder and found she couldn't be bothered. Crawling back onto the mattress, she pulled the covers over and drifted off realizing that, at least in Sombre, she was pretty damn powerful.

"Halliday's the shit," she mumbled.

§

The rite of passage ...

Even in her sleep, Hope hated this. She could feel her frustration as she watched herself being lifted up on to a door by the wedding horde. Eyeholes and open mouth filled with the stems of flowers. Her severed and butchered body lying in a pool of her own making; of flowers and thick, drying blood. She was walked out of the chapel and paraded down the street outside. The late afternoon sunlight shone down on her corpse. The weather was lovely. The horde below her chanted as they marched her on. "Hope the Unclean, Hope the Revol-ting! Hope all in red, the only good Hope's a dead Hope!"

§

Galloping out of The Funneling into the entry hall to The Office of The Menders, Halliday pulled Wilder to a skid.

"Halt nag, will you! This needs to work!"

Wilder lowered, tri-folding her mechanical legs down so her belly lay flat on the floorboards, she bowed her head obediently.

"C'mon Em," Halliday wrenched the limp form of Colonel Em Contusion from her horse, dragging her off like a bag of sand across the floorboards, she kicked open the big wooden door to the Office'.

"Hamish! I've had a go at this. Here man!" Halliday announced at the entry as if she were dropping off a parcel and everything inside was broken. She pulled Em up by the collar of her aviator jacket, "Come look at this girl won't you!"

The chief Mender walked up rubbing his hands on a bloody rag. "Looks like she's in one piece at least."

"There might be a bit of wind left in her as well, I haven't had the chance to check," Halliday said as two Menders came rushing up. Taking Em Contusion under the shoulders and ankles they lowered her onto a trolley.

Hamish eyed the Hell-Flyer as she was pushed past him. "She might be okay, Halliday, well done. I trust this didn't interfere with your drinking session at The Ruptured Spleen."

"Actually, no – I mean, it almost did. I was on my way up for my spirit when I had the presence of mind to check in on Em."

"You shouldn't have to *try* and check in on her, Halliday! She should always be at the forefront of your mind!"

"That's absolute rigmarole of the highest order, Hamish!" Halliday exclaimed, "I've got four bleedin' Other-selves to deal with already! I'll give Em what is left of my mind and that's it! She'll turn my brain into slaw, man!"

"Then you'll miss her more often than not! Do I need to remind you of the stroke rate of a Hell-Flyer?"

"No, you needn't! I saw them all falling down around me as I left the area with this one! What a bunch of dumb bells they all are! Do they ever catch a Nightmarer?"

"Not often," Hamish's mouth formed a grin.

Halliday looked over the chief Mender's shoulder and saw Em lying on a spot on the bench. She noticed that her twig-thin legs barely fit her aviator leathers. "Quite undernourished, isn't she?" Halliday mused, "Such a brittle little bugger."

"You need to look after her, Halliday," Hamish reminded her again.

"The girl crashes planes, Hamish," Halliday said as a rubber hose was placed into Em's mouth and a small generator was switched on. She winced as Em Contusion's body blew outward like a balloon, then deflated and convulsed. She muttered, "I will try."

"Good work," Hamish said giving her a pat on the shoulder. He left her and got involved in the endless and thankless cycle of mending Sombre's helpless citizens.

Halliday shut the door and entered the hall where her trusted Wilder awaited her.

"Come on my nag, let us go and have that drink. We have done well. I deserve it."

The clip-clop of hooves and the fizzing clicks of Wilder's gear work were soon replaced with the calamitous noise that was The Funneling. In seconds the two were spat out onto the dirt parking lot of The Ruptured Spleen. Halliday led her machanihorse through vehicles of the four wheeled and winged variety. There was no sign of Lucretia St Aimes bike - that was a good thing. Dave Bi-Planes' Bi-Plane was parked, wedged in between two Speed Trucks. This made her smile. A drink and a chat with Dave.

They continued on toward the dirigibles. "I shall leave you over near the balloons, as you are such a skittish thing at times," Halliday said to Wilder licking her lips. She was awfully dry. She let go of the reins and left the machanihorse alone to grunt and grumble to herself in the usual way she did when Halliday went for liquoring.

"Be a good Wilder and stay out of trouble won't you." She looked to the top of the mountain's peak. The Ruptured Spleen was as well-lit as its patrons; she could hear the familiar clinking of glasses and alcohol fueled laughter. With a light skip in her step, she made her way to the earthen entry, the metal elevator door at the mountain's foot. Every Halliday loved a drink a little *too* much. She made no apologies. She thought she would order a bowl of the Spleen's signature greasy chips as well, that would create that cushy layer for necessary absorption.

"She's more of a lush than I ever was," said an Other-self tapping her thoughts.

"I was quite fond of The Ruptured Spleen," another admitted longingly.

"It was our crutch. I know it cost me at least two of my strokes," another chimed in.

Grinning, Hope's Halliday pressed the up button and waited for the elevator to make its way down. "Up we go," she muttered under her breath and rubbed her hands together.

Then something ruined her good mood.

"Huh!" A sudden chill was at her back, she spun around. What felt like frigid icy fingers, were walking her spine, squeezing, and pinching at her nerves.

Ticking? She could hear ticking. She looked down at her chest. The Beating Clock didn't tick, if anything, it drummed - and it never sounded out so loud that it could be heard like this. Suddenly it had weight. It felt heavy. She had never felt her Beating Clock before. It was always just – there.

Halliday realized the ticking wasn't from her clock; it was in front of her.

There was a presence.

Instinctively, she pulled her blade from the holster and readied herself for combat.

"W-What is this? Come out of hiding, now! Coward!" She wasn't entirely sure if it was the correct way to address whatever *this* was – it was a *something* - there was no other way to describe it. It couldn't be seen, but it was there. She felt its chill. It was studying her, leering perversely, as if staring into her very core, at everything she was. She gulped. She caught her breath. The sword wavered in her hands and fell limp.

The elevator door opened. Shivering, she backed into safety, not able to look away until the door shut. The ticking stopped; the heaviness in her chest disappeared.

She ascended; The Ruptured Spleen would be her saviour.

Halliday slumped against the back wall of the elevator and hugged herself.

She had never felt as unsafe in Sombre as she had just then.

"What was that?" she whispered. Haunted.

∫

Hope woke with a start. She sat bolt upright in bed.

"Oh Jesus!" she coughed holding her chest. She gasped as she felt the pressure - she couldn't find her breath. Her eyes were wet. Had she been crying? Something had changed. Something was wrong. Really wrong. Grabbing a handful of her quilt she pressed her face into the linen and breathed - just breathed. She found some control.

Her room felt icy.

Chapter 17
The Coming Together

Chin resting on her palm, Hope played with a bowl of cereal, chasing the flakes around with her spoon. She actually felt like vomiting. She was dressed and ready for school, but not nearly ready, really. If any normal person had just had a night's sleep like she just had, they would be ditching school and calling in a 'mental health' day to rest and recover.

But how much real rest would she be afforded? The lines between her sleep world and her real world were starting to blur. That *was* ice in her room wasn't it? There was no mistaking it - that had been real. It was a 65-degree morning and her room was icy. She pictured Halliday at the foot of The Unexplained Mountain. Whatever that thing was that the Gatherer could feel but hadn't been able to see – that ice - Hope was sure that was new. Halliday's cocky demeanour took a swan dive there for sure.

She swallowed down another wave of nausea. With a sigh, she stopped playing with her breakfast and pushed the bowl to the middle of the table. She cleared her throat and croaked, "Are we leaving soon?"

Kate was in scroll mode on her phone as she absently chewed her toast. Hair was in a nicely organized plait that hung at her left shoulder. She raised her eyebrows in recognition but didn't look up. "I'm ready."

"Yep, five minutes." Their mother was in fine fettle this morning which for some reason made Hope feel all the worse. Evelyn Kelly had been humming and buzzing around the kitchen for the past hour. She put her hands on her hips, and exhaled, "Okay." She gathered her keys, "Your father will pick you both up this afternoon. I've got a thing on at The Social. I won't have a car."

"Afternoon drinks with the girls. Can't wait til' I get older," Kate said and got up from the table.

"Yeah, bet you can't - *try hard*," Hope said nastily and adjusted her glasses. She got up as well.

"Bitch."

"Hmmph," Hope mumbled and burped in retaliation.

Their mother wasn't listening; her mind obviously stuck six hours into the future where she sat at a table, with likeminded women, chardonnay in hand.

Grabbing bags from the floor, they all left the kitchen. The three Kelley women. A socialite, her apprentice, and dragging on behind, a nauseated troubled sleeper.

∫

Lunchtime had brought an amazing change in Hope's existence. She had been sought out by Parker. Both girls sat under the tree near the parking lot. She dared not call Parker a friend just yet. Thinking of such a notion might have made it not so. The only common ground they shared was based in Sombre - a nightmare world. The counterbalancing scale of her existence had tipped her way for once, and she wasn't about to test its merit.

As she ate her pre-packaged bean and tabouli, Health&Co wrap, Hope smiled between bites.

"So, you're like, my saviour," Parker said without a trace of sarcasm. "You saved me a stroke on my clock thing."

The cheerleader looked nothing like a cheerleader today. A bit sloppily dressed in jeans and a faded white t-shirt - her long, strawberry-blond hair was out - all over her shoulders and back. Hope noticed an unconcealed zit had appeared just under her bottom lip as well. 'Sombre acne,' she thought to herself as if 'Sombre acne' was actually a thing.

"Well, *Halliday* did," she modestly concurred. "I'll be surprised if she'll always be able to though. Colonel Em Contusion crashes planes ..."

"... like an idiot," Parker finished for her. "She's an idiot. Let's be honest. I've got myself a plane crashing, skull—faced idiot." She grinned and shook her head.

Hope laughed and thankfully so did Parker.

The older girl shook her head, "I find all of this so fucking scary. Do you?" She said as she sipped from a can of TITAN, a new super-high-octane-energy-drink a lot of kids were drinking. Hopes father had warned her ad-nauseam of the perils of energy drinks. Nodding her answer, she eyed the can.

Parker noticed. "Sombre has me drinking this bullshit as well. Need a pick-me-up. I'm *so* tired and sore all over the shoulders and down my front. Does that ever get better?"

"Hasn't got any better for me yet," Hope said and pushed her glasses up on her nose. She couldn't help but wonder about the social-suicide Parker was committing at this very moment. She was cooler and older. Hope didn't even have friends in her own year level. She thought she'd ask, "Do you have cheer practice later?"

Parker rested on her side and began picking blades of grass. "I quit. My mom never liked me being a cheerleader anyway," she sighed, "I just haven't got the energy at the moment – or the '*spirit*'." She made a curling hand gesture and rolled her eyes. "Besides, the cheer captain, Georgia, is an outright bitch. Can't deal with that crap at the moment."

Gaping at Parker relaxing on the grass as if she were an alien with a day pass from Mars; Hope took another bite from her wrap and swallowed. She had to converse with the girl. It just wasn't something she was used to doing. She cleared her throat, "Um, so what are they saying about Jerry Cowle?"

"He'll be out for the rest of the week. There's plenty of talk going round. His lips were sewn to his nose, he had no teeth left, someone had bit into his ear and his face was black and burnt looking ..."

"His lips weren't sewn to his ear!" Hope corrected.

Parker laughed cruelly, "not his ear! His nose! Ha! My God that would have been warped looking! Like some crazy Picasso shit!"

Hope laughed, realizing straight away that she shouldn't be. "Anyway, his lips weren't sewn. They were butchered pretty badly though." She pictured Jerry screaming through his cut-up mouth and remembered the colour of his face.

"His face was yellow, Parker."

The older girl peered up at Hope and her smile had disappeared, "like the yellow we see in our faces?"

"Yeah," Hope nodded slowly and screwed the balance of her wrap up in the packaging.

"Wow ... you sure?"

"It was yellow," Hope said with more certainty. She knew what she saw.

There was so much she wanted to share with Parker. But this was all so raw and new. She didn't want to freak her out and scare her away. Too much of The Hope Kelley Show had never worked for her in the past.

Parker sat up with a grimace and crossed her legs. "Feel like a sixty-year-old ..." She gathered her hair in a bunch then let it fall down her back, "So what are we gonna do, Hope-whatever-your-second-name-is."

"Kelley," Hope said and grinned.

"Two first names ..."

"Kelley's spelt with an 'e'."

"Okay. So, I'm not one to just sit on my ass and wonder what's going to happen next. I like to know what's going on around me. I am a control freak, Hope. Do you understand?"

Hope nodded. She liked where this was going.

"I want you to tell me everything you know about this Halliday. She's the shit. I want you to spill everything about what you see in Sombre. I need to know because I can't handle *not* knowing, okay?"

"Well I can't tell you everything right now, lunch is just about over," Hope said looking at her watch. Clearing her throat, she did her best to stifle a smelly garlic burp; the masticated contents of her wrap battling to make its way down to her stomach. She wondered if the older girl smelt it. She shielded her mouth with her hand just in case.

Parker pulled her phone from her pocket. "We need to swap numbers. Get your phone ..."

"Oh, it's at home."

"Really?" she gave her a quizzical look, "who does that?"

"I forget to bring it sometimes," Hope looked to the ground. She liked to tell herself she enjoyed being 'off the grid' – but in reality, it was a little sad, she had a total of four contacts and nothing social on her phone at all.

Parker's eyes were wide, "Well, can I just say that's so-fucking-strange, Hope Kelley spelt with an 'e'? Anyway, write my number, stick it in your phone and call me tonight. We have heaps to discuss," the older girl said and reeled off the numbers. She got to her feet.

Hope quickly grabbed a pen and pad from her bag and used her knee as a table. "Oh, yep got it!" she said breathlessly. She scribbled the number down in a rush.

The first bell rang to end lunch and Hope quickly got to her feet. She stood next to Parker and smiled awkwardly. Parker gave her a sideways glance and rolled her eyes. "Jesus, you need to learn to chill out around me, Hope.

You're a kickass warrior, remember? Surely a bit of this Sombre crap can rub off on you?" she smiled and nodded to herself. "*I'm* the gimpy pilot who can't string a decent sentence together and can't fly without crashing."

Hope didn't know how to respond. She felt a little giddy, actually.

The two walked toward their respective classes then parted ways.

∫

The drive home from school with her father and sister took too long. Dinner couldn't have finished quick enough. Hope showered and changed into her pajamas. She grabbed her notebook and phone and plonked on the bed with a bounce. Her phone was always charged. It rarely moved from her dressing table. She didn't use it. Her laptop was less of a strain on her eyes when she wanted to be online. Tapping into contacts, she entered Parker Wright in - name and number - then took a breath.

"Don't be such a try-hard, Hope," she said under her breath. "Call her and be cool for once." She tapped the number and listened to the dial tone. Chewing her nails, she looked at the clock. 7:46. Respectable time to be calling, she thought.

Parker picked up. "This you Hope? Wait. I'll call you back." The line went dead.

"Oh," she said with a delay and placed the Samsung on the quilt – then proceeded to stare at it while she waited ... and waited, she waited and waited, pulled at her fingers and sucked a wet patch on her pajama pant knee.

Fifteen minutes passed.

She wondered if she should go to the toilet.

Then she might miss the call.

"Jesus, just go Hope!" she chastised herself. Jumping off the bed she ran out of the room leaving her door open. She ran back in, part humming, part snorting some random song that probably wasn't a song at all. The screen was lit. "Shit!" There was a missed call. She dialed Parker's number again.

"Where were you?" the older girl said coolly at the other end.

"I had to pee. I didn't know when you were going to call back ... I had to," Hope said trailing off. She shut her eyes and shook her head slowly. Not a strong start.

"I just had a shower. Now I can relax. Now we talk - you good?" Parker started.

"Yeah, super good."

"Super good? Ha! Well that's *better* than just good I suppose. Although that sort of sounded like something my late father would have said."

'*This was going horribly!*'

Hope stammered, "O-Oh, sorry. I didn't know your dad was dead."

"He's not! Jesus, I wish! He's an absolute dickhead, though. Cheated on my mum three years back and has been trying to get back in our good books ever since ..."

"Oh."

"But seriously Hope Kelley, you need to relax when you're talking to me. I know you're younger, but not by much. And personally, I couldn't give a fuck. This shit we're going through transcends our ages."

'*My word she swears a lot,*' Hope thought to herself, '*be cool about it, Hope. Everybody does.*' "Oh, okay. I'll try."

"Good. I need *you*, remember. Not sure if you even *need* me. Even my numbskull dream person has worked out that you're a Gatherer, and pretty kick-ass with it. Now, take a deep breath and let's begin. Where do you think Sombre has come from?"

Hope felt a shiver run through her insides. They were about to talk Sombre. To say it was surreal was an understatement. "I really don't know. I only started going there when I moved to Pento."

"We do go there, don't we? I mean, I know it's only when we sleep, but it all feels too real, doesn't it?" Parker said without the usual edge to her tone. "I feel absolutely shot to pieces when I wake up."

"Probably because Em Contusion might have been -" Hope joked.

She got a laugh at the other end of the line. Turning round, she leant back against the wall and relaxed, rubbed her toes together through her bed socks. "Do you ever remember your rite of passage into Sombre?"

"No, what's that?"

"It's your lead in dream – your rite of passage. You obviously haven't woken from it yet. I have, once or twice. I think mine are always violent. I can never remember them once I wake from being Halliday, though. From what I can work out, they seem to focus on anything negative in your life and crank the volume up to 100."

"Jesus, I'd hate to think what mine are like if they focus on the negatives in my life," Parker sighed. "Let's move on. We don't need to get pulled into that pit this early in our friendship."

Hope grinned. This girl was her 'friend'. She cleared her throat and continued. "Well, Halliday drinks too much at a bar called The Ruptured Spleen. It's where all the Gatherers drink in between jobs."

"Bullshit! Really? You get to go to a bar? Jesus, you lucked out! How many Gatherers are there do you think?"

"Geez, lots of them. At least twenty, I've never really counted. Halliday's usually too drunk to notice. I think she sort of has a thing for one of them."

"Who?" said Parker well impressed.

"Dave Bi-Plane ... he flies a bi-plane."

"Ha! Course he does!" Parker giggled at the end of the line. "So why just you and me? I mean, this is pretty random, let's be honest; I wouldn't have given you the time of day had you asked me for it two weeks ago."

"Oh, I know! Nobody does!" Hope blurted and regretted it straight away. She'd almost sounded thrilled about it for god's sake!

There was a pause at the other end. "You're a weird girl, Hope Kelley. You know that, right? Likable enough ... but you do need to relax a little."

Hope sucked her bottom lip. "I think something big is about to happen to Halliday."

"Spill it."

"So, just about nothing fazes Halliday; you may have picked up on that."

"She's kickass."

"Ah, yep, she is. But something happened in Sombre last night that made her wet her pants."

"Oh no, literally? Poor thing, that's gross ..."

"No, that was just a figure of speech."

"Oh, good ... that could have almost ruined her for me."

"Anyway, there was an inexplicable chill that just about sucked the life out of her. It was like ice. It seemed to have a life of its own, it was evil and big, I have a feeling it was creepier than anything she had ever felt in Sombre before." Hope sat up and hugged her knees. "But you know, the frightening thing was that I felt the exact same ice when I woke up."

"You're room went cold?" Parker queried.

"Aha. I know you wake up feeling just as sore and as zonked as I do, but this was new, this was something else again. Next level."

Hope could sense Parker was hanging on her every word. She continued, "I went to a party with my folks on the weekend and there was someone there – he didn't feel real, you know? He was spying on me through some trees. I tried to confront him, and he vanished."

"Oh, fuck! That's trouble Hope! You were being followed? How come you haven't mentioned this before?"

"Well, we've only just started talking, haven't we?"

"God! You could have led with that, though!" Parker exclaimed, "That's some next level shit right there! You think there is someone else like you and me?"

"Maybe."

The line went quiet for a moment. Parker came back. "You said Jerry had yellow in his face, didn't you?"

"Yeah, he did."

"And you're sure you weren't imagining it?"

"His mouth was chopped up, Parker. That's not a normal beating. Not for a high school student. That would take time. That would take a knife."

"It reminds me of something from a gangland-mafia movie or something," Parker agreed and added, "I've seen lots of them. They do that sort of stuff when they want to send a message: chop off a finger or slice an ear. How could Jerry have pissed someone off so bad that *that* would happen to him? He could be a drug-runner."

"Doubt it," Hope said.

"I don't. I don't put anything past anyone. There are some very secretive bastards in this world, Hope. People are living double lives all the time."

"None of that explains the yellow, though," Hope countered, "That's got something to do with Sombre. I'm sure of it. I wasn't imagining that guy who followed me at the party either."

"But Sombre is just a dream world, isn't it? Did I mention that I am a staunch realist in a major fucking way? I don't even read fiction books ... Harry Potter is drivel."

"Please don't have a go at Harry," Hope said solemnly.

"I've seen a bit of the first film. All three of those characters could do with a foot in their asses. Ha! Cop that Hufflefluff!"

"So, we won't be talking books then."

"Not if you read that sort of crap."

"What do you read?"

"Not much. When I do, its bio's and true crime. Reality, Hope," she yawned and repeated, "reality."

Hope shook her head slowly and steered the subject back on track. "When do you think Jerry will be back at school?"

"In a week I suppose. You would have to give him at least a week for something like that surely."

"We need to talk with Jerry. Find out what he saw. Who attacked him," Hope said not quite believing that it was indeed she speaking these words. This was now a mission. "It could be one of great importance as well." She finished this thought out loud.

Parker yawned again, "What? Who're ya talking to?"

"Sorry. I was just thinking that it might be pretty important. Will you be able to organise a meeting with him?"

"Yeah, at least three of his buds have had a thing for me at one time or another. Should be easy." She yawned again, "Okay, as you can tell, I'm beat. It's time to go crash another airplane, Hope. Good talk. See you at school tomorrow."

The line went dead.

Hope Kelley and Parker Wright had come together.

Chapter 18
A Feeling of Utter Dread and Foreboding

Sleep came slowly to a buzzing Hope. Her mind filled with what it all could possibly mean. Sombre was seeping its way into her waking world. She recalled how adamant Hamish the Mender was that Halliday keep Em Contusion 'safe.'

Parker Wright's Colonel Em Contusion.

Why Parker? She was a random choice to say the least. They were two very different people. Hope liked her; her confidence, even her foul mouth. She could already tell Parker Wright said and did what she wanted.

To say she had needed a friend was a chronic understatement. Now she had the best kind: one that shared her nightmare world.

But why on earth was Jerry Cowle coming into her life as well? Was that what was happening? She turned over and over in the covers until she was hot and bothered. Clicking on her bedside light, she slipped on her glasses and picked up the book she had been plodding through for the past year; a well-worn copy of Watchers by Dean Koontz. She knew she should have been picking up To Kill a Mockingbird – but it was in her bag across the room and she couldn't be bothered getting up. Watchers – was a recommendation from her father. It was good, (she thought the aptly named dog, Einstein, very cool), but over the last month, getting through any book was going to be a struggle. She blinked and focused on the page, and true to form, the words soon got blurry. She drifted off, paperback in hand.

∫

Sleeping Hope had been afforded a birds-eye view of her nightmare.

Her death was being paraded. Pale white and bleeding red, her mouth and eyes were stuffed with roses, the rest of her body in bits inside her flower girl dress. Hope's carcass lay on an old wooden door as she was walked down the middle of the road in strange ceremony, by friends and family alike. They were quiet, and remorseless. Curiously, cars continued up and down the road on either side of the death procession, as if the wedding-party-horde-with-corpse was really nothing but a thing to make a little extra room for. Her makeshift pallbearers; mother at the front left, her father on the right, bared the weight easily with the others - Aunt Katrina, her burly new boyfriend, Tom, falling in just behind; scatty Cousin Bree from her father's side, a few more friends and colleagues all had a hand hold of the door. Her murderous sister Kate, seemed to have found control of herself – she appeared to be trying to find a way to hoist herself up onto the door to catch a ride – one hand on the shoulder of the groom, Stuart, (who held his new bride's Sophie's hand), the other on the edge of the door. It seemed everyone from the chapel had come for the walk. The tail of the wedding party was as long as it was motley; torn, partially burnt and bloodstained dresses and suits hung off and flapped around ... Great Uncle Eustis followed riding his motorized scooter.

The onset of evening brought its shadows as the day was coming to an end.

The procession continued on down the road.

∫

The Ruptured Spleen was always a welcome safe haven for Sombre's Gatherers. The heady combination of alcohol, tobacco smoke, deep fried potatoes (a special with ale) and well-worn Gatherer leather and dirt. With chosen beverage in hand, the bar at the top of The Unexplained Mountain numbed the senses nicely and eased the burden of being a professional crutch for the nightmare world.

Halliday needed much numbing this night in Sombre. On her third scotch, her lips felt nice and buzzy – anxiety from her earlier ordeal was slowly easing. She had no interest in heading outside to the balcony. She needed to be inside.

Across the table sat Recalcitrance Bexley, a very level-headed Ballooner Gatherer, and a very level-headed drinker, a rare one; the more the woman drank the more sense she made. She opened and shut a box of matches as she smoked a pencil thin, skinny-cigarette.

"Sombre throws all sorts of things at us, Halliday. You know this. Don't be surprised by a bleeding thing! I'm never surprised." She blew her smoke off to the side.

Halliday admired Recalcitrance's deep dark eyes, full of knowing and no nonsense.

"I *do* know this, but it chilled me to my core, Recalcitrance! An invader! An infiltrator! A bloody specter ... I'm searching for the words." Halliday swept her blond locks from her face and exhaled. She found her chin with her palm and leant on it.

"The drink won't be helping you with that," the Gatherer said with a knowing grin. She sipped her own vodka and raspberry.

"A-ha! Well that's just stating the obvious! You good thing of the air, you!" Halliday smiled gazing at the spiky tips of Recalcitrance's hair, then at the curious streak of silver just above the woman's ear. She wondered whether she could go for that kind of look at all. Would Hamish allow it? Her long blond locks were endlessly floppy and got in the way often when she fought.

She drained the balance of her drink. A hand was placed on her shoulder, making her startle, she turned.

"Halliday, can I get you another. I've just arrived."

It was the friendly face of Dave Bi-Plane. She gasped inwardly as she realized she wanted to embrace him - something she had never wanted from

Dave before. She went to leave her seat, then stopped herself, "Oh, oh yes please, my Dave."

He raised his thick eyebrows toward Recalcitrance who nodded her head.

"She's been drinking them quickly, Dave. Pull up a pew. We could use you in this discussion."

"One for you as well?"

"My word yes," said Recalcitrance.

Dave returned, skillfully holding the three drinks in his large hands, he took a seat next to Halliday. "What are we talking about my fellow Gatherers."

Halliday swept her hair from her face again, lisping a little, she spoke in a low tone. "Something's coming Dave, something big and ugly, cold and dangerous; an evil from somewhere other than here! Not Sombre! The more I think on it, the surer I am of it. It's ice, Dave! Cold as a thousand deaths! It spells major trouble! I'll bet Wilder's left leg on it."

Dave gave her a doubtful look. Then he gave Recalcitrance an even more doubtful one. "Well, this sounds like an interesting one to tip my dollar into." He said. Swigging his lager, he wiped froth from his upper lip. "Halliday, you are in clever company here. If we can't get to the bottom of this, I'll be amazed. I'm in a good state of mind tonight. Managed two clean drops to the Menders today," he gave himself two thumbs up.

"Right! Well done Dave Biplane!" Recalcitrance high fived her fellow air Gatherer, flashing him a winning smile, "Where were you at?"

"You're so pretty Recalcitrance," Halliday interjected, grinning.

"Thanks, Halliday! Where, Dave?" she said butting her stub into an ashtray.

"You're welcome," Halliday mumbled and hiccupped.

Dave smiled at Halliday, "Anyway. Yes, one in Minor Removed - plenty of land to drop the plane out there. A track jogger on The Never-Ending Rail; this one was having one of those mindless nightmares where he couldn't leave the track. Of course, The Black Spectral was about to run him down."

"You're good, Dave, you are," Halliday nodded to herself assuredly and gave him a wink.

"And you're well on your way, aren't you," Dave raised his eyebrows, "you'll fall off your bloody horse Halliday."

"I know. And she won't pity me even a little ... evil cow."

Recalcitrance lit another of her pencil cigarettes. "So where was the other, Dave? I do love to hear about clean gathers, it's the rigid believer in me." She shuddered, "My last Nightmarer had quarter of a head once I got him into the basket. Just a bit of jaw on a neck stump, terrible."

"You won't believe it," he smiled as if he didn't quite believe it himself. "The Twisted Fairground out in Bleeder."

"My god, man! That is a good gather!" Halliday said and shoved him in the shoulder.

"Woman or man?" Recalcitrance blew smoke into the air.

"A teenage boy, a speedy thing – thankfully. I had to shoot a few Psyclowns. You know what *they're* like. The kid had lost a hand, but I'm still calling it clean."

"As you should! That's an easy fix," Recalcitrance said clearing her throat. "I'm empty. We're all empty - think we need another round before we get into Halliday's fix. I'll go."

Halliday just sat and felt her face buzz. She was on her way to a wild sloshing, she knew this. Orty had been mixing them well tonight. She turned to her Dave Bi-Plane, found her chin with her palm once again and rested on it. "Scared me Dave, you know. I don't scare easy, do I?"

136

Dave considered this as he eased his heavy jacket off and placed it over the chair. "No, you don't as a rule. You have plenty of pluck Halliday."

"I have *plenty* of pluck, Dave," she affirmed, her eyes followed her scotch and dry as it came sliding onto the table. "Thank you, Recalcitrance, you are a spiky haired wonder. I like the spikes so much you know," she added.

"Thank you, my girl. Let's get into this now, Halliday," the balloonist gave her a wink, "You have two clever heads eager and ready to listen."

Halliday sat for a moment and sifted through the alcohol-fueled fog in her head. She was interrupted,

"She's as drunk as the town wino," an Other-self stated.

"How many has she had?" said another Other-self.

"Five without a pee. She'll need a pee shortly."

"Go away and let me concentrate, you lot!" Halliday said shutting her eyes tight.

Recalcitrance raised her eyebrows at the non-directional outburst. Dave nodded knowingly, "the Other-selves."

"Oh, I forgot she had those! Ha, ha-ha! Poor thing."

With a deep sucking in of air that made her feel a little sick, Halliday was finally ready. "It was bodied you know. It was a solid thing. It was ticking." She gestured to her Dave Bi-Plane placing her hand on his upper-arm, "Mr. Bi-Plane, I know I've had my share this evening, but I wasn't even partially sauced when this happened. Tonight's saucing is a direct bi-product of this event, in fact." She pursed her lips together and rubbed her nose.

"What was Halliday? We still haven't the information required from you to take it to this table we have here," Dave said rubbing his index finger on the well-scratched up wood.

Halliday found her mouth and sucked from her straw. "Empty, tell Orty."

"We will," Recalcitrance nodded.

"Well, everything in Sombre can be seen and felt, can it not, you always see the Beating Clock at least? This thing doesn't have one. It touched my back. It wanted me to know it was there. It was so cold! Deathly cold. A creeping violator! And it was causing a ticking in my ears like a time bomb!" Halliday shuddered.

Dave furrowed his brow, "so it was a ghost of some sort, that causes ticking? I'm finding it hard to imagine it, Halliday."

Recalcitrance lit another skinny cigarette. "I must admit that I have been drawing a blank as well."

"It's not a ghost, you two! It's bleeding well there! Sombre *has* its ghosts! You know this! Bloody 'Polter Town' is filled with them – but you can still see the blighters' clocks. Everything has a clock! Everything belongs – this doesn't!"

"The clock is a good point," Recalcitrance agreed as she stood up from the table to get another round. "And the ticking wouldn't have been your Beating Clock either. The clock beats, never ticks. A ticking clock would be so terribly typical," she rolled her eyes as she walked off, "Oh, the irony of it all!"

"I wonder what it could be?" Dave said stifling a burp with the back of his hand, "I don't think you would have imagined it. Halliday Knight doesn't make things up."

"I can't lie, Dave! Well, I can, just not very well. I fool only the very dim-witted." She gave him a coy grin, "never the likes of Dave Bi-Plane, though."

"Yes, definitely not the likes of me." He raised his brow and smiled. "Hmm ..." The airman went into quiet thinking mode. His expression changed. Nodding slowly to himself he looked at Halliday. "It's actually quite frightening, Halliday, I agree. To put a bit of a dramatic spin on it; this thing could be anything. It could be a sickness. It could be the start of a plague. What if it was to wipe us all out? If we can't see it, we can't really stop it."

Recalcitrance was back with the drinks. "I see the conversation has turned serious. Where are we at?"

Dave nodded a thank you to Recalcitrance, "We're at sickness and/or plague. Weighty stuff."

"A creeping death plague person. It had a body. It was as tall as I!" Halliday sipped from her seventh and mumbled, "Orty is mixing these well tonight ..."

"Did you hear anything, Halliday? Did said 'creeping death ticking time bomb plague person' make any noise?" Recalcitrance said through a puff of smoke.

"Not an utterance-Recalcitrance! O-Oh, I'm rolling out my rhyming words now! I best slow down on these or I won't be able to get a leg over Wilder at all!"

Dave flashed her a knowing grin, then darkened. "I think we need to consider this as something serious. Let's not spread the word just yet. It's all too vague right now. I think it might be best just to see if anything happens to either of us. It *could* just be Sombre throwing us a curveball, who knows? Sombre does do that from time to time."

"Hopefully," Recalcitrance said running her hands through her hair. She butted out her smoke and gave a clearing cough. "My clock is at five." She tapped the glass timepiece on her chest. "I'm trying desperately to keep it there - as we all are."

The conversation lulled, and Halliday finally realized how full her bladder had become, "too the loo for me."

She stood and her headspace was invaded. Swaying, she pressed on her temples. "Damn it! A job."

"Go get em' girl!" Dave called from the table with well-intended mirth as she hurried to the lady's room. As she pushed open the door, she heard him add in soberer tone, "but be careful!"

CHAPTER 19

RATS

Stepping out of the elevator at the foot of The Unexplained Mountain, Halliday was as filled with as much Dutch courage as she possibly could be – seven wonderfully well-mixed scotches filled.

She had a job to do – the creeping death plague person would just have to make way. This is what she told herself, (Dutch courage was such a wonderful thing.)

Puffing heavily, she paced toward the tree where she'd left Wilder. As was typical, the mare was nowhere to be found – but this time the reason was obvious. The familiar dull grumble of a revving twin exhaust.

"Oh, for all the rot in Sombre, woman! Leave my bloody horse alone!" Halliday yelled and ran east towards the exit. Dust was being churned equally by tyre and hoof as Lucretia St Aimes chased a distressed and kicking Wilder in circles around a Speed Truck. Raven hair flowing over the aptly emblazoned, 'Death-Witch' on her black leather jacket, Lucretia giggled like an evil child. Halliday pulled her Remington and fired a shot in the air. "Stop it you prig of a person! I'll fill you with bullets!"

"But she's such an easy stir-up, Halliday Knight! Such a spine-less nag!" Lucretia span up more dirt and raced the heavy bike closer to the machanihorse's rump.

Halliday had no time for this. Taking aim, she fired a shot, and with a loud ping, hit metal just below the tank. Lucretia skidded to a stop and instantly killed the motor. Kicking the stand, she jumped from the bike. Hair hanging over her face, arms straight down, hands were balled into fists.

"Ho-ho! My word, you must have a death wish, Halliday! No one takes a shot at my bike!"

Swaying a little, Halliday kept the Remington focused on the nasty piece of work coming her way. "Well, no one ever tries to run my ruddy horse down either - except you, idiotic woman! I haven't got time for this. I'm late for a job, I'm quite full of liquor, which always effects my judgement. If you don't want a bullet in that acid tongued head of yours, you'll hop straight back on your godawful contraption and leave us be!"

With unmistakable intent, Lucretia swept her hair from her face and pulled her own gun from a holster at her belt. "Ha-ha! You're a pretty thing, Halliday Knight – you have me covered there – but you are nowhere near the killer I am! Are we going to start this up properly!" Lucretia's barrel smacked Halliday's to one side and she fired a shot missing her right ear by an inch. She laughed savagely. "That was an intentional miss, Halliday. The next bullet I lodge in your forehead." Eyes wild, Lucretia's stark white features were fiercely pernicious under her black mop of curls. Her intent was obvious; her barrel didn't waver.

Sucking her bottom lip, Halliday held her ground. Sweat on her brow, she felt the sobering rush of adrenalin churn her gut. "Damn you woman! I just want to get on my bleeding horse and go do my job!"

"Apologize for the cheap shot at my bike!"

"Wilder! Here, nag!" Halliday called to her mare. With lots of snout clearing snorts, a very disheveled Wilder was at her back. Halliday eased her gun down. "Very well. *I am sorry.* There. That will have to do. Stop chasing my horse, you bully."

Lucretia lowered her barrel and gave Halliday a stony look, "no promises."

Halliday wondered what she got out of scaring Wilder. "You are a strange one, Lucretia St Aimes." Ramming her gun into Wilder's saddle holster, she jabbed her foot into the stirrup and threw herself over and on.

142

"Go have a drink and calm yourself down, you look pale and in need. Onward, my nag!" Giving Lucretia a final disapproving look, she kicked Wilder's sides and the machanihorse obeyed.

As Halliday left the lot, Lucretia caught her completely off-guard, hollering a question. "Halliday Knight! Have you ran into 'Ether' yet?"

"Who?"

The Death-Witch just laughed. Halliday couldn't stop ... but she wanted to.

The nasty piece of work knew something.

∫

A Gatherer couldn't pick and choose assignments. Sombre chose for them. Halliday and Wilder were on their way to quite the unsavoury town.

Steigler was a disgusting place. A town riddled with rats. Awful rats. Nightmarers ended up in the town often as these vermin were at the source of so many bad dreams. Sombre had towns with spiders, mice, reptiles in their all sorts, diseased dogs and mangy felines – *and rats.* Steigler had rats.

Halliday's thoughts weren't with the approaching, Steigler, at all. That wretch, Lucretia St Aimes, had a grip on her mind threads. Through the whooshing noise and movement of The Byway, Halliday yelled loudly to her galloping Wilder.

"That beast of a woman threw me sideways there, my nag! Ether. She said Ether! I hate speaking to her, we all do! But I must find out what she meant!"

The distorted rush of colors disappeared and with a loud bang, Halliday broke through onto a cobblestone road and eased Wilder to a stop. They were at the hilltop entry to Steigler. Halliday knew they were probably too late to spare the Nightmarer.

"Damn it, Wilder! Damn that obnoxious monster and her unctuous motorcycle!"

Her head felt only a little thick from the drink, she had recovered well. From a saddle pouch she grabbed Wilder's tin ankle covers and jumped down.

"These will stop the nibblers my girl," she spoke to her mare, "Ether. She said Ether. And have I met him yet? Or her? She didn't say ... it could be a her?" Halliday tried to focus, as she fastened the clasps, she eyed the half-eaten village below. Her flesh crawled as her eyes followed the grey, white and black patchwork of furry movement; a constant rodent epidemic running riot - squealing, hissing, and squeaking. Rats chewed everything, buildings were mere skeletons of limestone walls, open roofs and gaping, windowless frames.

"We're off to the vile rat-races, my Wilder. Sadly, I think we'll be left with only a Nightmarer corpse," she sighed as she mounted then added, "Positive, stomping movement, horse! That should keep our way clear and stop them running up your legs!"

Wilder set off in a busy trot with Halliday standing up in the saddle. As they approached, the four-legged, snively citizens of Steigler seemed to grow in number. The infestation littering the cobblestones, running on every rooftop, jumping from windows, magically spewing from underground boroughs in the drain work. The stench of faeces and rot was overbearing. "My word, that's offensive," she said.

Slumped in the doorway of a distillery building, a well-mauled corpse was being run through like a rat plaything; through the eye cavities and mouth, rats by the dozen discharged through a gnawed opening in the poor man's stomach. His shoes had been eaten off his feet, his feet almost completely eaten from his ankles.

"I shall name *him* Barry Shoeless, Wilder," Halliday said callously. "Poor fellow. I don't think he is our Nightmarer somehow, though. Rats work quickly, but not that quickly. Barry is quite the abused cadaver. He has been here for a time. I will mention him to Hamish when we drop this one off."

Halliday was hit in the side of the head by a rat.

She startled, "Uh! How-?"

Another landed on her leg, claws digging into her dress. Leaping from the rooftops, they were mounting an attack.

"Eeeeeeeek! Get off you smelly thing!" She tried shaking it off, but it dug in and began crawling. She writhed in the saddle. "Wilder! No! You dirty-!"

Rats were landing on the machanihorse's back. Rearing up on her hinds, Wilder began puffing steam into the air and whinnying madly.

"Whoa, girl! Whoa I say!" Halliday grazed her sword over Wilder's hinds flicking the vermin off.

Should she just turn back? Call in a failure?

"You can't, Hope's Halliday! I never ran, you coward! Get off your bleeding mare and show some gall!" An Other-self rang in her head like an alarm.

The Other-self was right. She jumped from Wilder and pumped three shots from the Remington to the bricks – this caused a scattering.

"Get to the high ground, Wilder. Go on, I will handle this one alone."

With a quick and tight turn, the machanihorse galloped back from where they came.

Wincing, Halliday pulled a wriggling rat from her skirt and threw it down. Now she was on foot and armed with her weaponry, she felt in control. Her Other-selves boastful wisdom sometimes came in handy. She fired more rounds at the cobblestones, her bullets the ultimate repellent. Kicking a well gnawed door open, she entered an old millinery supply shop. She took a quick look around at the shredded clothing material, the faeces stained benches and the few thousand rats running riot over the floor.

"A rat-queen!" Halliday exclaimed, taken aback by the state of the filthy looking female proprietor; Beating Clock stroking high in her chest, the woman sauntered around behind the sales bench, her split brown hair was down to the middle of her back, straggling rats climbed the strands. She wore a rat covered-fur coat. Occasionally she smacked her hand down on the bench and brained a rat for good measure. She had a long pointy nose and she sniffed it hard, a grinning mouth full of pointed teeth. White eyes were like liquid marbles – the woman was as blind as a bat and as mad as a loon.

"Woman! Have you seen a Nightmarer?" She tried and realized her folly straight away.

"Hope's Halliday, are you a simpleton? She's blind, you dimwit!"

"Blind as a bat with a head full of rats!" another Other-self rhymed quite skillfully.

The rat-woman slapped both her hands on the bench. Then she did it again, and again. She stopped and tilted her head to the ceiling. Her voice was a high-pitched squeal, "They're insatiable! Cheek-eaters! Vile contaminators! But I love them so! They hurt! Hurt me all the time! And I love them! Oh! Ha! Hhhhhhhaaaaaaa!" She de-entangled one of the rats from her infested locks and slammed it down on the bench. "NEXT!" she screamed, and spit sprayed through her teeth.

Halliday gulped. The woman was awful, and a lost cause. She suddenly felt very sick to her stomach.

"You mad witch …" she muttered under her breath and backed through the door into the main street of Steigler. The rats had seemed to double in number – it was as if they were all fornicating and birthing grown up rodents with production line speed. Halliday fired more bullets to keep her path clear. Skin crawling, feeling unclean and unwell, she kicked open doors to other hostels and hovels, scanning them quickly for a fresh-looking corpse, then continuing on.

As if being discovered doing all sorts of mischief, an avalanche of scuttling legs, quivering bodies, and sniveling snouts, cleared a lane. An open door revealed an outside toilet with one occupant on board.

"There you are! My dear fellow! You *are* an unexpected sight!" Halliday almost laughed.

The man sat, fully clothed (thankfully) on the porcelain's wooden lid. Rats covered every inch of his body. This was her Nightmarer. His body was slumped against the cistern from the sheer weight of vermin on his torso. Three rats filled his mouth, tails flipping from side to side, stout legs cycling as they tried to burrow further down into the man's throat.

"My goodness, you are in a state!" Halliday made her way toward the toilet-sitter. "I think you're actually still breathing! This has been quite the gather! I wonder how much of you will need a mend. Get off him, rats!" She pulled the three from his mouth.

With an outward exhale and a 'PUH!' from his lips, Halliday saw that the man was indeed still breathing.

"Oh, well done you! Oh! Woops!" He collapsed sideways, suffering an undignified fall from the toilet. Rats scattered from his person and Halliday used her blade to flick the rest away. Kneeling down, she pulled him up by the collar of his shirt and studied his face, eyelids were purple and bruised and shut for business, his mouth bled with tiny scratches from tiny nails.

"Can you stand? Say yes or no."

A rat crept onto her boot and climbed her leg, "Uh! Get out of it, you nasty little pestilent!" She pulled it off, threw it, and jumped to her feet. "Ugh!" She shuddered.

Deciding the man was either unconscious or dying slowly, she yanked him up and began to drag him from the lane. She called at the top of her voice, sounding almost chirrupy given the circumstances. "Wilder, my nag, you shall have to meet me on the street! I have a dead weight here!"

Remington tucked under her shoulder she cleared her way, firing round after round at the rats racing at her feet. She dragged her toilet sitting Nightmarer to the middle of the road and let him drop to the cobbles. The poor fellow's body was still covered in rats, but he was in one piece. Given her tardiness to the scene, that in itself was a small miracle. She watched her mare make her way down from the hilltop and smiled at the haughty, over-exaggerated stomping trot.

"Sometime this afternoon would be lovely of you, my nag!" She made another mental note of just another thing the machanihorse struggled to cope with – *rats.*

Halliday's eyes glazed as she thought again of that witch, Lucretia. Rarely did she say anything of interest. Ether. She hadn't forgotten the name. Had *she* met Ether yet? *That* was of interest, Halliday was sure of it. Other than the fact that the woman was quite awful, there was a lot she didn't know about Lucretia. She had always thought it best to keep things superficial with her. Most did it seemed; she was quite sure Lucretia didn't have any sort of relationship with any of the Gatherers. The woman forced herself upon the drinkers at The Ruptured Spleen. There was an unknown with her, that in truth, no one probably *wanted* to know about. "Hmm."

She refocused on the task at hand as a snorting and steaming Wilder pulled up at her side. Her mare was anxious, to say the least. "Rat's eh, my Wilder. Evil little gnawer's, aren't they?" She patted her nag then holstered her gun. "Calm, girl. We'll be out of here once I lift toilet-sitting-man onto your back. The rats don't want to give him up, leechy little blights on the world that they are. Get off him!"

She skimmed her blade across his back, clearing the last of the vermin. Grabbing the fellow by the shirt collar and pant belt, she heaved her gather past the front of Wilder's saddle, tucking his body under the horn and gullet, draping him across the machanihorse's broad neck.

Completely over rats, Halliday pulled a last runner from her boot leg by the tail and slung it. She mounted Wilder and kicked her mare's sides. With a grateful sounding whinny, nostrils steaming, the machanihorse stomped hard in the direction of the hill. Halliday adjusted toilet-sitting-man's body a little.

"Well, this was sobering to the say the least. I shall need a decent wash and some ointment; I am very itchy and scratched up. Then, sadly for you my nag, we must chase down that dark haired, horse chasing scoundrel, Lucretia." She added, "You'll be brave, I know you will."

Wilder snorted her distaste at the thought as the two left Steigler and its rats behind.

CHAPTER 20

ICY

Hope woke up itchy. Itchy *underneath* the skin, if that was at all possible. Especially in her legs around the knees, where the pull straps on Halliday's boots would have stopped. She tried scratching and regretted it straight away.

"Ow! Shit!" Applying pressure to the area, she held her breath. The itching was like an inner wound. Lucidly dreamt rat scratches hurt *a lot.*

"Well, that sucked ..." she reached for her glasses. She sat up and swung her irritated limbs onto the carpet. That could have been her worst Halliday mission to date. Rats. She could still picture them. The need to get to the shower had never been so dire.

There was a message on her phone from Parker, appallingly worded – 'not ded. no crash. fuck ay! c-u-at school.' Hope stared at the phone. It was official, Parker had befriended her, she just couldn't quite believe it.

And Sombre was responsible – their friendship a direct by-product of the nightmare world.

Her legs felt awful. She ran to the shower.

S

"They're all meant to be friends, but they're all bitches, mom!"

Kate had been in a talkative mood so far this morning. Hope divided her attention between her sister's rant and the breakfast team of Stacy and Jack on WZMP - Mayhem in the A.M.

"Don't call them that, Kate. Girls don't need to be calling other girls bitches," Evelyn Kelley shook her head. "But *who* exactly? You haven't told me - who didn't invite who?"

"Sky and Astrid, I guess," Kate sighed and shook her head, "their folks are hiring the bus."

150

"Ah, the twins ... oh well," Evelyn said as she turned into Centurion's drop off zone. "Well, have you been nasty to them at all, Kate?"

"No! I'm a good friend! You know that! Too damn good, obviously!"

Evelyn was rallying to her youngest's predicament. "Do I have a word to Jessica Woodworth? She's friends with Mandy Prentice. I could see if there's a seat left in the bus. Which arena are they going to again? Who are they seeing?"

"Los Angeles are playing Washington at Staples'. I couldn't give a damn about basketball, but it's not the point is it! I mean some of us are swapping schools next year. We're not all going to *this* hole!" Kate thumbed in the direction of Centurion High as the Jeep pulled up at the curb.

"Mind your mouth there missy, there is nothing wrong with this school, your sister has no complaints," Evelyn turned in her seat. "Okay, Hope. Oh-" She stopped herself mid-sentence and rolled her eyes. She turned the radio volume down, just as Stacy and Jack burst into laughter at another caller's not particularly funny story. "Jesus! Couple of dumb-bells, aren't they? Why do I listen?

"Sorry, Hope. Your sister has flooded the car with this problem this morning. Have a good day." She took her sunglasses off, huffed on the lenses and wiped them with a cloth. "Now, by the way, tomorrow after school you have another appointment with Doctor Marin, after hours at the clinic. You'll be sleeping there."

"What?" Hope stopped as she clicked her belt. "You're kidding me! I've had one visit and now I gotta sleep there? God, you could have given me some warning!"

Her mother shrugged her shoulders and gave her a pitied smile, "This is how it works, apparently... the clinic had a cancellation, and there wasn't another one for a month, so we fast-tracked. Doctor Marin gets his data this way. Should be interesting."

As Hope slid out of her seat and clicked the door open, she threw a verbal jab at her sister. "And you're worried about missing out on a stupid basketball match! Try sleeping overnight at some creep's lab so he can watch your brainwaves! Whiner!"

"Bitch!"

Hope shut the door hard. Her mother gave her a pleading *'why?'* look as she drove away. Adjusting her bag strap on her shoulder, then her glasses up on her nose, Hope walked toward the gate. The Halliday rat-itch was still in her knees, but it was fading. *That* happened in her sleep. How on earth was a monitored night of Sombre going to go down at a sleep clinic? She pictured herself in a white hospital gown, getting up out of bed, pulling cords and sensors along with her while she went on some sort of Frankenstein's-monster-like sleepwalk, arms flailing and legs kicking as Halliday fought off some beast on her latest mission. It was almost too much to contemplate.

Another pimple had formed just under her chin, big and blind and as sore as hell. She muttered an expletive as she spotted Parker sitting on a bricked partition, hessian book bag hanging off shoulder, chin up in smiley defiance. She was being 'talked at' by Georgia, the leader of the Sparks'. The discussion was a heated one, (well at least from Georgia's side). Parker looked like she was extremely at ease with it all. Hope kept her head down as she drew parallel with the two and then attempted to pass.

"Hope!" Parker called out.

Hope turned and watched uncomfortably as Parker the ex-cheerleader stood and stated calmly to the still-current cheerleader captain, "Georgia. If I wasn't so happy with myself right now, I would have slapped those fat lips of yours right off your face for that outburst. Take a pill and fuck off will you!"

With a broken sounding, "Huh!" from Georgia, Parker shook her hair and gave a few over-animated shrugs of her shoulders as she walked off toward Hope. She grinned.

"You're shunned, Parker!" Georgia yelled.

"Yeah, big deal," Parker called over her shoulder and then addressed Hope with an animated raise of her eyebrows. "I have the hospital Jerry's at. Visiting hours start after four – you game?"

Hope, still watching a fuming Georgia stare daggers at them both, hurried to catch up with Parker. A thrill caught in her throat as she answered. "H-How do we get there?"

"I've already texted my brother, Josh. He's got nothing better to do. He'll drive us. Make some shit up and text your mum. Josh will drop you home."

Hope's mind raced, "right."

The older girl rolled her eyes. "Tell me you have your phone on you Hope. Don't tell me you've left it at home on the charger. Old people do that. My gran does that."

"I have it," she felt the pocket in her bag just to make sure.

Parker grinned and nodded. "That's progress."

The second bell rang. "I better hurry, I have math first period," Hope stated.

"See you at lunch. Text your mom," with a friendly push in her shoulder, Parker left and headed in the opposite direction.

Hope pinched her arm just to make sure she was awake.

It was all real. The course of her life was changing. Veering off into the unknown.

"Awesome," she said under her breath as she raced to class.

∫

"Josh is a total dick about his car, Hope." Parker said as the two walked toward the main gate at schools end. "He's 19 and working part time at a shitty pawnbroker in Lamont. He's up to his neck in debt with it. Best just to sit and not touch anything, I'd rather keep the drive civil."

The silver Mustang started up as the two approached. Hope waited for Parker to open the door to the coupe. The two were bombarded with an aural explosion of death metal as they slid into the black leather seats.

Parker had to yell, "Josh, did you just turn that up as we got in?"

"Deal with it, Parker. Who's your friend?"

Josh Wright turned and removed his sunglasses. Hope gulped. Parker's brother had a dangerous air about him. Dyed, jet black hair swept over his blue eyes. She noticed the chiseled jaw-line. Like his sister, he was well put together – but he seemed to be fighting against it. Hope tried a smile. The older boy gave her the blankest of looks as he slid his glasses back on.

"Josh, meet Hope. Hope meet Josh. He thinks he's tough, but he really isn't. He sure tries hard though."

Hope mouthed a, "Hi."

Josh didn't bite back at his sister, just threw the Mustang in gear and revved the motor hard. They pulled away slowly.

"He's at the Mercy, Downtown – second floor, room **315!**" Parker announced to both occupants, yelling to get over the rumbling death metal. "Oh, turn this shit down will you! You're not impressing anyone with it!" she turned in her seat, "Sorry, Hope, this abysmal rubbish is what he listens to 24-7."

Josh ignored Parker as he stopped at the intersection, turned right and floored it.

"What did you tell your mom?" Parker queried.

"That I've been invited over to Tran's to study for an English exam," she called back as she began pulling at her fingers with vigor.

"She a friend?"

"No."

"But she is in your class, right?"

"Yeah."

154

"She cool?"

Hope swallowed. "No, not particularly."

"Should you have used someone else?"

"There's no one else to use," Hope admitted, not overly comfortable with this conversation. (Particularly in front of Parker's brother who she was sure she saw smirk.) Parker had picked herself up a younger 'dud' to hang round with. He would be wondering where his sister's head was at? He was picking up the stench of Parker's social suicide. Hope knew the car suddenly stunk of it.

Parker gave her brother a sideways glance, then turned down the music.

"Hey! I didn't say you could do that!"

"Just a bit. I can't hear myself think, nerd!" She pulled down the passenger visor and looked at herself in the vanity mirror, then began rubbing a hand over her left cheek. "Friggin zit-fest lately. So' run down. I did have the best skin in my class."

"Mine used to be okay as well," Hope offered as she felt the car change gear and slow down. A cream-colored building came into view. Indicating, Josh pulled into the Mercy Hospital drop off zone.

"Don't go far, Josh. I'll text you."

"You owe me for this, Parker," he said and ran his hands through his hair as he pulled to the curb.

"Yeah, whatever. Stay close, we'll be about twenty," she cracked open her door.

Hope did the same. Josh Wright was intense; she was more than happy to be getting out of the sedan.

Lending well-timed authenticity to the occasion; Hope caught a glimpse of the yellow in Parker's cheeks as the two stepped out onto the path, the late afternoon shadow-light giving the older girls skin a strange, deathly glow.

Perfectly tempered air filled her senses as she followed Parker into the entrance of the Mercy. "Straight to the elevators," Parker said licking her lips, clearly enjoying herself. Hope was her giddy accomplice, two Sombre-affected teenage girls about to visit a beaten Jerry Cowle; like two detectives on the most random of cases: a mystery with next to no semblance in reality. The older girl jabbed the 'up' button and they waited.

"I think I'd better do the talking to begin with. He knows me enough to not be freaked out," she raised her eyebrows and grinned. "Fuck, Hope! How's this! You nervous?"

"Shitting myself, actually," Hope said grinning. She pushed her glasses up on her nose. The elevator door opened, and they stepped in.

Parker studied Hope's face. "You need contact lenses, Hope. You have nice eyes behind those things, the friggin lenses are so thick they look like frosted glass."

"Contacts make my eyes itchy."

"Get some drops then, make it work somehow. If it was me, I'd be saving those things for home. The whole Millhouse from the Simpson's thing you have going on there needs a rethink."

"That's not very nice, Parker," Hope said, a little dismayed by her new friend's need to take an observational crap on her good mood.

"Yup. No, it wasn't. But *very* true, Hope ... I *did* say you had nice eyes."

Parker Wright shot from the hip - something to get used to.

The elevator stopped at the second floor.

Parker sucked on her bottom lip. "C'mon, this is us. We don't have to worry about the front desk. It's room **315**."

The two paced through the ward. Hope remembered how much she hated hospitals. She had spent more than her fair share in them when she was younger. Her Great Auntie Elle had suffered through a bout of pneumonia that she ended up dying from. Hope was seven at the time and visiting with her mother, daily. She learnt from a young age that hospitals couldn't fix everything. Not able to help herself, she peered into every room they passed.

"This is it. Wow, he's got a private one," Parker announced in a gruff whisper, "you ready?"

Hope just nodded as she fell in behind her friend. It wasn't her intention to hide behind Parker – but it was only now that she realized how awkward this was going to be – they really had no right being here at all.

"Shhh - shit!"" Parker exclaimed stopping just inside the doorway. She held Hope back with both arms. "Who in the hell-?"

Hope peered in over Parker's shoulder.

Jerry was asleep, his hand resting on a mini iPad.

He had a visitor.

The man was sickly gaunt under his black raincoat. His long, thinning dark hair barely covered his scalp. Hope couldn't tell if his hair was wet or just greasy. Beneath the strands, an over-elongated neck was sickly white. Back turned, with long fingered hands clasped behind his back, he stood over Jerry at his bedside, leering, as if daring him to rouse.

"It couldn't be ..." Hope croaked.

He had been partially obscured by trees at the party, but she knew this was the same creep who had been watching her.

The chill in the room was crypt-like. A replica of the other morning in her bedroom. The same chill Halliday had felt at the foot of The Unexplained Mountain.

"Are you going to go in? He's due to wake up soon."

Both girls startled, as a young nurse entered the room. Heading straight to the clipboard at the end of the bed, she studied the monitors and began penning notes.

Hope could see that the nurse was completely oblivious to the other presence in the room.

Satisfied with Jerry's readings, she turned and walked back toward a wide-eyed Parker and Hope, giving them both a gentle, tired smile. "You know, he'll be fine. A beating like the one he had will take some time to recover from. He's had some internal bleeding that caused us some concern ... are you friends from school?"

"Y-Yes," Parker said. It was a miracle she could say anything at all, as only feet from the nurse's shoulder, the man in the raincoat stood watching both of them, mouth set in a knowing smirk. In stark contrast to his sickly pale face, his eyes were an unreal luminescent black. Arms rigid at his sides, his almost powder white hands were turned outward, as if imploring both girls to come closer.

The nurse continued on, "We have Jerry on calmatives, those things make you sleepy." She gestured to two chairs at the wall. "You can sit and wait if you want."

With a curious, but friendly smile, she left.

The two girls were left staring at the stranger.

"Fuck! What do we do? He's a ghost, isn't he? That nurse couldn't see him," Parker hugged her arms, "It's so friggin cold in here! She couldn't feel *that* either! Do we go in?"

Hope couldn't peel her eyes away. "No! We're not going any further. He's dangerous, Parker!"

"Do you know this freak? Who is he?"

"Uh!" Hope gasped as searing pain shot from her left temple and coursed across her forehead. "I think ... oh god, what's going on ... I think I'm going to collapse!" She took hold of the older girl's arm to steady as her legs folded beneath her. Her eyes glazed. It was the party all over again.

Parker braced her fall, "Shit! No, you're not! I won't fucking carry you out of here, Hope!" She shook Hope by the shoulders. "Sorry, but this has to be ..."

Parker slapped her face hard, dislodging her glasses from her nose.

Hope's vision was filled with stars, but the slap had done the trick, broken through the pain.

Parker pulled her by the arm toward the door as the strangers mouth widened; he produced a thin tongue. A guttural murmur rose from deep down in his throat; he sniffed up a snot-full, coughed and laughed as ticking filled the room, filled everywhere.

Hope felt like she was being punched continually in the chest – it was her heart – she could actually feel it; its size, its weight.

She gasped, "Can you feel that, Parker?"

"What? Like I'm about to have a heart attack? Yeah - I can!" the older girl cried.

Hope's hand went to her breast, an attempt to cushion her precious organ, as it pounded along with the ticking.

The ghoul moved closer, mesmerizing them both. Black eyes shining wet, he snorted excitedly, as his focus went directly to Hope. He spoke in a whisper, his tone full of gravel. "Oh, how she's known! What an intricate path she is to walk. How she impedes upon the spaces as she lives her burden. A burden to all!"

Hope felt his chill pinching her spine, pulling on her nerves. Was this what Halliday had felt?

Losing control, she fell forward. The pain in her head was back. "No!"

"Oh, fuck this!" the ghoul's spell had broken on Parker, she burst into action. "Good luck Jerry! Come on!"

She dragged a shivering, convulsing, Hope out of the room.

$\int$

Parker and Hope sat in the back seat of the Mustang in silence. Parker had offered a still-shaking Hope a comforting arm. She held Hope's surprisingly weighty glasses in her right hand, figuring they would just get in the way as she recovered.

Both had hardly uttered a word. Sensing the mood, Josh's non-stop death metal attack was at an acceptable volume. In contrast to the onset of their journey, the muscle car's motor could now be heard and not just felt.

Hope had finally stopped shivering. Retrieving her arm, Parker sat up. Rubbing her hands up and down her jeans she called out to brother,

"We'll need fifteen, Josh. Pull over."

"Why?"

"Hope and I need to talk."

"So, talk - no one's stopping you."

"We need privacy, dick!"

"This favor's almost out of gas, Parker! I've got things to do you know! Jesus!" he slowed down and pulled the car into a curb. "*Ten* minutes, I'll be timing it!"

"Yeah, whatever," Parker pushed open her door. "Come on Hope."

Hope looked up at Josh's rear-view mirror as she slid along the back seat - he was watching her. Hope Kelley was turning out to be a real pain in Josh Wright's ass.

She met Parker sitting with her legs crossed on the warm, dry patch of nature strip. It was summer, and there was as much dirt as there was grass. She glanced around at Channel Drive. They were a few streets away from her house. Some kids were having a noisy game of Nerf guns, while their mothers spoke in the driveway. She found the sight soothing.

160

"Quick, sit down, Hope," Parker said ripping up some yellowed lawn with her fingers. She spoke hurriedly, "What are we going to do. All of this has just gone up a gear. Who in the hell was that? What was with the ticking?"

Hope sat and shut her eyes; she was still lightheaded. She pictured the creep's smiling face, the black eyes. The long neck. She shuddered. She could still feel how his chill pulled at her nerve-endings.

"Halliday hadn't been able to see him. She could only hear and feel him," she said. She stared straight at Parker, "He was the stranger from the party who followed me into the trees ... he's from Sombre. I - I can't believe it."

Parker nodded and grinned. "Why can't you believe it? I can! We went there to see something. We saw the show. Of course, I didn't think we were going to run into that freak ... shit! What a rush!"

Hope nodded. "He has to be the one who attacked Jerry. So, Jerry has seen him. We have. Halliday hasn't yet ..." She paused as a flashback from her previous night in Sombre flooded her thoughts. "Lucretia has though! She asked Halliday if she had ran into Ether. Ether! That was the freaks name. It has to be him! I wonder what it all means?"

"What do you mean what it all means? It means that our freaky dream world is crashing our reality, Hope! That creep has broken through!" Parker stopped and gave her a curious look, "Hang on, back up a bit. Who's Lucretia? You just dumped a random in there."

"Another Gatherer – sort of Halliday's nemesis. A nasty piece of work. Rides a motorbike, has black hair and black lips, she wears a black leather jacket, says 'Death-Witch' on the back."

"God, I'm so jealous your character is a Gatherer. Stupid Em can hardly string a sentence together," she threw grass at Hope. "You suck."

"Ether is dangerous, Parker. You heard what the nurse said. Jerry had internal bleeding! It's taking him days to recover. What if he comes after us?

He's already followed me! Why was he in Jerry's room? It was like he was waiting for us! He said something as well. Can you remember what it was?"

"No. The lunatic was rambling, we were trying to leave," Parker said. "Hm ... actually, you're right about one thing. He didn't seem surprised to see us."

Josh hit the horn.

"Yeah, okay!" she shook her hand at her brother and held up two fingers for two more minutes. She turned to Hope. "Call me tonight about this. I think we should talk before we hit the hay. Let's keep right up in each other's business now. We need to stick together as much as we can when we're awake."

"What am I going to do tomorrow night?"

"What do you mean, friend?" Parker said as she got to her feet. Josh hit the horn again. "C'mon," she pulled Hope up by the hand. "We don't want him to drive off on us."

They both walked to the car.

"I forgot to tell you," Hope continued. "My mother has me going to a sleep clinic. I'm going to be monitored as I sleep."

Parker laughed, "Oh shit, that ought to be fun! Couldn't you get out of it? What's going to happen do you think?"

"No, I can't. And who knows? I'm not looking forward to it. The doctor guy is pretty lechery as well."

"But you'll go to Sombre, won't you? How's that going to work?"

Hope waited as Parker cracked the shiny passenger door to the Mustang, she answered her without a single trace of humour. "It might be quite a show."

CHAPTER 21

IMPOSSIBILITIES

"If we see him, I suppose we'll just have to run."

Hope said yawning, she craned her neck to look at the clock. It was after ten. She had been laying on her bed and talking with Parker on the phone for just over an hour.

"As chickenshit an idea as that is, Hope, I think you're right." At the other end of the line Parker also yawned. "Gee, I'm beat. Anyway, it's not like we can go to the police – no one can see him," she wound things up,

"So, what do we have so far: we're fairly sure he's this Ether fucker. He's beaten up Jerry Cowle to within an inch of his life, for reasons we're not sure of. He's like some sort of dream ghost? We have no clue why he's here. We're just waiting for that Gatherer, Louella-what's-her-name, to feed Halliday some information in Sombre once she chases her down."

"Lucretia," Hope corrected the older girl.

"Yeah right, much better than Louella. Louella makes her sound like someone's overweight aunty – Aunty Louella! Ha!"

Hope giggled. "I couldn't see Aunty Louella riding round on Lucretia's motor bike!"

"We still need to talk to Jerry, though," Parker said. "See what he knows about this freak. There has to be a reason he's been targeted. For all we know, Jerry could be someone in Sombre as well. He's got that same nasty yellow in his face like we do."

"Maybe," Hope said unconvinced. Parker had come to her through Halliday. Hope's Halliday had some almighty purpose with Parker's, Colonel Em Contusion. Hamish the Mender had said so. Halliday had nothing to do with Jerry as far as she could tell.

The line went quiet at the other end for a moment before Parker yawned and said, "Hope. You know you can end this phone call if you like. I mean, I'm tired, you're tired – I won't be hurt if you want to go. I shouldn't be the one to always have to end the phone call. It's all a bit nasty of you, really." Parker yawned again. "Do you hear how tired I am."

"Oh. Okay, sorry," Hope said not knowing if she had really pissed the older girl off or if she was joking.

"It's alright. You're not well versed in phone call etiquette. We can't text all this stuff – we have to talk it out. You're like a new teen-alien, learning the ways of our strange society," she huffed, "You need to be able to say, 'Parker, I'm tired, see ya,' or 'well, I'm bored with your boring shit – *later*."

Hope giggled, "well I'm not going to say that last one, am I?"

"Why? I'm your friend. I won't get offended. I *might* bore you occasionally, it happens – as sparkling as my personality is."

"Good night, Parker. Sleep well," Hope said.

"Oh, you're hanging up on me now?"

"I am," Hope said grinning.

"Good. Later."

∫

Hope drifted then fell heavily into sleep, wraithlike hands came searching for her subconscious, dragging her back into her rite of passage, into the nightmare world ...

Her butchered body, in bits under her bloody bridesmaid dress, slopped around on the wooden door as the wedding-turned-funeral procession walked her corpse through cemetery gates. Her sister having found a way up onto the door, rode with her, she was checking her phone, scrolling through some social media.

164

The relatively clear afternoon disappeared as an unreal mist came over the grounds – a particularly fake looking mist, as if pumped in by dry ice machines for special effect. Her mothers head appeared at the edge of the door, she smiled evilly at Hope's corpse, her eyeshadow ran ghoulishly, bringing out her impossibly bloodshot eyes.

"Gonna drop you off now, Hope. There's a hole ready for you, you wretch! Ha!"

A single gull landed on Hope's corpse and began to peck at her carcass with its beak. Her dead nightmaring soul cried out at the indignity of her ending, the unfairness of it all. What had she done? More gulls flew down and landed on the sliding mess that was her body, joining in the blood feast. Her sister didn't seem to notice.

The procession continued along the winding gravel path, past rows and rows of cement headstones; the bride and groom, and twenty or thirty soiled and bloodied guests, walking in slow motion, (in her Great Uncle Eustis's case, scootering) all wanting to see her soon to be bird-defiled, corpse gone.

∫

Halliday Knight had never had to seek out Lucretia St Aimes – *never.* The very thought of it left an acidic taste in her mouth. After dropping 'toilet-sitting-man' off at The Menders, her time was now her own. Well, at least it was, until Sombre gave her a next mission, or the quite hopeless, Colonel Em Contusion, decided to crash another plane. Aboard a galloping Wilder she travelled through The Byway and watched and listened to Sombre's movements. The Byway at this speed was pure distortion; comically unreal and horrifying at the same time. Endless forms of towns and their citizens came and went, terrible and disturbing to the eyes. A discordance of shouting voices screamed in anguish, thrill and pain, murderous rage and wild laughter. One could hear distant missiles and tea-kettle-like whistling, bombs and explosions and a variety of roaring motors.

Halliday listened for just one motor; an obvious twin exhaust that she thought she knew quite well. And if *she* didn't, her mare certainly did.

"There is something wrong in Sombre, my faithful steaming nag. Crooked! Damned well bean shaped! Mark my words!" Wilder pumped wet vapor up and into Halliday's face as she whinnied her disapproval of this venture.

Her rider wiped her forehead and laughed hard. "Oh, snort at me if you want, you stroppy cow, but this will be for the greater good! Just listen out for that abominable contraption of hers."

"Halt, Wilder!" A rumbling motor caused them both to slow until they heard the air horn. "Speed Truck! No! Move on!" Halliday yelled licking her lips, deeply invested in this new challenge. The endless thoroughfare that was The Byway went on and on. Time passed. With a high-pitched whinny, Wilder skidded to a stop.

Halliday kicked her mare's sides in the stirrups. "Yah! Ha-ha! That would be her! Well done, my nag!" Machanihorse and rider charged through the entry into the town where Lucretia St Aimes had been summoned.

ʃ

It was the edge of the night. They stopped on a road of loose asphalt. The skies cracked and flashed with heavy gunfire - lots of it.

"Where are we Wilder?" Halliday said genuinely confused. "And how on earth did you hear Lucretia's bike through all of this?

"She's gone and chased that witch into Battallion," said an Other-self, *"bad move."*

"If to get yourself shot to pieces was your aim, this is where you would go!" said another with a huff. *"But Hope's Halliday is a bit of a simpleton. We have established this, and she just keeps proving us right."*

The current Halliday shrugged and pulled her Remington, she gave Wilder a squeeze with her legs and spoke under her breath to her mare, "C'mon let's go find her."

Halliday was intruding, she knew it, this wasn't her mission. What she was doing now would be frowned upon, but she didn't care. Deep in her core she knew this was right. This Ether, had to be found. If she had to break a few of Sombre's unwritten laws, so be it. Another burden to add to her growing list, she would have to wear it like a badge of honour. Things were changing. Hamish had told her this again and again.

As if a light had switched on inside her, finally, she now believed it.

Battallion had a depressing air about it. A World War II situation; its creator had a very elaborate nightmare indeed. He or she had dreamt up a coastal war scene, a war-torn city as well. Ocean spread out to Halliday's left; three Higgin's boats were ashore; two massive aircraft carriers were anchored in the distance. Faceless houses and equally faceless, multiple storied buildings, were spread out around the inland in clumps of uniformed rows, as if taken from a World War II edition of Monopoly. A central city was the target of heavy attack. Flash-fire and bombing throughout the streets lit up the bomb-bitten buildings.

Halliday sighed, "this will be a challenge, Wilder."

There was a heavy metal shake and rumbling of tracks and Halliday gave way to two rumbling tanks approaching on the road from behind. An open topped jeep followed and swerved to miss her. One of its two occupants shouted at her, his voice young, full of hopped up inexperience. "Get outta' the way, you stupid dame!"

She retaliated. "Barbarian! Mind your manners, soldier! You rude little prig!" The serviceman turned and leered at her as they overtook the tanks and continued into the city. She shook her head and addressed her mare. "I'm not hugely opposed to slander as a rule, Wilder. But I will not be called a 'dame'. Such terms are unbefitting and unnecessary!" Wilder went into a jaunty trot, heels high - she understood - and agreed. Left hand on the rein, Halliday's right held the Remington ready at her hip. Smoke filled her nostrils as they entered Battallion's main city dwelling. The random fallout of war was everywhere. Grimacing mothers with tear-soaked faces ran with children in hand, scampering for cover. A lost dog whimpered, a black Mastiff, on the loose from its home, tip-toeing in indecision. Fallen civilians and soldiers were being rushed away on stretchers.

Strangely, a dozen well-dressed servicewomen, Beating Clock's gleaming, hair perfectly coiffed, marched through the town singing a stirring rendition of the Andrew Sisters anthem, 'Boogie Woogie Bugle Boy.' Saluting the action with smiling, lipstick smacked mouths, voices smooth and jazz-filled;

> *'He was a famous trumpet man from out Chicago way*
> *He had a boogie style that no one else could play*
> *He was the top man at his craft*
> *But then his number came up and he was gone with the draft*
> *He's in the army now, a-blowin' reveille*
> *He's the boogie woogie bugle boy of Company B!*

The group of women continued through the street, seemingly untouchable.

"Woe Wilder!" Halliday shouted as she spotted a slew of aerial bombs fall and a building capitulate in fresh explosion; slabs of concrete rubble falling, dust and smoke blanketing the area. Rounds of gunfire flashed and echoed through the streets. There were shouts from soldiers from opposing sides, and subsequent screams of anguish as direct hits claimed more victims.

Halliday pulled Wilder to relative shelter; a laneway between the walls of a barbershop and a cinema. "This place is quite volatile, Wilder. Not my wisest decision," she said jumping from the saddle. Her boots splashed into the lane's guttering.

"Rightly or wrongly, we are here now. I shall guard us with my gun until we spot Lucretia." She patted Wilder on her steam-soaked nose. "We'll be out of here soon my mare."

Squatting, back against the wall, she peered around the corner of the cinema to her left. Another wave of action was elevating as tanks rolled through the street blasting holes through the facades of every building. A burning bomber fell from above, spiraling down like a drunken phoenix. It landed heavily in the centre of the street in an impressive display of combustion.

"BACK WILDER!" A grenade rolled in front of Halliday and she threw herself backward. The blast lifted her high in the air, she somersaulted further down the laneway. Landing hard on her front, she heard her clockface crack. The dust cleared; she opened her eyes.

"My god, this place is all sorts of painful!" she said and spat grime from her lips. The grenade had blown a large chunk from the wall she had just been using as a shield.

Her legs didn't feel right.

She felt a moment of panic. Had they been blown off?

"No, no, no!" Pulling herself up into a sitting position, she looked down. They were there, just numb. Blowing out a massive breath of panicky air, she put her gun down and tried rubbing some feeling back into them. Wilder's snout was suddenly nuzzling her neck "You're a clever thing, my mare. Are you scathed?" Halliday turned on her backside and faced the machanihorse. "You are!" Wilder's Beating Clock-face glass had been cracked, as had her oil pressure, water and steam gauging windows. She was wet and greasy between her shoulders. Halliday shook her head, "You're leaking a little. This needs to be over, so I can get you back to the Office'. My transportation needs repair."

Wilder flinched and whinnied.

"What? Do not be offended. That is a wasted emotion for you, Wilder. You *are* my bleeding, leaking transport!"

At her back, Halliday heard a revving motor. It filled the lane.

"Oh, I see ... that was for Lucretia."

A hot tyre was suddenly pressing into her back.

Lucretia St Aimes revved her motor again and then killed it. Halliday twisted round and craned her neck, she peered up past the heavy front suspension and the illuminated head lamp of the cycle. Raven black hair hanging like rope, Lucretia leered down at her. Halliday gasped. The woman's face was monstrous! Not unlike her own Morphia! Wild red eyes were set deeply into her skull, spidery veins covered her cheeks, her mouth was open, an animal-like scowl, baring broken teeth. She spoke gutturally,

"What are you doing in Battallion, Halliday Knight? Don't give me any bullshit about Sombre giving you a mission here, either!"

Feeling having returned in her legs, Halliday stood up. She pointed accusingly, "You! You have your own Morphia!" She furrowed her brow. "How is it you're not ripping me apart now?"

The beastly woman's crooked smile said it all.

Halliday had a lot to learn about the Death-Witch, Lucretia St Aimes.

CHAPTER 22
The Death-Witch, The Hell-Flyer

Two Gatherer's, one machanihorse, one motorbike (with headless Nightmarer tied to back seat), stood in the lane of Battallion as the nightmare town's endless war continued on around them.

"You haven't answered my question, Halliday. What are you doing here?" Lucretia let her features slide back to her usual dark beauty.

Halliday got to her feet and dusted off her backside. She blew her fringe out of her face. "I have sought you out. I need to speak with you about this Ether person. You piqued my interest for once, Lucretia."

"And you'd risk another stroke for *that*?"

"As it turns out, I would." Halliday folded her arms. Lifting each leg up and down gingerly, she shook her feet and grimaced. "Now, if you could please tell me how you control your Morphia like that? And why you have one at all? That would be nice of you."

Lucretia's face darkened. "You really think you can encroach on my mission and throw demands in my face, Halliday? I know you think Sombre's sun rises and sets at your bootheels, woman, but you can pretty well piss off! I don't have to tell you a thing!" She smiled and raised her eyebrows.

Halliday despised the smugness. The woman loved this! Why had she expected anything different?

Lucretia eyed Wilder. "Your skittish companion seems to be leaking. You might want to get her to The Menders, can't have her insides drying out. I'd imagine that would cost her a stroke." Lucretia went to kickstart her cycle. Halliday grabbed the handlebar. "You can't just leave, Lucretia. We really need to talk."

Lucretia pushed Halliday's hand away. "Actually, we really don't. I need to get headless Jim here back to The Office."

"Jim can wait!" Halliday said shrilly. She was on the backfoot, this was all about to become a complete waste of time. She had to go somewhere she didn't want to go with this damnable woman – there would be pleading involved. "Please Lucretia, please give me ten minutes of your time. I need to know who Ether is!"

Lucretia gave her a hard laugh, "Why should I give you anything, Halliday? I know what you and the other Gatherer's think of me." She struck the kickstand and parked the bike.

"We all speak to you. I don't know what you mean?"

"Puh! Rubbish, woman! You're lying to me and yourself!" As if it were a mere after thought, Lucretia pulled a heavy revolver from a side-sack at the bikes saddle. She turned just as a half dozen soldiers rounded the corner of the lane.

Instinctively, Halliday readied her Remington.

"A dame! Two of them!" A very youthful looking soldier boy stared wide eyed, mouth agape, as his helmeted compatriots fell in behind. He wore his silver rimmed Beating Clock under his service coat, Halliday noticed his strokes were at nine.

"Corrr! Ebony and ivory, boys," said another slightly older one with a confident grin. "Sight for sore eyes. Wildcats too, by the look of em!"

Halliday's blood boiled, she couldn't help herself, "I am no dame, you stupid man!" Before she could say more Lucretia unloaded and shot the soldier in the middle of the forehead, splitting the skull wide.

"Jumpin' Jesus, boys! She shot Davey!"

"Lieutenant! What do we do? This isn't the enemy is it?" Heavy Garand rifles were raised as the men spread out across the lane. "BACK DOWN! DROP YOUR WEAPONS!"

Halliday opened fire, with an incredibly controlled and focused Lucretia St Aimes. The soldiers were dead in an instant.

Lucretia lowered her revolver and smiled to herself. "Beauty is such a weapon, Halliday. Did you know that?" She returned to her motorcycle and swung a leg over. "I suggest you get out of here, Battallion isn't good for anyone." She kicked life into the motor, revving hard.

Halliday wouldn't let her go. With her arms out wide, she stood over the front wheel of the bike. "Meet me at the top of the hill, at the entry, where it's safe! Please, Lucretia! Just ten minutes!"

She gave Halliday the hardest of stares and then a nod. She backed her bike around the dead soldiers. The Death Witch was giving her a chance.

Halliday ran for Wilder.

∫

"This won't take long, girl," Halliday spoke to a trotting Wilder as she stood in the stirrups. Remington in hand, she covered them both through the smoky Battallion street. She watched the skies, as directly above, planes circled the city, ready to drop bombs with about as much thought as a flock of gulls clearing their colon's. Battallion was dangerous, but a rather senseless place, Halliday surmised. Then again, a lot of Sombre was.

At the top of the hill, Lucretia waited. Halliday knew she wouldn't wait long. She eased her mare around two more passing jeeps. There was a hissing sound and wet steam on her mare's neck. "You're not well, Wilder, are you? I'll be as quick as I can, this has to be I'm afraid."

"Quickly now, Halliday Knight! I want out of here," Lucretia called out as they approached, "I notice your mare looks ready for the butchery." The woman's smile was needlessly savage.

"She'll be fine," Halliday said and jumped from the saddle. Wilder didn't move from her side, she nuzzled into her owner's neck. Halliday felt around Wilder's leaking nostrils, she was losing a lot of fluid. "She has a decent tank."

"One that is in dire need of a fix and replenish!" an Other-Self piped up in her head.

"She'd rather talk to this awful wretch than tend to her mare! Stupid Hope's Halliday!" said another.

"Shut up all of you!" Halliday clenched her fists.

Lucretia looked sideways and sat up straight on the bike. "Who're you talking to, woman?"

"My bleeding Other-selves!" she admitted. "Do you have those as well?"

"What? You have voices in your head? Oh! Ha-Ha! No! Oh, for all that's wrong in Sombre! That's rich that is! Halliday Knight rides a scared horsey and has a head full of naysayers!" The Death-Witch held her chest and laughed until she coughed.

"Are you finished? I'm sorry I told you, you devil's hex!" Halliday said screwing her face up. "Let's get this over with. Firstly, how do you control your Morphia like that?"

Lucretia smiled smugly, she gathered her long locks, pulling them round to her back. "I'm resourceful Halliday. I use everything I own to do my job. My will is strong, stronger than my Morphia ... you have no idea *how* strong."

"So, there is no trick to it?"

"No. It's not a trick," she rolled her eyes. "You need strength. You have to be stronger than your monster. It makes you the ultimate."

"Oh," Halliday said wondering straight away why she couldn't do this. She could feel Wilder moaning gently. She thought she had better get to the point.

"Who is this Ether? How do you know of him?"

"He's an 'it', and 'it's' not from Sombre. And 'it's' bad news for us all," Lucretia's expression changed, her mouth tightened. "Well, accept for me. I've been chosen as a point of contact."

"Why you?"

"It sees me as it should. Superior. An autonomous warrior-type."

Halliday watched the woman's black lips speaking the words; then the woman's eyes believing nothing of what she herself was saying. Were her dark blue peepers even darker than just a moment ago. Halliday felt a twinge of pity.

Was Lucretia worth this type of emotion? She didn't think so. She cleared her throat, "How is it I could only *feel* this Ether, not see it? It was like ice!"

"It was observing you, obviously. I have a good feeling that every Gatherer will cross its path. When they do, they might know it, they might not as well." Lucretia went about retightening the ropes around the torso of her headless Nightmarer. She obviously wanted to leave.

"Where's the fellow's head?" Halliday queried.

"I have a flat pack of mush in a satchel. A tank ran it over. You don't need to see it."

Just as Lucretia went to kickstart her machine, Halliday tried for one more question. "Where does it come from?"

"The Isolate, Halliday. It comes from The Isolate. It's cold there." Raising her eyebrows, she smiled smugly and kicked the motor over. With a rev, she turned and pulled away.

Halliday watched the Death-Witch, slip into The Funneling, black hair flying. It was over.

She turned and faced Wilder with her hands on her hips. The mare's whole front was now soaked with her leaking fuels.

"Well, my dripping, oily companion, I need to get you-"

'I'm coming down hard, Commander Acker! CRASH AND BURN BABY! This Woeful dove has a death wish! I'm riding her home! Tonevereturn!"

Halliday shook her head, "Oh, good lord, not now, Em, you pathetic wretch!" She turned on her heel and peered up. The junker was spinning madly, with one wing left intact, black smoke patterning the sky - it's deluded occupant taking the ride to the ground. She looked to her ailing Wilder, who snorted and nodded her head. "We have to. I'm sorry, my nag. Damn this dopey woman!" Halliday boarded Wilder and the mare set off toward the centre of Battallion in a lethargic trot, steam puffing from her joints.

'Ka-Ching! I've touched down with a cerrrrunchhhhhhhh! Eerrrrrrr...!'

"Oh, for all the stupidity in Sombre, Wilder! What a bane this Em Contusion is!"

Halliday and Wilder entered the main street to a rampant battle royal – a fresh new wave of soldiers shouted commands in a European tongue. The grey coated fought the tan coated, their gun fire deafening. Hunched soldiers ran from one building to another, covering fire echoed through the area. Three tiger striped Panzer tanks blew random holes in one multi-storied establishment in an effort to topple the structure and create a barrier between the two warring factions.

It was foolhardy, she knew it, yet how could she avoid it? This was her cross to bear.

"I'm coming Em, hold on!" Halliday shut her eyes as Wilder galloped through a hail of gunfire. Em Contusion's burning bomber had dumped nose first into the cabin of an army jeep. She was alone. "They allowed you a solo flight, Em?!"

Exasperated, Halliday looked skyward. The wreckage sat in the shadows of the very building the tanks were trying to topple. Every shot was finding good purchase – it didn't look like she would have long.

"Find some cover, Wilder!" she bellowed leaping from the saddle.

"Ughhh!" a stray bullet lodged in her shoulder. Biting her bottom lip, she caught her breath as she peered through the cracked cockpit cover. She could see Em's shocked, ghastly face. Her neck was not on a good angle. "Broken neck ... Hamish can fix that right up, Em."

Flames licked the one good wing, her only avenue up to the cockpit. With one eye on the capitulating building above, Halliday braved the blaze, and boosted herself up by the wing.

"No! You blasted thing!" Fire caught the hem of her dress, she slapped at it. The heat was ferocious - she would burn up fast. With fumbling hands, she pulled at the cover and it broke open. Reaching in she snapped the clips on the safety harness and freed Em from the belts. She pulled at Em from under her arms. Her dress caught alight again as she attempted to wrench the Hell-Flyer from her seat.

"Damn it all to hell, Em!" she cried slapping away at the flames. There was an obstruction. Em's scrawny knees were caught under the throttle. "Wonderful! How the bleeding hell am I going to-!" Halliday was about to burn up, she had to do something – fast.

"Break her legs! Use your weight, Hope's Halliday! Stomp on them!" an Other-self piped up.

Gasping with exertion, feet boiling in her leather boots, Halliday grabbed hold of the aerial mast and swung her herself into the cockpit. She jumped up and down on Em's knees until she felt them crack.

"You're a broken bugger now, Em! Sorry!"

Coughing, Halliday swung herself back out, and pulled Colonel Em Contusion free from the remnants of her abysmal solo flight. Overbalancing on the wing, both women fell awkwardly from the wreckage and hit the ground. Halliday rolled free from Em, slapping at what was left of her charred dress. Lying on her back, Halliday watched as a bout of concrete rained down from above. The panzer tanks had just about done what they had set out to do - demolish the core. The structural integrity of the building was breaking.

"Wilder! Here, nag! *'Hack!' 'Hack!' 'Hack!'*

Halliday rolled over and got to her feet. Wilder trotted up and nudged her head with her snout. "Get down will you, girl. I haven't the energy to climb you." Halliday lifted Em up by the collar as Wilder folded her piston driven knee joints down – hydraulics wonky and tired. The machanihorse was on her stomach. Halliday flopped a very deceased Em over the front of the saddle and then got on herself.

She called out to Sombre, "Please bring The Funneling!"

Hind up first, front up second, with a 'phshhhhh' from her knee-work, Wilder was upright and galloping away from the scene. Halliday coughed and spat in a most unflattering fashion, as she looked over her shoulder. An explosive, catastrophic boom enveloped Battallion as the building finally toppled.

A battle-weary Halliday, a lifeless Em and a very ill Wilder vanished into The Funneling.

CHAPTER 23
SCRUTINY

"So next year I've got the stupid prom. Wouldn't say I'm looking forward to it," Parker said swallowing a mouthful of egg and salad roll.

Both girls were sitting under their designated tree – the new Centurion lunchtime spot. The temperature was good and hot-Californian, hovering around 90'.

"Why? You'll have your pick of dates, won't you?" Hope said trying her best not to study her friends face - she had more of the mysterious Sombre acne.

"Because it's an absolute twit-fest. Frocked up girls parading around like peacocks. Dumb assed jocks doing their best to get down your pants, just so they can say they did it on 'prom night'." She rolled her eyes, then gave Hope a look. "Oh, and subtle by the way ..."

"What?"

"Stop looking at my zits, bitch! Your face is no better," she grinned at Hope. "My skin would wanna start clearing up soon. It better not scar-up, or the only date I'll get will be with Lenny the Leper from band! He's got some godawful bowel issue and farts himself stupid!"

Hope burst out laughing.

Parker laughed with her. "I've actually seen him lift his butt cheek to give his ass-wind proper clearance!"

Doubled over, Hope put her lunch bowl down on the grass and fought for breath. She proceeded to cough. Reaching for her mineral water, she took a long swig.

She rubbed tears from her eyes with the back of her hand, "Oh god, don't *do* that!"

The older girl folded up the balance of her roll in the paper bag and changed the tone, "Jerry's back tomorrow. I reckon we'll need to watch him."

Hope nodded. "I wonder what sort of shape he'll be in?"

"Physically he'll be fine. They wouldn't let him go if he wasn't. I'm curious to see what this Ether person has done to his head though. *He's* the spookiest asshole I've ever seen."

"Agreed," Hope said. The two had already discussed Ether. The relatively small amount of information Halliday had managed to find out from a reticent Lucretia left a gulf of unanswered questions.

"Where was it Ether was from again?" Parker said stretching her legs out stiffly on the grass. With a free hand she rubbed her neck, "Man-o-man, I'm sore ..."

Hope watched her friend grimace with her aches and pains. "Well, you know Em's neck was broken, don't you? And Halliday had to break Em's legs to get her out of the plane as well. She jumped up and down on them!"

"Savage thing, isn't she?"

"She can be. Gets the job done, though," she smiled wanly at Parker. She wasn't about to apologize for Halliday's antics. The aches and pains – and the *pimples* - an unjust part of it all that had to be suffered through. "And getting back to your original question, Ether is from The Isolate. It's cold there." Hope said repeating Lucretia's words from the night before.

"So now there's another place we have to know about? Fuck! It's not like Sombre isn't more than enough!"

"Like you said, our worlds are crashing."

"Yes, I did say that," Parker said.

Hope sighed, "I've got the sleep clinic tonight. Not looking forward to that."

"What if you do a Sombre flip out and trash the room or something!" Parker chuckled. "I'd pay good coin to see that!"

"Yeah, real funny. What if I can't get to sleep?"

"You could try and stay awake."

Hope yawned. "Actually, I doubt it, I'll sleep. I'm already tired. As you know, Halliday had a big one last night."

The school bell rang. Both girls got to their feet and dawdled back to class.

"You couldn't save Em's stupid ass though, could you? She's on two strokes now," Parker huffed. She looked down at the ground and shook her head. "It's bizarre, and more than a little fucked up, but there's a disturbing part of me who likes being her, you know."

"I know, I'm the same. I'm worried about Halliday's strokes as well. She's a ticking time bomb."

"Ha! Don't even put her in the same stall with Colonel Em Contusion, my friend! The colonel is in an entire league of her own!"

Parker gave Hope a shove in the shoulder. "Halliday needs to look after her better is all!"

∫

"Have you packed some pajamas, Hope?" Evelyn Kelley looked sideways at her daughter. She pulled into the sleep clinic's parking bay. Daylight was on the decline. They were running a little late. Her mother had all but forgotten about the sleep therapy booking. Such was her busy social schedule – to Hope, the therapy now felt like an intrusion.

"No. Should I have?" Hope pulled her seat belt free.

"Well I would have thought pajamas would help you relax a little. I forgot to remind you."

"I'll be fine."

"Jesus, *I* wouldn't be ..." Evelyn muttered as she cracked her door open.

It wasn't quite true, she knew it, but Hope couldn't help feeling like an unwanted bag of clothes her mother was dropping off at good will. Evelyn Kelley had an annoying habit of having well-meaning and helpful ideas, setting them up, then not particularly caring how things panned out. If this worked – good. If it didn't work, she would be quick to wash her hands of it. She didn't dwell on things, she moved on.

They both walked the parking lot in silence until Hope pushed on the tinted door to the Marin Sleep Centre. She read Doctor Marin's bronzed lettered credentials. She spoke with a sigh, "Go through, mother. You're paying."

"Cheeky." Evelyn raised her eyes as she pushed through.

The air-conditioning in the reception was frigid. As they approached the front counter, Hope saw Dr Marin meandering around behind the receptionist, obviously awaiting their arrival.

"Ah, Hope and Evelyn Kelley! How are we this evening? Damn hot outside! Are we ready?" He stepped out from the counter, pursed his lips and tapped his chin in mock contemplation. "No pajamas, no blanket, no pillow? Nothing from home at all?"

"No, I'll be fine."

"I did remind her," her mother lied. She gave Hope an encouraging rub on the upper-arm.

"Yeah, as we were pulling in," Hope said.

"Where do I sign." Her mother said heading to the counter. Keen to purchase her first born a ticket to sleep away from home with wires and monitors.

"I sense a bit of anxiety here," Dr. Marin chaffed, eyes darting between the two Kelley women. He rubbed his hands together. "Totally understandable. Although there's absolutely nothing to fear. Cognitive therapy is quite gentle. Once you get used to the wires. We find most patients adjust very quickly."

"Okay, see you then ... in the morning," Hope waved to her mother.

Evelyn looked up and smiled, she held eye contact with Hope for a few seconds.

"Yes Hope, 6 a.m. sharp. You'll be better for this!"

Hope allowed herself to be guided through into what she ghoulishly assumed would be a Dr. Frankenstein-styled laboratory. She assumed wrong. The rooms turned out to be quite civil.

Dr. Marin spoke softly,

"We have four rooms, Hope. The other three are already occupied. Here we have what we affectionately call the Nightingale room. Do excuse the furnishings, the walls, the fluffy toys ... this is normally used for infants. Our cancellation has a bout of chicken pox," he smiled then pursed his lips as he gestured her into the already open door.

She really wished he'd stop using his kissy-lips – they were so off putting. She stepped in and looked around at the walls; dark, night-time blue, emblazoned with 'cow jumped over the moon, the dish ran away with spoon' wallpaper. Two technicians were preparing the bed, a full hospital bed, with side rails and white sheets. They both looked like students or interns to Hope; the woman was youngish with glasses, long blond hair in a plait; the man was tall around the same age; dark, he wore his thin moustache well, had a nicely shaped jaw. A wide screen T.V. hung above playing a game show at a low volume. Hope eyed the various machines beeping intermittently, L.E.D. lights flashing. There was a trolley with a jug of iced water. This was just like a hospital stay. A small wave of nausea came over her. What if she did have a Sombre flip out? Her sleeping world was about to be delved into by scientists! She hadn't thought hard enough about this at all.

"So, Hope Kelley, meet Jessica and Taj. They'll be in charge from here."

She was greeted warmly by both.

"How are we feeling now?" Dr. Marin cupped his hands together oddly, as if he didn't want to touch anything and possibly infect the area.

He was a weird one, thought Hope, "okay I guess."

The two younger assistants, seemed to be either used to Dr. Marin, or too nice to register his weirdness as anything other than the norm.

The doctor looked at his wristwatch. "Okay, Hope. So, I'll leave you in Jessica and Taj's quite capable hands. I am wanted at home. By the morning, hopefully we'll have plenty of data that we can analyze. This therapy is quite enlightening." He smiled and nodded, "Good night."

Hope sat on the bed and pulled her trainers off. Picking up a clipboard, the doctor walked to the door and ran through a few things with Jessica, then left.

"You good, Hope?" Taj smiled at her as she lay down on the bed. "I can boost you up a bit if you like. What do you want to watch? We've got everything."

"Whatever, I'm not that fussed."

He looked up at the monitor sour-faced. "This game show is pretty crappy, though. We can do better." He began flicking through the channels.

"Hi, Hope," Jessica said at her bedside giving her a tight but friendly smile. "You ready? Time to hook you up to the gadgets. Andy, can you bring me the tapes please."

The two worked quickly; Hope found herself covered in wires at her throat and temples, nose and forehead; everywhere up her arms. Jessica did a lot of the talking and Taj nodded and said 'it's all good' a lot.

"Hope, this is Diagnostic Sleep Therapy. Dr. Marin has told us you can't remember your dreams, correct?"

Hope nodded and lied, "I just wake up super tired."

"Oh, well. I guess we'll just have to see. With a bit of luck, you'll have some crazy dreams tonight and we'll get heaps of data!"

"Hmm ... not too crazy, I might blow up your machines," Hope joked uneasily.

She realized how serious all of this was getting. In the centre of her chest, the box all the wires were plugged into suddenly felt heavier than it actually was - like a symbolical reminder of Halliday's Beating Clock. She had to catch her breath. Making a grunting noise she tried to stifle but couldn't, she pulled the box down closer to her stomach. She fidgeted nervously, and Jessica put a soothing hand on her wrist.

"Just relax, Hope. We do these all the time. You have nothing to fear. Take in some water, hydration is very underrated, *everyone* forgets to drink enough, before and after sleep."

Hope sat up and Taj poured some water into a tall glass, he reassured her once again. "It's all good, Hope. Take a drink, take a breath. It's all good."

Taj was nice, but actually giving her the shits. It was like he was in some sort of bedside manner training.

With a final check of every taped wire with her index finger, Jessica seemed happy with her work. "Okay, Hope, I think we're done. We'll leave you to relax and watch T.V," she looked up at the monitor, "Beetlejuice!? Really, Taj! Couldn't you have found something a little more relaxing? The whole film's like a nightmare."

"It's a good film - it's funny," Taj said and shrugged his shoulders.

"Don't worry," Hope said. "I'm a fan. I've seen it heaps of times."

Taj dropped another, 'it's all good.'

Jessica rolled her eyes and pushed him in the side. "Have a good sleep, Hope. We'll be watching. If you need anything just ask."

The two left the room.

CHAPTER 24
THE COLDEST PLACE

Hope's eyes glazed as she watched a shrunken Beetlejuice threaten the deceased Maitland family in the mini cemetery – her favorite scene. She'd seen it so many times but couldn't help but giggle as he swore and grabbed his crotch. He was a disgusting thing.

She licked her lips, the room felt too cold. She didn't think it was something worth complaining about though, the whole building would be set to the same temperature. Hunkering lower into the covers, her eyelids felt a little heavy. There was an itch underneath a sticker tab she did her best to ignore. She looked up at the screen again and admired Geena Davis's portrayal of Barbara Maitland; she'd had a massive girl crush on her when she was younger – she thought her a brilliant actress.

The room fell colder again as she lost sight of the movie and drifted. Teetering on the edge of sleep, her thoughts went to Sombre. What would happen? What would Jessica and Taj see once she became Halliday? She pictured needle thin Gamma waves fluctuating across the clinic's screens, crazy signature-like patterns drawn by an out-of-control digital hand. Her semi-conscious state delved further. She imagined flashing computer monitors overloading, sparks shooting from consoles, big messages of 'SLEEP STATE OVERLOAD' 'PATIENT SAFETY ALERT' 'WAKE UP HOPE!'

With a spasmodic jerk that startled her semi-awake, Hope opened her eyes. She was on her side, right eye covered in pillow, her left stared straight at the shimmering form of Ether. Black eyes watching her intensely, he squatted down at her bedside. His wet fringe came down past his eyes in thin strands. Beads of water dappled his cheeks and nose.

A big grin came across his mouth as he put an index finger to his lips. He breathed a spit filled "shhhhh," through his teeth. Peering down at the floor, eventually the ghoul shut his eyes.

Hope shut hers as well.

ς

There was no lead in nightmare. No rite of passage. There would be no Sombre tonight. Hope knew this to be true. She knew this, even in the unconsciousness of sleep. This was as horribly tangible, as physical, as any Sombre-led dream or nightmare she had ever had. She was definitely here. Dressed in stark white pajamas, she stood barefoot. White and blue and grey vapor filled her senses, blurred her vision. A dribble of water cascaded down a set of stairs to her left. The air was beyond cold. An unreal and persistent wind pushed against her cheeks yet didn't ruffle her hair. Bitterly cold water drifted up to her ankles. Her frost-bitten fingertips felt pain in its purist form.

A dirty blood red pulsed in the pale vapor ahead – the only sign of anything resembling life – living or dead. Hope felt something at her back, spider-like fingers ran up and down her spine. Gasping, she turned. There was no one, well, no one in body anyway - just a well-formed outline of an open mouth sucking in the wet vapor. The mouth hung in the air. She had an urge to see if it was real and poked it with her finger. It broke into particles, then instantly reformed when she pulled it away.

The mouth whispered to her.

"Hidden. This is the hidden place, Hope Kelley. This is The Isolate. You should already know this. Your isolated self becomes real here. Here, you cannot hide who you really are. This is your stilled heart ... your stilled heart ... your stilled heart ... stilled heart." The mouth coughed, and watery-spit exploded in her face.

Hope felt a sudden, sharp, heavy pain in the centre of her chest. She doubled over and inhaled the cold - like a knife slipping down her throat.

"Stand up straight, Hope Kelley, you of the pathetic! You of the slovenly! You of the spiritless!" The mouth threatened, no longer a whisper, now a metallic waspish growl.

Trying to stand, Hope's body felt impossibly heavy; like a crane with multiple tons on its boom. She tried to speak and all that came out was gibberish. The gibberish turned into a gargle and she felt a liquid escape her mouth, "ugh!" Instinctively she caught the blood in her hand. The pain in her chest worsened. Peering down she saw a gaping wound had formed through her pyjama top. With one hand cupping the blood dribbling from her mouth; the other searched the hole between her breasts – it was large, her hand fit inside easily. Ice had crystallized the plasma, stemming any blood flow from the wound.

"Look at me, Hope."

Hope lifted her head. As if standing in front of a mirror, she now stood face to face looking at a fully formed reflection of herself. A horrific looking reflection. Her eyes were seeping blood under her glasses, pink open cracks had formed over her cheeks and nose. The reflection's speech was dry and croaky.

"Never come here again, Hope. The Isolate is terminal. Do you hear me? Worlds end here."

Her reflection reached out and covered her face with her hand.

Hope left The Isolate.

∫

Hope woke facing the wall. Staring at the dish running away with the spoon, she momentarily forgot where she was.

"Oh ..." she croaked through the driest mouth imaginable. Clearing her throat, she reached for her water. There was another presence in the room. She felt the bed rise up.

A smiling Jessica stood holding the beds remote yawning. "Well, that was interesting, and not very at the same time. Let's get these wires off your person, shall we?"

Hope lowered the glass from her mouth. "What happened? What did I do?" Fearing the absolute worst, she felt her heart rate go up. The monitor, still plugged in, picked up the elevation and beeped quicker.

"Ha! Relax Hope. All is well, girl! Too well, actually..." Jessica proceeded to pull the wire-tapes from Hope's skin.

Hope rubbed her chest after Jessica unfastened the diagnostic box. "What do you mean, 'too well'? What happened?"

"A whole lot of not much," the technician shrugged. "You slept like a baby, Hope. The data that I will give to Dr. Marin will show lots of good average sleep patterns, oxygen levels and near perfect brain activity. You slept better than most people do, actually."

"Wow ... awesome I guess," Hope said cagily, not knowing exactly how to feel about it all. How could the dream she just had not have affected her brainwaves and things? Dreaming in Sombre was always chaos, bed rolling; waking exhausted and sore. The Isolate was what? Nothing at all? She *felt* like she just had a good night sleep as well - odd.

Jessica yawned again. "It's been wonderful to meet you, Hope Kelly. I have called your mother and she's on her way. Best get your shoes on."

The technician gave her a warm smile and left the room.

Feeling numb, Hope slipped her trainers on and grabbed her glasses. On her way out, she stopped and looked back at the bed.

She was mystified.

CHAPTER 25
ON JERRY'S RETURN

"Well it looks like I just blew three and a half thousand dollars," Evelyn Kelly said as she pulled up at Centurion High's drop off. She let out a short and bitter laugh, "Shame our insurance didn't cover it."

"*How* much?" Kate said looking up from her phone on the passenger side. "Shit! Who spends that much on me?"

"Mind your mouth, Kate, please. Besides, you have braces coming up. That'll be at least three thousand, and that's with insurance." Her mother stared straight ahead, hand on the wheel. She sighed. "Oh well, Hope. You had your one shot on that ride. If you still have problems with your sleep, we'll get you some sleeping pills."

"Drug her up," Kate chuckled.

"Okay," Hope muttered. She had no idea the therapy cost that much. She was still dumbfounded by the results.

"She doesn't sound that grateful," Kate said.

"Jesus! Shut up, Kate!" Hope yelled and pushed on the door. "Sorry, okay! Shit! It's not like I could do anything about it!" Suddenly desperate to get out, her bag got hooked on the seatbelt denying her the fast, dramatic exit she wanted. Her glasses slipped down her nose as she wrenched the bag out. "Uggghhh!" She pretty much fell out of the Jeep onto the footpath. She half-shut the door. Her sister giggled at her.

Her mother rolled her window down a few inches and stated coolly. "Please shut it properly, Hope."

Hope shoved the door closed. The Jeep pulled away.

Gathering herself, Hope walked through the gate and had the presence of mind to pull her phone from her bag. There were three messages, all from

Parker, all sent within an hour - 'Heya, let me no x!' 'WTF? – giv me something!' 'usuck! x'

A new one flashed onto the screen - 'I can see u!'

Hope looked up, Parker stood leaning against the cream coloured, bricked archway of the main entrance. "Are you some sort of stalker, or what?" There was no humour in her delivery – she regretted it straight away.

Parker raised her eyebrows, gave her a mock smile then a frown. "So, it didn't go well, then?"

Hope stopped and looked her friend in the eyes. "I went to The Isolate. I saw Ether."

"Oh, shit! That's some serious shit ... shit! I can't stop saying shit! What happened?" Parker licked her lips hungrily.

The first bell rang for class.

"That's the bell," Hope said.

Parker waved it away as if shooing a fly, "Fuck the bell. This is more important, what happened? What's there?"

"Just Ether. And The Isolate is just like Lucretia said to Halliday. It's cold and wet and white – not much else. But I can tell you one thing. Ether didn't want me to be there at all. It said it was where all world's end."

"Wonder what that means?" Parker searched Hope's face as if it could hold the answer. Realizing it didn't she then looked her straight in the eyes. "What did he look like in The Isolate, the same?"

"No. There's no he, it's just a thing. At first it was just a mouth speaking to me through mist. Then it became whole and it was as if I was staring into a mirror; but my face was all broken and my eyes were bleeding. I had blood in my mouth, a big hole in my chest."

"A hole in your chest, you say? I'll bet you that's meant to signify something."

The second bell rang. Parker hoisted her heavy looking bag up high on her shoulder. "Best get going, eh?" She grinned. "So, did you smash up the room? Have a conniption?"

"No. I slept like a baby apparently – completely normal."

"Wow! Really? You couldn't have!"

"I did," Hope nodded looking down at the ground. "Mum's pissed off. It cost her thousands."

Parker actually clapped and laughed. "Oh, that's funny!"

"No, it isn't, she's hating on me pretty bad."

"She'll get over it. You're family seems to be going okay for a dollar. I'll see you at lunch. We have to stalk Jerry." Parker paced off.

"He's back?" Hope called out after her friend. Parker had made her feel a hundred times better.

Pulling her hair over her left shoulder, the older girl chimed spookily as she walked off. "*He's backkkkk!!!!*"

∫

Hope's lunch consisted of a Health & Co carob and muesli cake, a fat slab of dried nutrition that boasted no nuts, eight kinds of seeds and as many fruits. Her mother had forgotten to pack her anything else. It turned out to be a bit of a blessing as she wasn't sitting down to eat, she was on the move.

"That bar looks cumbersome. Is it any good?" Parker said as she crunched an apple.

"Filling," Hope concurred.

"'*Where-o-where are you Jerry.*" Parker sang to herself as the two girls strolled the grounds.

The day was overcast, a cool change looked on the cards, a break from the heat Southern California had been enduring for over a week now.

Parker dipped her sunglasses and cased the bleachers. "I actually haven't seen him today – but I know he's here."

"Ah, why wouldn't he be catching up with the rest of the guys from the football team?" Hope asked wondering if that was indeed who Jerry Cowle actually hung out with. Apparently, it was.

"I would have thought so as well." Parker stopped and nodded toward the bike racks in front of the library. She hissed triumphantly, "There! Got him!"

Cutting a lonesome looking figure Jerry stood in shorts and a loose t-shirt, leaning against the side wall of the single-story building. Hope could see his colour; looking like he was made of aged newspaper, his entire body was covered from head to foot in the pale sickly yellow.

"My god, he's covered in Sombre. He might be dreaming like us, Parker!" Hope said excitedly through a mouth choked with muesli cake.

"Wonder if he's got a face-full of zits like us as well?" Parker observed.

"What do we do?"

Parker walked her mostly-eaten apple over to a nearby bin. "Well, I wasn't expecting him to be alone. Chuck the rest of that birdseed bar and let's go see him."

"Should we though?" Hope said dumping her lunch and brushing her hands clean. She was as desperate to see Jerry as Parker was. But everything was going to the next level – fast.

"Of course, we should!" Parker licked her lips. "He looks weak. This is when we pounce."

"That's nasty."

"Yes, it is. C'mon."

Hope kept behind Parker as they paced toward Jerry Cowle. He stood hunched, peering down at his phone.

Partially under her breath, Parker commented on his form to Hope. "Wow, he's lost a lot of his bulk in hospital. He'd probably struggle as a Running Back right now." She blurted, "Hey! Jerry. How're you doin'?"

Clearly not expecting company, a startled Jerry looked up. "What? Parker?" He pocketed his phone.

With all the subtlety of a freight train ramming a broken-down car, Parker lined up her target. "Were you looking at porn just then, Jerry? Um-Ah, Jerry Cowle! You know that's not allowed!"

"I wasn't looking at porn! What do you want, Parker?" Jerry moaned. Clearing his throat, he folded his arms and looked off to his side.

"A word. That's all," Parker said taking a fierce stance.

Hope instantly felt for the guy. A verbal load from Parker was the last thing he needed. He was so pale. The bruising around his mouth reminded her of a three-year old's hot chocolate mouth halo. His eyes were bloodshot and rimmed with shadow. The pale Sombre-yellow of his skin was making her feel a little sick to her stomach.

He gestured toward Hope. "Who's she?" He dabbed his mouth with the back of his hand.

"The girl you ran into that day," Parker said. "You *hurt* her Jerry."

"Oh, sorry. I didn't know what was happening."

Hope just nodded. Parker was being pretty rough.

"How's the mouth?" Parker said screwing up her face. "Saw you dribble a bit."

"P-Piss off, Parker! I don't need your sh-shit okay!" Jerry stammered and gestured around. "Do you see me hanging out with anybody else? I just want to be alone!"

Hope put a hand on her friends arm and hissed. "Don't push it! We need this!"

She was probably overstepping, but she took over,

"Jerry, you don't know me. My name is Hope Kelley. Sorry, I can see you don't feel up to it. We were just hoping you could help us out. Do you know who attacked you that day?"

"Like I've told everyone, I can't remember – wait. How in the hell would it help *you* two out? Did you get attacked as well?" His eyes darted left and right.

"No." Hope said shaking her head.

"Well, what does it matter to you then?" Jerry said putting his hands in his pockets.

"Do you really not remember? Can you see our skin, Jerry? It's the same colour as yours. Does he make your chest hurt, like your about to have a heart attack?" Hope prodded surprising herself with how even she sounded.

Parker took over as bad cop, "We reckon you *do* remember, Jerry. You're just too chickenshit to own up to it! We need you to man up!"

What was Parker trying to achieve! Hope desperately wanted to tell her to quit it. What was stopping this guy walking away from them? Parker Wright had a way she spoke to her peers, and an image to portray - and with anyone else on any given day, it probably worked - but not with Jerry Cowle, he seemed far too broken. The guy was obviously overcome with anxiety.

Ether had gotten to him, was probably still doing so.

She shot Parker a look. She had a few scathing words poised on the tip of her tongue. Instead, she breathed, pushed her glasses up on her nose and changed tact,

"Look, Jerry, we'll leave you alone. Can you just answer two questions for us?" Hope didn't wait for a yes or no. She could see he just wanted to get away.

"Where do you go when you dream?" She realized as soon as she said it how strange it sounded out loud.

"What? What sort of question is that?"

She lowered her eyes. "Do you know someone called Ether?"

Jerry didn't answer. He coughed like an old man. With a shaking hand he dabbed at his mouth again.

"My god!" Hope blurted under her breath stunned. She pressed her hand to her lips so she wouldn't say another word. She realized that the guy was actually stone cold. He was freezing. On a ninety-degree day; Jerry Cowle was shaking like newly born foal in winter. He stared Hope in the eyes. His glare said what his mouth wasn't about to say. Was too scared to say. Clearing his throat, he muttered an almost inaudible. "No. I gotta go."

Head down, he walked.

Hope looked to Parker. "He knows! What do we do?"

Parker lowered her eyes and huffed, "Nup. This is bullshit." She followed and called out after him, "Why, Jerry? Where are you going to go?"

"Leave it, Parker!" Hope tried grabbing her arm.

Parker shrugged her off. "You know him, Jerry Cowle! Fucking tick-tick, Jerry! You need to talk to us! We can help your stubborn ass!" Her voice echoed throughout the grounds. Jerry only walked faster.

Parker was drawing attention. The ex-cheerleader and Hope the geek – causing a ruckus. Hope caught up and stood in Parker's path. "Dude, stop it! Leave it alone. We'll have another go tomorrow."

Watching Jerry until he disappeared, Parker shook her head. "He's being a dick."

"He's frightened! Who knows what Ether has said to him?" Hope added, "He won't know what's good for him. We just need to take it slower."

Parker smiled. "Since when do you use the word 'dude'?"

"I was under pressure. It slipped out."

"I'm influential aren't I," She raised her eyebrows playfully and grinned. "I'll warp you for the better, Hope Kelley. Watch. You'll be speakin' your mind and droppin' cusses with your big sister, Parker, in no time!" She raised her arms in the air and sang to the skies. "Come, come down to the gutter with me, Hope Kelley! The air's surprisingly clear, the headspace is fucking righteous!" She turned round and round as they walked.

Eyes were on Parker and her younger friend as they walked to class. Parker reveled.

Hope could only shake her head and laugh.

They were freaks.

CHAPTER 26

THE FIRST REAL SIGN OF TROUBLE

That night, Hope lay in bed, mind racing as it travelled down her increasingly complex, cerebellum highway of human emotion and bizarre circumstance. She tossed and turned as she wondered at the sheer scope of it all.

She pictured the bruised and broken Jerry Cowle and his Sombre-sick, yellowed skin, not just his face – everywhere. His hands that had shook from a chill, as if suffering from a bout of pneumonia. Her thoughts skipped to Parker Wright. A new, completely unexpected, enigma in her existence. She was her easy-to-trigger, almost completely uninhibited, foul-mouthed companion of Sombre and Centurion High. The girl shocked her and made her laugh when she probably shouldn't. She giggled as she recalled some of Parker's greatest verbal hits.

She thought of Ether; the new ticking, maniacal presence who made her heart feel as heavy as a medicine ball. Who filled her head with pain so unbearable she could hardly stand. Who seemed a threat to everything and everyone, everywhere – on earth and in Sombre. She pictured the disembodied ghoul standing in the cold of The Isolate. She shuddered as she remembered his chill filling her to her core, like frozen, deathly electricity.

Thinking of Ether led her to an even darker place – a place where she couldn't rule out the whole thing killing her – it actually seemed more likely now. Halliday's *Beating Clock?* That had to mean something more, surely. Was she herself living on borrowed time? Halliday to use up her twelve strokes and - bang! Hope Kelley to perish right along with her?

Did The Isolate mean her demise?

Everything seemed destined to collide at some kind of terminal intersection. But who knew when?

It should have had her gasping for breath in a fit of anxiety. Instead, a disturbing part of her psyche seemed to want to embrace it all – have it all for herself.

She drifted off this way.

A mess.

∫

Bird shit. Her corpse had been shat on almost as much as it had been pecked and pulled at.

The macabre wedding party stood flanking the wooden door that had been lowered down into the hastily made hole – eight foot by four – and six feet deep. All looked down on Hope, eyes judging. There was no word strong enough that could begin to describe the hatred. As pitiful as she now was, a vile mess of splat on the door, there was no condolence, no words of regret. In fact, no one spoke at all, until her sister Kate piped up with, "My phones dead. Can we get back to the car now? Need a USB port. This bitch can rot."

Using all his skill as a leader in business and in life, Hope's father proceeded to take care of things. Shoulders up, chest out, he announced with a warm smile,

"Family and esteemed guests, children, Uncle Eustis ... thank you for all your help with the disposal of our eldest daughter, Hope. I know the circumstances have been less than ideal."

He clapped his hands together and flashed his pearly whites, in an unreal Cheshire cat-style,

"From the bottom of our hearts, can I just say that we - Evelyn, Kate and myself - love you all and appreciate you coming to wish good riddance to our bad rubbish. May she forever taint the dirt."

With a guiding hand he gestured to the congregated. "Now, can I have you all move to one side, please."

A bobcat's motor grumbled, and a bucket of dirt was tipped onto Hope's corpse.

∫

"I know its cold comfort, my nag, but you *are* low in your strokes still. And you *did* die in the right place at least ... very fortunate."

Halliday sat atop her newly rebuilt machanihorse as she reflected on the last visit to The Office of The Menders. The two travelled The Common Ground. Halliday's mood was light. The Common Ground felt comforting to her, its earthen, canyon-like path of fallen stone and rock wall seemed to safely embrace her and Wilder.

"It was quite the shemozzle, I know this. The excursion to Battallion was a taxing one, for sure. Em was well and truly busted and broken. And to have you just burst open like that? All over the floor? My goodness! It was quite the eye-opener - cogs and gears and meat and muscle ..." she shook her head in bewilderment. "You're such a complicated thing, you are. Fizzing steam keeps you hydrated and oil feeds to your bits and pieces through these thin lines that reminds one of black spaghetti. You know there's a buckety looking thing in your gut, Wilder? I learnt so much about you from Hamish. He is a know-it-all and a bossy-bore, but the man knows his business, that is for certain."

Wilder snorted and shook her head.

"Now, I will have you know, my nag, that while you were on the table and not useful, said Mender, Hamish, shared a few new things about you and your makeup." She patted Wilder's neck. "Your skittishness needs to be nipped in the bud now. Apparently, previous Halliday's didn't allow this side of your psyche to show nearly as much as I do."

Hope's Halliday cocked an ear and waited for the jibes. None came. "Ha! Ha!" She was well pleased with this. "For once, the Other's must be asleep in their Other's-boxes,

"He also showed me a few trigger points on you that he would have thought I would have worked out for myself. And as much as I didn't appreciate his smart-alecky-tone, these things do sound handy. They make you faster, Wilder, more instinctive. A zone-hopper! You are a tool I should be putting to greater use."

"Dopey Hope's Halliday is finally talking about Wilder's Inbred Reflexiveness."

"Ah, and there we have it. The Others' finally come to ruin a perfectly good ride," Halliday rued.

"She hasn't asked nearly enough questions of Hamish. He is a wealth of information, not to mention, quite easy on the eye. We used to speak for hours ..." said another Other-self.

"So, you used to waste the man's time!" Halliday snapped defiantly.

"Oh, what the jolly, bloody god of Sombre that man is! How we used to wistfully pass the time. What a relationship we once had!" piped another, Other.

"I don't believe any of you! The man's far too-"

About to try and engage in what would be a fruitless conversation with the four members of her psyche, Halliday faltered as she happened to look on ahead.

"Stop, Wilder."

A very familiar, yet surprising figure was on foot on The Common Ground. She was confused. "Dave Bi-Plane?" she mouthed under her breath. "Where's the man's transport, Wilder? He's just standing there. Take it slow, girl, he may have had a few too many ales at the Spleen'."

Goggles pulled up high over his forehead, the Gatherer stood with his arms down at his sides, legs evenly spread. He appeared to be watching Halliday on her approach, then she soon realized he wasn't. The man seemed to be in a state of catatonia.

"Dave Bi-Plane! Are you okay? What has brought you to The Common Ground?"

He didn't answer. Eyes glazed, mouth in a tight grimace, he continued to look past her. She wondered, was he waiting for something to happen? Something seemed very wrong.

She dismounted Wilder and stepped toward the man with caution. Peering into his eyes, she sucked on her bottom lip. "Er, what are you on about, friend? Are you drunk?"

She had a rather awkward question next, but thought it needed to be asked, she whispered, "Do you need to be taken to a toilet?"

Suddenly she could hear ticking in Dave. It then filled her ears. She could feel her clock's weight again, heavy in her chest.

He continued to look through her. In a haunted tone, most unlike Dave, he finally spoke, "Halliday, I've met Ether."

"When?" Halliday said.

He croaked, "Now."

His body proceeded to shake uncontrollably.

"No Dave!" Halliday had an urge to hold him in a tight embrace - risk the unchartered territory. She reconsidered; a hand placed on the shoulder would have to suffice.

"Calm down friend! Dave, listen to me! You need to get a hold of yourself! Uh! ... Oh dear!"

Her hand left his shoulder and she recoiled as his skin split bloody red at his hairline. She stepped back. The man's goggles popped off almost comically.

"Errrrrrrrrrr... Halliday!" he moaned.

Dave's cheeks began to split open in the same manner. He shut his eyes. The splitting crossed through his mouth and tore through his neck. Blood spattered her front. She heard his Beating Clockface crack under his aviator leather. His chest was expanding. The man was like some sort of shaking, overloaded generator.

Genuinely frightened she yelled, "What is happening! Dave? Dave!"

She turned and ran to her horse. "Wilder, I think he's going to explode! Get back girl!"

Halliday could only watch on stunned as Dave Bi-Plane burst open like a gore filled balloon, spraying bits and pieces of his everything, everywhere.

The ticking stopped.

ʃ

"This is Halliday Knight, please bring The Funneling. Quick! Gatherer down! Dave down!" she called out to Sombre's Menders as she squatted and surveyed the mess. Dave Biplane was scattered all over The Common Ground; his torn limbs had been thrown like projectiles. His blood painted the rock walls.

"What does this mean? I've never seen anything like it! Never!"

She felt sick in her stomach as she eyed what remained intact of her comrades body; a limb-free torso sitting on a sideways lean with a smashed Beating Clock face, a bottom third of a head. His lower mandible sat proud upon his stump of a neck, like some sort of makeshift cranium-table. She found it terribly macabre and hard on her eyes.

"Dave," she uttered miserably and faced the other way. "The Mender's are taking their fiddling time, aren't they!"

Her mare nuzzled her cheek, and Halliday sighed in resignation.

"I suppose it doesn't matter how long they take, my Wilder. He's all bits and pieces anyway." The machanihorse snorted in agreeance. Halliday gave her a scratch under her chin.

"I know. You like Dave as well don't you ... poor bleeding sod of a man. He saw Ether, Wilder. Did Ether do this? I'm sure Dave tried to say as much."

She hugged her arms. The air was icy. There was an unreal denseness to the chill, as if it were somehow solid.

"A remnant of the scoundrel if ever there was one," she stated feeling a mix of anger and wonder.

A sudden shimmer of silver appeared ahead. The Funneling birthed the forms of three Menders: two males, one tall and one short, and a familiar female Mender. Halliday knew her as Janice.

The three surveyed the scene. They all looked as lost as they should have with what was on offer.

"He just exploded," Halliday said hopelessly.

"Hello Halliday," Janice said giving her a judgmental glance. "Yes, we can see that. He's causing a bit of trouble for us at the moment, is Dave Bi-Plane."

"What do you mean by that?" Halliday queried the Mender. Dave was generally one of the most solid Gatherer's she knew of – in every sense. He was a veritable rock of a human. To even think that he was any sort of regular patient of The Mender's was quite imaginary.

The small but strong looking woman stood with her hands on her hips. With a pensive expression she watched on as her two male companions began bagging up as much of Dave as they could.

"Halliday, this will be his second complete rebuild in as many days. Something is going on with him. He is out of control. He's definitely pissed off someone. Ha! Or maybe even Sombre itself, who knows?" Janice nodded her head slowly as she watched the tall male Mender spray a liquid substance at the Dave-stained walls of The Common Ground. "But I can tell you, The Office of The Menders needs this sort of thing like it needs a bout of dysentery. Complete rebuilding just saps our resources."

"Oh," Halliday said unhelpfully.

"We're about done here," the mender shrugged and walked off. The conversation was over. "Hey, Geoff, you missed some!" Janice called out to the short male who dragged the bag of Dave. She bent down and picked up another small chunk of head and one solitary torn finger. Giving Halliday a nod, she stepped into The Funneling and disappeared. The silver shimmer warped sideways and was gone.

A disillusioned Halliday stood with her machanihorse and gazed at the wet stains on the sandy gravel. Wilder nodded her head up and down. Halliday let go of her bridle. The mare went for a walk.

"The man is so quietly proud of his stroke rate as well," she pondered. "That will take him to four on his clock ... more than mine."

She peered down at the body spatter on the front of her dress and shook her head. She pulled at the tough fabric. "Good god! I look like I've had some sort of surgical fit! Would have been nice of them to offer to clean a girl up - nasty sods! Wilder, we need to find us a water source."

Then, as they so often did, her hands went to her temples. She was called upon,

"My nag, we have a job to do."

Chapter 27
A Market, in Ginnifer West

For some untold reason, having new work gave Halliday release. With her attire still stained red from her good friend's exploding innards, she and Wilder hit The Byway with a vigor that felt like rebellion.

"It is official, Wilder. This blasted, Ether, has definitely arrived in Sombre – and he has targeted the wonderful Dave Biplane!"

She could feel bits of the man's blood crusting on her face as it dried.

"Dave is a proud fellow, exploding into bits is definitely not his style! This spook is powerful, that is for sure. To have that much control over Dave is as impressive as it is terrifying!" She went to lick her lips, then thought better of it. "Indeed, to somehow coerce Dave to get out of his plane and be on foot at all is an achievement in itself!"

It suddenly occurred to her that maybe she was *meant* to see the eruption of her friend. It was a boastful display and far too coincidental. She recalled what Janice The Mender had told her.

"Twice, Wilder. Ether has done this twice to Dave! My, my! This time I was around to see it!"

A nicker of agreeance came from her mare. She pictured Dave's face, his demeanour, before he blew apart. "The man was listless, Wilder! Beyond stupor!"

It was turning into a lengthy run through of The Byway. A plethora of disturbing imagery from the nightmare world flashed by on both sides as they continued at high speed through Sombre's never-ending thoroughfare; of monster, of machine, of manmade structure, the completely unreal.

"Faster, my nag! We must be getting closer to this Ginnifer West."

With her patience at its wits end, Halliday finally had her entry. A chasm full of natural light appeared in The Byway wall.

"My word, what a too-long journey that was!"

Halliday and machanihorse burst into a sun-drenched valley of green. Far into the distance, hills rolled away lazily.

A cloudless blue sky held a single dirigible, on its way to wherever. It looked slow, but Halliday knew this to be an illusion. Air travel was fast; and even faster in Sombre. Flames shot up to its eggshell coloured balloon in gassy explosions. She cocked her head to the left and read the black logo emblazoned on its sides, big and proud, 'FEISTER'. Captain Andrew Feister. A fellow drinker. An absolute warbler of a man.

"I've never noticed that boorish fellow's balloon before, Wilder. It's quite the impressive thing isn't it?" Wilder slowed and Halliday watched it sail away on its slipstream. "Magnificently simplistic, aren't they? Driver, basket, balloon ... quite the wonder.

"So, nag, where are we?" She focused ahead. "There seems to be not a lot out here. I think we forge ahead over that first hill and see, eh?"

With a whoosh of fresh steam, Wilder took off in a trot across the secluded valley. Halliday smiled as she listened to the wet mechanics of her faithful transportation. Making quick work of it they scaled the first hill; they were then faced with a second. They pressed on. Halfway up, again, she felt the heaviness of her Beating Clock.

The ticking from The Common Ground returned.

"This is an interesting new thing, this ticking, isn't it, my Wilder?" She drew a deep, tight breath and rubbed her hand along the glass face. "I don't like this feeling at my chest though! Very uncomfortable!"

Upon reaching the second hill's peak, the two were finally rewarded with something other than grass. A large rustic looking pavilion. Stalls were set up on tables under its tin roof. Sellers stood in the shadows as market-goers perused their wares.

"Ah, so this is more like it. But it's all a bit odd isn't it? Are we already in Ginnifer West? Is that little markety thing all there is? Is Ginnifer West *just* the markety thing?"

Halliday steered Wilder toward the secluded market with practiced caution, but without any true concern.

"Don't people dream up all sorts of things, my Wilder? One can't help but wonder what happened to the original Nightmarer of this one. How troubling can a common thrifty flea market be? And how has our new Nightmarer ended up here at all? Sometimes, the situations Sombre chooses baffle me to no end!"

She waited for some advice from an Other-Self, but none came.

She berated her mind invaders under her breath. "When they could be of use, they choose to be quiet. When I don't need them, they hang around like blowflies on a bloody carcass! Shit's of things they are ..."

She pulled on the rein. "Halt girl. Wait here, this shouldn't take too long."

Halliday pulled the Remington as she dismounted. Wilder wandered off and pecked at some grass.

On closer inspection, the market's pavilion resembled a farm shed; the weathered tin roof, metal cross beams and posts. She passed sellers tables, all loaded with equal parts trash and treasure. It was all typically random: clothing to hand-tools, wristwatches to well used electricals.

She actually spotted an old scuffed up saddle complete with just one threadbare stirrup. This made her laugh. "Oh, imagine that thing on my nag! She'd never forgive me!"

The ticking was louder here. Her Beating Clock felt even heavier.

Still perplexed as to how this was all a nightmare in any form whatsoever, she made her way to the market's centre.

Then it struck her.

Where was the haggling and chat and barter? In fact, other than the incessant ticking, the whole place was silent.

"What in Sombre does all this mean?" she said out loud.

She walked over to a stall of grimy crockery and dusty looking magazines. The two customers looked up on her approach; a balding middle-aged man dressed in sports jacket and slacks, his wife in a white cardigan and a green ill-fitting short skirt.

"Oh! In all the-!" Halliday recoiled. Their mouths were horribly cut up, open knife slits exposed bloody redness. The couple's eyes were devoid of any expression, *zombified,* as if existing in body only. Choosing not to engage the couple, instead, she addressed the stall owner. A squat, grey haired woman knitting with black wool, sat hunched over in a foldup chair.

"You there! Proprietor!"

Peering up at Halliday, she continued to knit, her dark ringed eyes just as lifeless, mouth just as mutilated.

"This place is absurd, woman! Who was it that ruined your mouths?"

Why hadn't she noticed the state of these people when she first entered? In a fruit and veg stall across the way, the rotund male owner stood staring at Halliday as if she were a ghost; his mouth a bleeding mess.

"What is the meaning behind this mutilation?" Halliday turned to face the woman, who put down her knitting and stood up. She proceeded to unbutton her cardigan, revealing a large bleeding hole in her chest. A hole where her Beating Clock should have lived. "Oh no!" Halliday said dumbly and turned to the couple that were both showing her the holes in their chests as well, a bloody trail ran down their abdomens.

A feeling of dread came over her.

A woman's laughter, echoed through the pavilion.

The Nightmarer.

A chill swept the market.

She gulped as she saw the warm green hills outside turn to white ice.

"What is this witchery!? Wilder!"

Halliday turned to where she had entered, fearing the worst. She could see her mare's rump; a flick of the tail told her the machanihorse seemed at ease. Halliday licked her lips and shivered. She had a job to do.

Lifting the Remington to her shoulder, she went searching for the Nightmarer.

∫

Was this just what happened in Ginnifer West? Did everything flip on itself? Warm spring sunshine one minute switched to bitchingly cold winter the next? The mute citizens of the market wore cut-up mouths and holes in their chests? Halliday didn't think so. She had never known Beating Clocks to ever come out of any citizen, ever! Well, barring the citizen's demise.

As she paced down each of the markets aisles, a pang of uncertainty hit her - she wondered if she might not be in Sombre at all. The ticking was unnerving; her Beating Clock seemed to be getting heavier. Her teeth chattered.

There was movement at every stall, but it was robotic and laboured, slow hands sifted and sorted and perused the wares on each table. All were disengaged. She imagined in regular Sombre-circumstance, that these people would have turned on the Nightmarer in a joint marauding, pulling the unlucky sleeper apart limb from limb. That was how it always went in Sombre. Not this group of broken, dull-eyed, dopey dwellers, though. She couldn't imagine these people able to do much more than scratch their noses. Where was the spirit?

It had been cut out of them.

Something had taken them over. Had taken over the whole of Ginnifer West.

Another thing gnawed at her mind material. For some inexplicable reason, she recognised the cut-up mouths. She couldn't put a finger on where she had seen it though.

She flinched as the laughter came again, a woman's. The Nightmarer was close.

"I can't see you!" Halliday said helplessly. Spinning around she got down low, eye fixed through the Remington's sight. Would she even need to shoot? She wasn't sure. She wasn't sure of anything.

"Damn this place!" she said and sniffed up the cold. Ginnifer West was getting the better of her. Sidling passed a large group of marketgoers; she saw more gaping holes, savagely cut through their backs to their fronts. This seemed a popular stall. Peering through shoulders, she realized with horror that this group were sorting through a table full of blood drenched Beating Clock's. Long entrails and detached, Mender-wired apparatus, were sprawled all over the surface.

She spoke out loud, "How can any of this be? It goes against every rule! How can these citizens be upright and living at all? They should all be floating in The River!"

A blur of vivid red hair flashed by to her left.

"There!" she cried. She switched, reeled back, aimed - then lost sight. "Damn!"

A distinct feeling of dread filled her to her very core. All was not right here. The ticking was getting louder and faster, as if it was racing to an end. Her clock now felt impossibly heavy at her breast. She coughed and let out an involuntary whimper.

Willing herself to remain in control, she uttered. "Come on now, Miss Knight ... keep it together."

Clenching the Remington, she stalked her prey.

As if appearing from a magical pocket of air, a young pale-faced male, was lifted high then thrown down on a table of magazines.

Halliday got a good look at her vicious Nightmarer. Holding thin knives in each hand, the woman was tall and heavily built, wearing a most unflattering prison issued jumpsuit. Through the long, flaming red hair, Halliday could see that her hard face was turning a deathly blue.

"You there, halt!" Halliday bolted in her direction.

There was no screaming and no fight-back from the Nightmarer's victim. Submitting like a frightened pup, the citizen was every bit as pitiful as a Sombre citizen could often be when put to the test.

The Nightmarer playfully turned the blades inches from her victims face.

"Halt, I say!" Halliday aimed at the woman's leg and pulled the trigger. The bullet ripped a hole as it lodged. The shot achieved nothing as the Nightmarer set to task; her expression of pure, cold concentration not faltering in the slightest. She was incredibly quick as she worked. One hand sliced the boys lips with cursive strokes - The Beating Clock was cut out cleanly with other - then flicked out of its cavity with indifference. The timepiece hitting the table with a thud.

Halliday stood mesmerized, her gun barrel wavering. She had no idea how to play this out. She had never seen a Nightmarer as brutal as this one; had never seen such indifference shown to the Beating Clock. How was Sombre allowing this to take place?

The boy rolled himself off the table, lips incised, a freshly bleeding pit at his chest; red wet spreading down his denim shirt. He walked off showing no trace of emotion, as if resigned to the fact that his chest was now hollow.

"You abomination," Halliday whispered at the Nightmarer.

The red-haired woman turned and faced her, laughing darkly, showing the whites of her teeth, stark against her increasingly ghastly complexion.

Halliday looked round at the bedlam this woman had just caused in Ginnifer West; breathed in the chill. She licked her bottom lip. Sombre would never had allowed this. Halliday felt those invisible fingers crawling down her back once again.

"Ether," she murmured under her breath. The ghoul - was only feet away from where she stood. She knew it like she knew who her own name. How it could be here and have just done what it did to Dave Bi-Plane was anyone's guess. But it *was* here. She looked to the woman's left and right, above and behind. It had somehow possessed and guided this Nightmarer to do the unspeakable. But how?

"Where are you? Show yourself!"

The woman just stood watching her, silently taunting, blood dripping from her knives.

As confused as she was, Halliday sensed an opportunity.

"Leave her, you dirty infiltrator! The Nightmarer is a product of Sombre!"

She aimed the Remington just above the woman's head and took a shot. Just a warning shot. *Preserve the Nightmarer* - she had to try and keep the poor thing in one piece, not riddle her with bullets. In a deep voice full of bombast, she hurled another warning. "Come out you coward! Show yourself! Let me sink a bullet between your eyes!"

Then the strangest thing happened.

The woman opened her mouth and four fingers appeared from within. A thumb pushed against the inner skin of her cheek and she made the vilest of retching sounds. The fingers then wriggled as if gesturing Halliday a hello. More fingers from a second hand appeared and wriggled on top of the others.

"The hocus!" A stunned Halliday breathed the words and her gun fell limp in her hand. She was being mocked. The Nightmarer's body began to lift and convulse.

Ether nodded her head viciously.

A horrible realization dawned on Halliday – of just what the ghoul had done; ripped the Beating Clocks out of all these citizens, left them with holes, butchered them and somehow had kept them all standing upright and in motion. It had turned the weather from hot to cold. And now, it was inside this poor woman. This thing was always going to be a step ahead, always, because it came from outside Sombre.

"Unstoppable," she said in awe.

Ether finished nodding the woman's head. Pulling her jaw wide open, one hand on top, one at the bottom, he stretched the mouth's skin as if it were mere rubber. Halliday was speechless. She could only watch on as the jaw snapped with a sickening 'click' and the woman's lower mandible was thrown to the ground like a piece of unwanted offcut. Her body was then stretched and pushed savagely outward from within, bones cracked with the contortion as cartilage made way for another someone from inside. Tearing the whole body apart like a skin jacket, Ether stepped out from the Nightmarer. Covered in blood and inner goo, as if newly born from its victim, Ether stood in a human form. He was smiling at Halliday, hair wet and congealed with gore, the thick strands coming down passed the eyes, black shining eyes.

She hadn't known what to expect, but it was a very unremarkable figure. Other than the eyes, he was an average joe if ever there was one. Dressed in a black - hip length coat and slacks, and a pair of knock-off shoes. Was it the hair? Ether looked down on his luck, not unlike a common street bum.

"What will stop me shooting you dead?" Halliday said grimacing as Ether's stench attacked her nostrils. She lifted the Remington and took aim, set right between the filthy leeches eyes. "I know you, you tainted scar! Before I shoot your unfortunate face off your oddly long neck, tell me, what brings you to Sombre?"

There was no answer, at least no answer that made a skerrick of sense. His smile just widened. The ticking hurt her head. Her Beating Clock began pushing hard against her; as if it were burrowing into her chest. The pain excruciating, she fought the urge to double over and cry.

"What is this peculiarity, you p-pig of a person!"

Ether stepped toward her and snorted with excitement.

In a reed thin voice, all she could muster, she yelled, "Confusing creeper! Take a barrel full of lead!" Holding her breath, she pumped the Remington. Bullets ripped open Ether's cheeks, punctured through the man's throat, and she screamed a "YAHHHHH!!!!!"

She shot the freaky man in his smiling mouth, exploded his right eye socket. There was relief, the pain in her chest lessened and she yelled in triumph. "Wickedness from the unknown! Taste your comeuppance!"

The aberration was to meet his end right here in Ginnifer West! She would have such a story for everyone at The Ruptured Spleen! She licked her lips, suddenly craving her Scotch and Dry from Orty.

Amid her gunfire, she noticed the ticking had stopped - along with any motion from the monster. Halliday's trigger finger slowed as she realized that more gunfire was pointless.

"What? Where? You blasted snake!"

Lowering her gun, she pushed on what was left of the head. The body was light, like a termite scavenged log.

Ether was gone. He had left his shell.

She poked his chest with the barrel of the Remington. The remains toppled and very un-ceremoniously hit the ground, breaking into pieces.

Each and every one of the hollowed-out citizens of the market followed suit in a mass-collapse. Lifeless bodies folded over in unison.

Ginnifer West fell silent.

"Damn," Halliday muttered.

Chapter 28

Hamish, A Clever Fellow

The marketplace of Ginnifer West resembled the aftermath of a massacre. Bodies lay strewn every which way, drunken looking in their deadness; some slumped over tables, others bent sideways in chairs. A lot were face down on the ground, arms folded underneath them on dislocated angles.

Sunshine and heat had returned to the town, as had the lush green hills surrounding the market. Halliday stood with Hamish the Mender as a dozen other Mender's mindfully lifted corpses onto gurneys and pushed them back into The Funneling. Like the bloodiest of bric-a-brac, the gorily extracted Beating Clocks gracing the market table were being gently placed into a blue tarpaulin bag.

"I'm still a little confused, Hamish. Is this all there is in Ginnifer West? This market? Is this Ginnifer West a town or just a market? Is there more?"

The chief Mender gave her a bemused look and shook his head. "I do often wonder, Halliday, what it is that triggers your thought patterns? Here we stand in the middle of a catastrophic mess of corpses and, let's face it, an obliterated Nightmarer, and your focus is the makeup and origin of Ginnifer West?"

Halliday peered down at the poor opened up woman; like a woefully performed autopsy from the heaviest of hands, exposed internal organs were squashed, ribcage split into two. Halliday thought it looked like someone had left the twin doors open on some sort of carcass closet.

Hamish rubbed his chin and shrugged. "It's okay I suppose. Quite sure your other versions were the same – callous, with more than a sprinkling of a common sociopath. It makes you the Gatherer you are."

She found herself quite angry at the whole situation, "Ether took my Nightmarer, Hamish. I didn't even have a chance to get this one to you in any sort of reasonable state!"

Hamish nodded and sighed. "Walk to the office with me Halliday, bring Wilder, I wouldn't mind checking on the piston work we did in her knee's, anyway."

"Nag, here!"

∫

"How can Lucretia call herself a Gatherer, Hamish? How can she be one of us and be in league with this miscreant as well? She's a bleeding wretch of a woman!"

Halliday held Wilder by the stirrup, guiding her through The Funneling with Hamish walking alongside. Fast moving gurneys were being pushed by complaining, harried Mender's. The doors to the Office' had been chocked open to allow easy access.

"And you have had this discussion with her, she's admitted to it?" Hamish rubbed his hand through his thick black hair. Getting his fingers stuck momentarily, he yanked them free then gave Wilder a pat on the nose.

"Yes! Twice, man! She's in league with the creature!"

Inside The Office of The Menders the scene resembled a war time hospital. At the walls, waiting bodies were piled two and three high. All gurneys were in use as makeshift bench space. The usually spotless and ammonia-cleaned floors were stained red, a male Mender wrung a mop out into a steaming bucket, slapped it back down and tried his best to clean the blood from the floor. Intense expressions were worn on faces all-round as delicate and intricate procedures were being performed amidst total mayhem.

"What a meat factory you have here at the moment, Hamish!" Halliday said dumbfounded.

He looked at his office with a hardness. "We can't keep this pace up. Something has to be done. To say it's all on top of us is an understatement. It's never been so bad. This is meant to be a facility to configure new Nightmarer's. Standing citizens are meant to come second, and you bloody Gatherers, a distant third! You know we've had Dave Bi-Plane in here twice in three days, don't you? He's at four strokes. Dave at four! One our most solid performers."

Halliday frowned and brought up something that had been niggling at her. "Is it a man? Ether? Lucretia said it was an 'it'. I saw a man in Ginnifer West."

Hamish rubbed his chin. "No, I don't think so. I think it takes on a bodied form when it needs to. As you know, no real human, animal or monster can exist here in Sombre without a Beating Clock."

"Well, that's why Lucretia being in league-"

Hamish shot her an exasperated look. "Halliday, my god! Stop it with her will you! What does it matter?"

"What are you on about, man! Ether is the cause of all this! And she speaks to him! Goes to this other place as well!"

"No, she doesn't," Hamish huffed and shook his head.

"Oh, she doesn't? How would *you* know? That's quite a stupid assumption coming from the gob of such clever man!"

The Mender gave her a wry smile, then he walked to Wilder, squatted down and set about pressing his thumbs into the piston joints of the machanihorse's mechanically muscularized legs. He didn't look up as he spoke to her. "It's not an assumption, Halliday. It's a fact. The only type of transportation *from* Sombre is to an entity on earth. Through sleep. You know this. We simply can't exist in any other kind of place or world. If it did

220

happen to Lucretia, I would imagine her combustion would be instant and infinite."

"Then how does she know of The Isolate?"

"This is what she calls it? The Isolate?" Hamish considered, "legitimate sort of name, I guess ... Oh, I don't doubt she's had contact with Ether, as you have had. She may have learnt of this place. She definitely didn't go there though; maybe she's just trying to impress you with her dark ways."

"She does try and do that a lot."

"I'm sure she does. Every Lucretia St Aimes has had a problem with every Halliday Knight. This isn't new. She has always had a bug in her backside about your beauty and light; your wit and charm - as misguided as it all is sometimes. And you, Halliday, have always thought of her as Sombre's only real devil." Hamish appeared from behind Wilder's rump, he rubbed a cleaning solution into his hands, "Wilder is good ...

"Anyway, don't forget that Lucretia is just another Gatherer, Halliday. You aren't all on some sort of sporting team, you know. Every Gatherer is an individual. Just because you all meet at The Ruptured Spleen and get bombed together, it doesn't make you any kind of joint conglomerate at all, in any way. You are all working for Sombre, you are not working together."

The Mender hesitated and gave her a searching look, as if trying to find the answer to a question he was about to ask before actually asking it. He raised his eyes and rubbed his chin in consideration, "Hmm."

"What?" She didn't like the cut of his gaze. "What, man? Spill it! I don't appreciate your leer!"

"Okay, well, now I'm going to contradict everything I just said to you." Leaning back on the bench he sat on his hands and sighed. "This could be the dumbest thing I have ever had to set in motion ..." He shook his head. "Just know that I really don't know if you'll be able to cope with this at all, and if it all goes awry, I am sorry. But, Halliday, if this Ether is to be stopped, I feel at least some of you may *have* to work together. Form a working alliance. Everything you see here," he gestured to the room, "This is all unprecedented. We've never had anything like this before. Ether is something else. And if there is one thing Sombre won't stand for, it is something it can't understand or control."

Halliday picked up on his meaning straight away. "A band of us to go and stop Ether? Is that what you're suggesting?"

"Yes."

Her mind began to turn the idea over. She folded her arms and shrugged. "We could do it I suppose. But we will all be called in for missions, Hamish! You know that. Sombre never leaves us to ourselves for long."

"I think Sombre will leave you alone whilst you take *this* on."

"And Em'? She's quite hopeless, Hamish! Sombre won't be able to stop her crashing her plane! I can't be there for her!"

"It might be a good idea to make Colonel Em Contusion part of your 'band' as you put it. You need to be able to keep her under control while you do this. She will be of little use, but then, you never know, she might surprise you.

"You best pick your Gatherers. As soon as you name them, they will know they're needed, Sombre will see to that. You need to begin planning how to stop Ether. I don't have too much advice. This isn't a normal human, but it needs to be one while it's in Sombre. The shell it left behind in Ginnifer West was an impressive anomaly – like some sort of calcified ghost – something I can't explain. But a body is a formation of bone, skin and organs – we have to hope that while it's in this form it can be destroyed."

"Well as you saw, I tried shooting the scoundrel! It didn't work!"

"I would think it will need more than a mere bullet from your Remington, Halliday." He gave her a dark look. "You have the biggest possible weapon at your disposal - The Morphia. As random and untamed as it is, it is an incredible killer; faster than a cheetah with a jaw like a metal trap. Your cohorts will hopefully be able to help you to keep it under control, so it can be used efficiently."

"Lucretia can control hers'," she frowned.

"Her Morphia isn't as powerful as yours," Hamish said flatly. "The Morphia Affliction is an imbalance in the psyche that relies on Personality Differential. You, Halliday Knight, are very different to The Morphia – once you engage the beast it works from the complete opposite end of a long range. In layman terms; day becomes night. Freezing reaches boiling point," he shrugged, "good becomes evil, if you will."

"So, it's because Lucretia is such a nasty prickle, that her Morphia is weak? Right, good to know," Halliday nodded to herself smugly.

"Well, yes, although I wouldn't say weak, Halliday, just not as strong as yours. The differential isn't large enough. She has a darkness to her personality that she will never shed - and will never want to.

"Anyway, the speed that Ether uses will have to be matched. What seemed like just moments before Ginnifer West, you alerted us to Dave Bi-Plane's felling at The Common Ground. Ether seems to be able to use Sombre's Byway's with incredible efficiency. His *killing* efficiency is even more impressive. The dissection of our Beating Clocks actually scares *me*, and I don't scare easily."

Halliday tapped her bottom lip and pondered. "But I've never tried to use The Morphia's speed. It's mind is an out-of-control Whirly-Gig, Hamish. I'm surprised I can run in a straight line, let alone jump through The Byway's chasing a smart monster like Ether!"

Hamish nodded, "You'll have to use your Gatherers to help you control it. Pick people of use. You'll need speed and ingenuity on land. You'll need to be swift in the air as well. Wilder can stay here." He patted the mare on the nose, "she can have some well-earned time off."

Straight away Halliday thought of Recalcitrance, her Dave Bi-Plane – that would cover the air and ingenuity. The thick moustache, reddish-blonde hair and sideburns of Drew Drucker the Speed Trucker came into her mind. The Australian man had the best of the Speed Trucks. He wore too short-shorts and a ratty blue singlet – she didn't know him so well, but had always seemed a genuine fellow, if not a little roughly spoken. He would do for anything necessary on land.

"This is a lot to ask of me, Hamish. Why me? Why not another Gatherer? We all have similar skills?"

"Because you have been chosen and you'll do what your told!" Hamish said like a father. He shut his eyes and rubbed his temples. He was agitated. "This needs to be stopped! Look around you! The current rate of resident attrition can't continue. This department cannot cope as it is. Sombre can't destroy it! It isn't from Sombre! Sombre can only control its own. You will use your Morphia and you will like it!"

Feeling well scolded, she mumbled an, "okay."

In a soberer tone, Hamish continued. "Oh, and one other thing. Captain Andrew Feister is missing."

Halliday was confused, "No, he isn't, Hamish. I just saw his balloon pass over Ginnifer West! He appeared to be on a mission."

"No, he is gone. He's flying, but he isn't on any mission. He's nowhere at present. We need him back here, so we can put him down, put him right again – reconfigure his clock and mind. He has lost sight of who he is. This is bad for a Gatherer. Everyone in Sombre knows their place. This is especially bad for Andrew Feister."

"Oh, agreed. He is a loopy individual. I'm not at all surprised," Halliday nodded.

"On his last drop he was all over the place, Halliday. Now he is missing. I am only speculating, but I can't help but think that Ether has gotten to him in some way. He isn't the strongest in personality, you know."

"What? Are you kidding me man! He is a headstrong and overly verbose, dill! An extremely unattractive chauvinist! Even worse when liquored up!"

"I think you'll find that most of that is show. Andrew Feister suffers from incredible anxiety. He needs regularity. If he has had any sort of run in with Ether, he may have fallen to pieces."

"So, he is really just a wobbly sort of fellow? Hmm ... I wouldn't have thought," she mused.

"It's all brittle bravado. You'll need to look out for him."

Halliday stretched, performing a mock yawn, she scratched Wilder on her snout, who had nuzzled into the crook of her neck. "Well, Hamish, anything else why we're at it? You seem to think you can just keep showering Sombre's problems all over me."

Unfolding his arms, he stood and placed a hand on each of her shoulders, looked straight into her eyes. "Halliday Knight, I told you, you were meant for more – this is more. You are Hope's Halliday, for better or worse. I think you can safely assume that your Hope Kelley is feeling the effects of Ether as well."

"I *know* she is," Halliday admitted. "I recognize things I shouldn't. Things that I haven't seen in Sombre at all." She pictured the butchered lips on the citizens of Ginnifer West. She had seen the cuts before – just not in Sombre.

"Best to assume that everything you see and feel from now on, Hope will be experiencing some sort of form of as well, in her daily existence."

Taking his hands from her shoulders, Hamish raised his eyebrows and a smile formed on his lips. "This is quite the burden on you, Halliday."

"Yes, it is! Do not be so smug! It is not appreciated!" She fumed. "It's all very well for you, isn't it, clever man? You are the cleverest of all! From the comfort of this office you set me these tasks!" She threw out a hand in exasperation and accidently flicked Wilder in her left eyeball, the machanihorse whinnied and snorted her disapproval. "Sorry, nag."

Hamish gave her a quizzical look.

"Good god! From the comfort of this office you say! The same office being bombarded by death and mutilation minute after minute! Of complaining, overworked menders? Yes, quite the vacation I'm having here, Halliday!" Shaking his head, he began rubbing a thick solution into his hands, his focus had turned to the benches. He'd had enough of her. "Remember, I'm working for Sombre, just as you are. But you are special, Halliday. You are something else again, not just another run of the mill Gatherer ... take it as a compliment."

"And I will ask you again - why me, Hamish?"

"You happened upon Hope Kelley."

S

Hope woke up on the floor, staring at her bed.

CHAPTER 29

Jerry Cowle, Signing Out

Parker Wright had changed - changed a hell of lot.

In what had only been a handful of days, she had all but completely ostracized herself from the old Parker.

It had all been an exercise in letting go.

She had let go of that impossibly high rung she used to cling to on Centurion's social ladder; she'd let go of judging the world so indifferently; let go of thinking her shit didn't stink as well. The biggest was letting go of that hideous, cheerleading, rich-bitch persona. And it *was* just a persona after-all; she wasn't rich, she was lower middle class at best. After her parents split, things tightened up and her mother, store manager at Stiletto Shoes, rented the tiny, three-bedroom unit the Wright's called home. The dwelling was stuck behind a group of the crappiest shops, in the absolute anus of town, Lower Pento.

Indeed, a lot of what she had brought to the Centurion Sparks was an act, a forthright acknowledgement that she could match it with those girls physically and socially, and she did, but now she couldn't have given less of a shit about them if she tried. Her attitude was still undisputed, and forever would be. Parker Wright still had plenty of bitch about her, and she loved it, she owned it.

But mostly, she loved her surprising new friendship with Hope Kelley. Bizarre and unexpected; the chances of the two of them being brought together was as likely as a spaceship crashing into the Centurion school bus. And as messed up and random as Sombre was - had it all been for the better? Bet your ass it had. As strange as it was to even think it, she had something to believe in now. She had Sombre. The nightmare world was something out of the ordinary. Ordinary was boring. Ordinary made her angry. The *extraordinary* threw plenty of curveballs. Curveballs were real. A part of life.

Jerry Cowle. Now, that was a curveball. What was his part in all of this?

Any contact with Jerry was a possible opportunity to try and find out. She had math with him.

She'd told Hope, to keep an eye on her phone.

Parker had chosen a seat a few rows behind him; next to Josie Myer, a 'Spark', who gave her a cool glance, crossed her legs and hid behind her blond hair.

Parker was an above average math student. Math was black or white, right or wrong, one correct answer, which you either understood or you didn't – no bull.

Miss Tandecker addressed her classroom of twenty-five,

"So, students, looking at the ordered pairs below, is the relation between these numbers considered a function?" she drew bracketed numbers and arrows to the domain and range, with a well-practiced hand on the white board. "I need you all to figure out the range and a positive output in order to find the negative." Capping her blue marker, she turned to her class and smiled, she flourished her hand, "go to it, you have 15 minutes before lunch."

Parker gave her calculator a glance, then the equation on the whiteboard, then Jerry. Thankfully, he had been quiet all through class. She texted Hope - *nothing yet*

She picked up her pen with her right hand and began keying in numbers on her well-worn Texas' with her left.

Five minutes in, the relative silence of the room was interrupted - well, it was for her and Jerry.

She felt the chill that no one other than her and Jerry would have felt. She heard the ticking that no one other than her and Jerry would have heard.

Dressed in his black parka, wet pale face and dripping hair, Ether slipped across the floor. Jerry let out a low cry, "... no!"

The class looked up in unison.

"Shut up Jerry, we're trying to concentrate!" Wade Rig, the blond burly quarter back said to a few nasty giggles. The new Jerry Cowle had demons and his classmates knew it, and typically, it didn't stop them from being assholes.

"Shhh!" Miss Tandecker shot from her desk. "Ten minutes left, I expect a correct answer from everyone." She gave Jerry a look that read part pity and part concern. The class settled.

Parker watched on with her heart racing as Ether leant over Jerry's desk. Leering at him expectantly the creep showed Jerry a blade and pointed it at his mouth.

"No," Jerry whimpered again, this time lower.

Ether whispered, and Parker could hear every word, *'come captain, time to go, bring Jerry or I'll slit him open right here in front of everyone.'*

Jerry's hand shot up. "Miss Tandecker, could I go to the bathroom, I've answered the question."

The teacher nodded. Jerry stood. In ghostly silence, Ether led the way to the door.

Parker watched on and gulped. For a moment she wondered who in hell this 'captain' was? Then realized she was stalling. There was no time to waste. She had to move. Quickly penning her answer, she got up, slinging her bag over her shoulder.

Miss Tandecker put her hands in the air in a gesture of 'what gives?'

"It's almost lunch, Parker. What are you doing?"

Parker walked toward her teachers desk, pinched at the fabric of her skirt awkwardly and whispered, "Monthly girl emergency. Heavy flow on."

Miss Tandecker shook her head, "lovely."

Parker rushed out the door. In the hall she whipped her phone from the side pocket in her bag and tapped hurriedly – 'Jerry on the move!'

§

"Please hand in your 'To Kill a Mockingbird' essays at the end of tomorrow's class, my wonderful students," Miss Sparrows sat at her desk and lowered her glasses. "As I've mentioned numerous times, this will contribute a big chunk to your end of year score."

The bell rang for lunch and the room rose as one.

Hope made a mental note in her very cluttered mind. She had to finish the stupid book then scratch out something that resembled an essay. Well, it wasn't a *stupid* book; it was a classic. She just had far too much going on at the moment and this was just another thing to do.

Last night's adventure in Sombre was a taxing one, and she had a bruise on her hip to prove it. She had no idea how long she had slept on the floor after rolling off her bed but was surprised the impact hadn't woken her. Although she shouldn't have been surprised. She seemed to only wake up when Halliday needed the toilet. Sombre sparing her the indignity of wetting the bed.

Miss Sparrows peered up from her laptop as Hope passed her desk. "On top of things are you Hope? I expect fifteen hundred meaningful words. On Word, pen on paper, iPad. This will be your first major thing you've done for me since you've arrived here. I'm looking forward to reading it."

Hope's phone pinged in her bag. Parker was already on the move.

"Uh, yeah. Almost finished, just a few paragraphs to go," she lied as she cleared her throat of a whopping great phlegm-ball.

Miss Sparrows wrinkled her nose at Hope's ill-timed dislodgement. "Yes, good, well don't get sick will you."

Smiling awkwardly, Hope left the room. She rummaged in her bag for her phone. Her hand shaking a little, she read the last of Parker's messages.

'meet me at the water tank hes here'

Reaching for the salad wrap in her cool pack, Hope palmed the hallway door and hit the one o'clock sunshine, heading straight for the uninhabited outer boundary of Centurion. Shaded by a clump of fifty-foot Alder trees planted just past the fence-line, the big grey circular water tank sat right alongside the groundskeeper shed – an area absolutely no one went. Jerry Cowle must have *really* wanted to be alone.

Hope saw her friend leaning on the wall of the tank. She waved. Parker kicked off from the wall. Hope's senses searched for a name for the smell that suddenly hovered at her nostrils – she settled on hot grass and public toilet. Parker walked toward her, pinching her nose, she kept her voice low. "Bit stinky here isn't it? Couldn't imagine anyone but birds and pedophiles hanging this far out."

"Where's Jerry?" Hope said.

"Behind the shed. Pretty sure Ether led him here. The fucker came into the classroom and asked him to leave, just like that!" she added and grabbed Hope by the arm. Dragging her a few feet to the right she pointed. Hope could make out an arm and a pale leg in tan shorts.

"What's he doing?" Hope shoved the last of her wrap in her mouth and stuffed the Health & Co, paper-cellophane packaging in the hip pocket of her shorts. She rubbed her hands together and moved toward the shed, hunched over and tip-toeing.

Parker followed her. "This is stalking isn't it? We're stalking this dude, aren't we?"

Feeling the danger, Hope cleared her throat and answered in a hushed tone, "We have to. This could be big. I think Jerry could be someone in Sombre. Halliday just had a massive talk with Hamish the Mender about how closely our dream lives and real lives exist to each other's."

"He probably is. That'd make sense," Parker agreed, "but why Jerry? And not that I'm complaining, but why me, for that matter? We're nobody in relation to you, Hope. Well, I am, I suppose. I mean we hang out now ... we're friends."

Parker's words may as well have been an embrace. Hope felt a tiny flutter of happiness in her chest; she wasn't about to make a thing of it, though. She breathed the moment in just for a second, then moved on.

The two reached the edge of the shed. Hope picked at a splinter in the wooden paling wall and listened in. Jerry was sobbing. Pretty pathetically, it had to be said. Faint words were being spoken between sniffs.

"Poor guy," Hope said.

"Bit piss weak ..." Parker shrugged. "Needs to toughen up a bit."

Jerry cleared his throat and coughed. He bent over and put his hands on his knees.

Hope couldn't bring herself to share in her friends callousness. Jerry had been through a lot. He had lived through an attack from a ghoul from another existence, was still obviously being taunted by said ghoul. Sombre had scathed him badly.

She whispered, "Halliday went to a town to gather a Nightmarer and everyone's lips were cut up just like Jerry's were."

"Oh, shit! Really?"

"Really," Hope answered whipping her glasses off. She huffed on the lenses and wiped them on her shirt.

"Jesus! He's spotted us!" Parker hissed.

Hope rammed her glasses back on, almost impaling her eyeball with a temple tip in the process. "Ow, shit!"

Jerry was facing them.

A weird smirk crossed his lips. He fixed his gaze squarely on Parker and rubbed his hands together. Jerry was staring at Parker as if for the first time and spoke as if he had never met her – but really liked what he saw. He opened his hands in an imploring fashion.

'Oh, and who are you my swan? Did that scoundrel scar you in anyway – hurt that beautifully etched chin of yours!'

"What?" Parker said lifting an eyebrow.

"I have been ripped down from the skies on nothing more than a flukey-fluke of a whim, by a miscreant of the lowest form!" Jerry fluttered his eyes and flashed some badly maintained, plaque-stained teeth, in what was meant to be a winning smile,

"But my fortune has changed for the better, because you, land dweller, are a catch of the uppermost picking!"

Jerry took a step toward Parker, who in turn took a step backward.

"No one *picks* me, asshole."

She looked to Hope bewildered. "Shit! Jerry's lost his fucking marbles! Do I need to slap him?"

Hope could only give her an unhelpful shrug and an equally unhelpful, "ugh ...?"

Jerry continued on earnestly,

'Have you ever courted an airman, my swan? My craft boasts speed, flame and firepower. Falling to your knees, you would surrender to the skies, guided by the most dexterous, yet tender hand that would ever touch your skinny-skin!'

"Ew! That all sounds completely lecherous, Jerry. Back away, now! Scuzz-ball!" Parker threatened and uttered to Hope, "What are we going to do, he's going to touch my skinny-skin! Ha!" She laughed in spite of her situation.

Hope suddenly knew who this was. "Oh, god! You're Captain Andrew Feister!" she blurted taking a step back. "So that's who-"

As if Hope had only just arrived on the scene and had a voice worth listening to, Jerry paused in his pursuit of Parker and swung his attention her way. He didn't speak, he just stared. Lowering his eyes, his shoulders dropped. He then turned and walked back in the direction of the groundskeepers shed.

"That stopped him," Parker said. "Who's Captain Andrew Feister?"

"A balloonist Gatherer, bit of a chauvinist, harmless though. Hamish has just told Halliday that he's missing – that he's MIA."

"And now he's here? In Jerry Cowle?"

"I guess?" Hope said mystified.

Hope and Parker watched on as Jerry walked straight through the boundary fence, as if the wire mesh was merely a mirage. He headed into the trees beyond.

With a telling look to each other, they followed.

In a dramatic turn, daylight died in an instant and a fog swept the area. The familiar chill was back. Ticking sounded out in the distance like a calling.

"This is all sorts of trouble, isn't it?" Hope said to Parker.

"Yup," Parker said and grabbed Hope's lower arm.

The two walked straight through the boundary fence.

Chapter 30

A Hope Shaped House

Jerry Cowle had completely transformed.

Hope and Parker now followed the gawky form of the aviator, Captain Andrew Pfeiffer. The Sombre gatherer ambled through the Alder trees like a phantom, glowing in the foggy gloom. He was taller than Hope remembered from Halliday's meetings at The Ruptured Spleen. His balding head looked shrunken - like a decorated hard-boiled egg - sitting within the high collar of his brown leather flight jacket. She noticed how bow-legged he walked; as if someone had kneed him hard in the balls.

"Don't even ask me what this is all about, Parker. I have no idea." She rubbed her bare arms and took a quick look back at the very much still intact boundary fence that they had both just walked through, just as Captain Andrew had.

"I know. Crashing worlds. Things are getting fucked up, friend." Parker nodded to herself, not taking her eyes from Andrew Pfeiffer. "He looks like an ugly uncle on his way to a fancy-dress party, doesn't he? Why is he walking like that? Does he ride a horse in Sombre at all?"

"No, he doesn't. He flies a balloon."

"Yeah, right, you said ..." Parker trailed off.

The Alder trees came to an end and the woody path dipped to a lonely roadside. Jerry Cowle/Captain Andrew Pfeiffer stumbled down into the middle of the road and kept on going. A round orange light shone through the fog like an eclipse as Hope and Parker followed. Hidden by haze, a flat land of nothing rolled out to the left and right of the road. The ticking was getting louder.

"Where are we? This isn't Pento, anymore, is it?" Hope said shivering a little. She licked her lips, tasting the air. It was so cold.

"Captain 'o' captain, where the hell are you going," Parker sung under her breath, then yanked Hope by the lower arm. She pointed ahead, "Keep up Hope. Answers are this way. We're meant to see this."

Hope quickened her step. "Parker, have you stopped to wonder where Jerry is?"

"No, not really. He's in our very unappealing friend up ahead of us, isn't he?"

"I guess," Hope answered not sure that Jerry actually was. She wasn't sure of any of this. Nothing was meant to exist outside of Sombre. Yet this had Sombre's stamp all over it. They weren't sleeping, weren't dreaming – they were both very awake. She poked Parker in the arm to make sure. "And we're not dead."

"No, we're not," Parker confirmed giving her a smile and a playful raise of the eyebrows. Hope could see her friend was clearly enjoying herself.

The road veered left and a single house materialized in the distance, a big black, monolithic shadow. Captain Andrew left the road in an ostrich-like sprint, heading straight for the front doors. The ticking got louder when he entered. There was a distinct thud as the door shut. The ticking softened.

The orange orb in the sky, dropped down on their approach, aiding light. The residence was now in full view.

"What the f-!" Parker stood frozen. In a thinner voice she then uttered, "Hope, what is this?"

"I-I don't know," Hope answered pitiably. She stood in awe.

"But that's you?" Parker said in a tone that bordered on the accusatory.

Built with weathered grey wood, the two storied residence was impossibly sculptured. Sloping tiles on either side of a flat-gabled roof top suggested a head. Two large, nautical styled circular windows resembled Hope's glasses. In line with the second floor, a protruding patio roof supported by C-shaped bracket columns housed the twin doorway; the wide entry was the mouth - a wooden step running the width of the doorway was the chin. Curved, boarded fascia on each side of the entry created cheek-shapes.

Parker was right. It didn't take much imagination to see that the house was meant to resemble her. Her being Hope Kelley; the girl who lived the best part of her life in a dreamworld. The girl who up until recently, had not really had a proper friend; actually, epitomized the social leper. The girl who's waking life sometimes felt so insignificant, she could simply vanish, and no one would notice.

That girl was now being made a big-deal of. Here sat a house shaped like her! She didn't know whether she should be frightened or be gushing with pride.

"It's like some sort of freaky monument," Parker said in awe, then added, "no offense."

"None taken – it *is* freaky. Do we go in?" Hope peered up at the disturbing eye-glass shaped windows and felt a need to adjust her own.

"Oh-we-o-so-fucking-do! Jerry has! Well, the dorky aviator version! C'mon."

The older girl grabbed her by the arm and marched her toward the doorway. Wearing a grin that Hope found a bit savage given the circumstances, Parker grabbed the two copper doorknobs and turned.

Parker and Hope entered the Hope shaped house.

S

Hope Kelley lived in the now.

She had never been that big on recalling the past. She found there was never much point. Her past was generally filled with indifference and instability and acceptance of that indifference and instability.

The Kelley's had always been the family on the move – seemingly forever uprooting and moving to new destinations. Health&Co started from nothing. When her father had to chase more business, he chased it like a hungry dog (albeit a well-dressed one, always). Her mother, rode her beau's curtails, trusting the path he was on implicitly. She would package up the two Kelley girls with barefaced, smiley indifference. Any sort of life Hope and Kate may have had on the go at the time would be gone.

Hope *learned* to live in the now. The Kelley's lack of foundation as a family never made her sad, just numb.

So, what she was faced with now was a curiosity, to say the least.

"Jesus, this is a head-spin, eh? You were a cute little mutha. That *is* meant to be you, yeah?" Parker said with her arms folded. "If I wasn't so used to this sort of bizarre shit now, I'd swear I'd been drugged."

Hope couldn't respond. She could only try to process what she was seeing.

She and Parker both stood on an entry landing of weathered, hardwood floorboards. The first floor of the house was just one room, twenty feet wide; just the one set of stairs to the left and what appeared to be one implausibly long, airy hallway. If there was an end to the hallway, Hope couldn't see it. Dim, yellow-lit wall lamps intermittently flickered in the small portion where she and Parker stood. Beyond this point, all lights were off. The ticking was incessant.

A few feet from the landing, a dark-haired baby dressed in a pink jumpsuit lay on a change table. She peddled her legs in the air and grizzled; pulled a foot toward her mouth, let go of it, then grizzled some more.

"Do you think that baby's meant to be me?" Hope mouthed to Parker.

238

"Well, it's not me. I had hair as white as rice noodles when I was younger," Parker said and added, "and we *are* standing in your house. One can only assume."

A small circle of crumbling yellow flame appeared in the dark hall.

Hope gasped as she heard a familiar song start from somewhere within the house. Beautiful strains of Mama Cass's, 'Dream a Little Dream of Me' filled the air.

A younger, paler version of her mother materialized out of the gloom. Her blond hair was tied up in a messy bun. She was dressed in slobby home gear; sweatpants and slippers. Butting her cigarette out in an ashtray, Evelyn Kelley walked toward the change table, picked baby Hope up and took a whiff of her bottom. She then popped her on the floor with a buttoned-vested, no-pant-wearing teddy bear.

Baby Hope rolled onto her front and tried to commando-crawl in the direction of her mother, who had walked off into the gloom, lighting up another smoke. A fridge materialized, Evelyn flung the door open and pulled out a bottle of beer. Shutting it with her shoulder, she cracked the top off her bottle with an opener.

She began to sway. She flung her head back and sung drunkenly at the top of her voice to 'Dream a Little Dream of Me',

> 'Stars shining bright above you
> Night breezes seem to whisper "I love you"
> Birds singing in the sycamore trees
> Dream a little dream of me'

> 'Say nighty-night and kiss me
> Just hold me tight and tell me you'll miss me
> While I'm alone and blue as can be

Dream a little dream if me'

She then disappeared. Baby Hope was left on the floor.

"Real nice ... but I won't judge, my mother wasn't much better," Parker said.

"She loved this song. Gee, I don't remember her ever being like that? Ever." Hope said feeling more than a bit exposed in front of her new friend.

Materializing from the dark, a two-year-old version of Hope then came sliding in on her knees. She wore shorts, a thin cardigan and lime coloured gumboots. She was playing with a Sesame Street school bus along the floor. Big Bird's yellow head popped up and down through the roof as tiny Hope pushed and made strange sucking noises with her mouth. She had a saliva rash on her chin. Her glasses were strapped around her head like swimming goggles.

"So that's how all you blind little fuckers kept your glasses on? Right. Makes sense," Parker said.

Hope watched her miniature selves rooting around on the hard wood floor and wondered what in the hell was going on? What was Sombre trying to show her? That she used to be a baby?

Her mother returned from the dark again; this time she had no cigarette or beer in hand. The baby-bump in her belly showed that she was pregnant with Kate. Her eyes were filled with tears, she had the sniffles. Evelyn Kelly looked down contemplatively at toddler Hope. She wiped her eyes and cheeks with a tissue that she pulled from the pocket of her sweatpants.

"Jesus, she looks sad, Hope," Parker said, "hormonal as hell ... where was your father?"

"Working," she answered without pause. Hope looked on with a hardness that was well practiced, the Kelley concrete resolve.

Her mother's phone rang, its little blue screen lit up, she walked off into the dark and answered it.

Another, slightly older Hope came rolling into the room, kneeling on a thin red skateboard. Hope guessed she was around four. Her glasses were way too big for her head; her hair was tied back in a ponytail. She was wearing shorts and pink gumboots. The skateboard stopped and she pushed off again with her right foot.

"My god, I looked like a crazy person," Hope said shaking her head.

"What's with the gumboot fetish?"

"My mother couldn't get me out of them."

Like a knife strike, a wild scream cut through the strains of Mama Cass's soothing *'night birds'* and whispered, *'I love you s'*.

"Fuck! What was that!" Parker grabbed Hope by her arm.

Hope stumbled forward as the same bolt of pain she felt at the hospital flashed across her temple. She couldn't speak, the pain was unbearable. Her tongue felt fat in her mouth. She gulped and tried clearing her throat; choked down a wave of nausea. Shutting her eyes tight, she breathed deeply and tried to gain composure. She then opened them again - just in time to see her four-year-old self speed unnaturally across the floor on the skateboard, hit the wall and wipe out. Her little body smashed to pieces like globe-glass.

Baby Hope began shaking as if she were being electrocuted. Liquid ran on the floor under her body. Toddler Hope suddenly got tired and dropped to her side next to her Big Bird's bus.

"Shit!' Parker dragged Hope back toward the door. "We gotta run, Hope! This is all sorts of wrong! We shouldn't have come. No, this was bad by me! You shouldn't always listen to me! No sir ... I'm too fucking gung-ho all the time!" Parker tried the twin door handles. "Ho! And that'd be right wouldn't it! Locked! Ass-hole!"

Another scream, an unhinged, banshee-like wail started in the dark hall and came at them fast in the form of a sprinting, wild eyed, Evelyn Kelley. Like a fast Running-Back, Hope's mother bent down, gathered baby Hope by a leg and flung her straight at Hope and Parker. Hope's former baby self hit her square in the face and exploded like an over ripe tomato; ectoplasmic blood spatter filled Hope's glasses with red.

"Jesus!" Hope yelled and wrenched her glasses off her face.

She turned to a shell-shocked Parker, who stood open-mouthed and appalled, neck and torso-covered in baby gore. "Crazy, fucking bitch! Sorry. But she is!"

On her knees, Evelyn Kelley laughed madly and slapped the floor with both hands. Hope knew she was looking at the hate-filled mother from her rite of passage nightmare.

Sombre wanted her to see her this way. Why?

Hope looked back pleadingly at her friend as if she had been caught telling a lie. The biggest. As if this house was revealing the true ugliness of her life. But it wasn't true! None of it was!

"Parker?"

"What?" Parker answered. "This is so fucked up! But it's not real!"

Crawling on her knees, both coughing and laughing, Evelyn Kelley slammed her hand down on the back leg of Hope's suddenly listless, two-year-old self. She stood, holding her child upside down like a ragdoll.

With a tired-looking back swing, she threw toddler Hope back into the darkness and walked in after her. Her laughter turned into pissed-off-sounding yelling; yelling along with Mama Cass.

'SAY nighty-night and KISS ME!

JUST hold me tight and TELL me you'll miss ME!

While I'm alone and blue as can BE!

Dream a little dream of me ...'

Savage thunder crashed through the music and the ticking; an aural barrage, shaking the foundations of the house. Heavy rain poured down throughout the hall.

The orange sky orb that had guided her and Parker to the house was back; dramatically illuminating the black coated figure of Ether in the darkness. A submissive Captain Andrew Pfeiffer was on the floor. Ether rammed his blade into the airman's shoulder. Andrew's howl of pain rang out with the deafening thunder. Andrew Pfeiffer was Jerry Cowle. Jerry Cowle was Andrew Pfeiffer.

He was about to be executed.

∫

The driving in-house rain cleared Hope's head.

She felt a gust at her back.

She turned. The front doors were wide open. Was the house testing her morality? She now had a way out. It wanted her to take it. She eyed the knife wielding maniac in the hall. She took another look at the exit; then at Parker. Sombre was playing a game with them both. Or was it just her?

She looked to Parker. "We can't go."

Parker shook her head, eyeing the exit longingly, "I know, we get Jerry and then we go ... but the creepy fucker has a knife! What do we do? What if we die?"

"We chance it! We have to, Parker! *Jerry* will die!" She turned, Ether stabbed Captain Andrew again, this time further down and in a slicing motion, to the left side of the abdomen. Ether was going to kill the Sombre airman slowly.

Drenched hair stuck to her cheeks, Parker licked her lips, "then we just run at him ..."

"... and we'll see what happens," Hope finished for her.

Hope turned and faced what was now inevitable. "We go."

Running into the driving rain, Hope led the attack. She jumped from the landing with Parker at her boot heels; charging into the dark with eyes only for Ether.

She screamed.

Parker screamed as well - adding a nasty barrage of abuse about his lack of manhood for good measure.

Splashing through what felt like at least two feet of water, Hope lost her footing and fell, ploughing into the ghoul's side. Parker either jumped or fell over the top of her, she couldn't tell, screamed a "MOTHERFUCKER!!!!!!" and hit Ether with open arms in a tackle. Parker was flung off as Ether toppled over; his blade left in Captain Andrew's shoulder.

The attack was woefully executed but seemed to be enough.

Hope was on Ether; she felt a scrawny chest of protruding ribs under his raincoat as she recovered and scrambled up his long frame on her hands and knees. What was she was going to do to complete her attack? Scratch his eyes out? Sock him one on the nose? She hadn't a clue. Drawing level with the ghoul's face she saw that he was smiling. Black eyes peering into her own.

"Hope Kelley, welcome!"

With the raspy greeting came a transformation – a facial reconstruction. Under the wet, greasy licks of fringe, Ether had made a change, it had taken on Hope's face. She looked directly into the eyes of her replica.

Ether rolled Hope's eyes to the back of Hope's head and licked Hope's lips. He hissed. "Wake up, Hope Kelley! Wake up or die a thousand deaths! It's all for you. Only you! Time! Time will eat your existence!"

Ether grabbed the back of her head and wrenched her in close – nose to nose.

She felt her own lips tasting her own skin; her own open mouth breathing deathly cold air as her face was sucked. She wanted to cry out loud, but she couldn't.

She couldn't move.

The violation was so dominate, so *personal.*

So final.

A hurricane wind blew violently through the front door.

As if made of nothing more than dust fragments, Ether eroded from underneath her, and blew away.

Suddenly everything was dust.

Everything blew away.

Blinding daylight returned.

Jerry Cowle hadn't.

CHAPTER 31
LOEW AVION

"So, when are we going to meet this Parker girl?" Hope's mother topped up her wine and gave her a deliberate raise of the eyebrows. "You're skipping school with her. Catching lifts home in her brothers car! Not thrilled with that at all."

The school had rung her mother reporting Hope's truancy. When she hadn't turned up to third period, Centurion had responded as if there had been a prison break. An annoyed Evelyn Kelley had come home from the salon early. She had been waiting for Hope; and had seen her guiltily squeeze out of Josh's two door silver Mustang.

"She's older than you. Where does she live?"

"Lower Pento," Hope answered as she sliced through her gravy-soaked veal. The day's events hadn't upset her appetite at all, just the opposite, she had a cavern in her gut that just had to be filled.

"Hmm, Lower, eh?" Her father raised an eyebrow. He cleared his throat. "She do drugs?"

"No! She's a cheerleader, well, she was ... she's awesome! You wanted me to have a friend!" Hope said swallowing a large mouthful of meat.

No one had reported Jerry missing yet. They would, it had only been five hours since he vanished. Was he dying a slow death in Sombre somewhere - or worse still, The Isolate? There was a lack of Jerry Cowle on planet earth. She was under no allusion that today would be the end of it. The school knew she and Parker had left the grounds; they would know Jerry had as well. When there he was nowhere to be seen, the authorities would come calling.

A disturbing mental image invaded her thoughts; what she saw of Jerry /Captain Andrew Pfeiffer before everything blew away in the wind. Bleeding from his side and from his shoulder, his lips had been re-mutilated. His eyes were sunken in his pale face; distinct black shadows in the sockets gave him the appearance of a failed, masked comic book villain. She wondered how much more of Ether's brutality Jerry could possibly survive.

"Parker sounds like an epic bitch," Kate said wrenching her from her thoughts.

"She's not!" Hope said pointing her fork at her sister. "Better than most of the idiotic cattle you hang out with!"

Devan Kelley chuckled and had to cough. "Sorry, I like that - *idiotic cattle...* but Hope, you need to be careful. No skipping school please. And as your mother said, we'd like to meet this girl. Size her up. She's older. Generally, an older friend will have some influence over you."

"She's only a year older," Hope said.

"Ha. A year's enough, Hope." Her mother said pairing her knife and fork on her empty plate. "You do a lot of growing in your 16th year, let me tell you - in all sorts of ways. I was a shocker."

"Really? What ways? Give us the juice, mother!" Kate raised her eyebrows, rested her chin on her palm and waited expectantly to hear about all of Evelyn Kelley's sins of the past.

Their mother looked sideways. "That can wait until you're 16, I think."

"Yes, I think that would be best left at least 'til then ..." their father said and took a sip of his wine.

A wave of tiredness hit Hope, the day's events taking their toll. She yawned, lifted her glasses and rubbed her eyes. "Parker will be happy to meet you all I'm sure. I'm beat, no dessert for me, thanks. Can I be excused?"

Her mother nodded. "Tomorrow, Hope. I would like to meet her, tomorrow, okay?"

"Okay," Hope agreed.

Her mother's past had just been spoken of. It suddenly occurred to Hope to ask. "Mom?"

"Yes?"

"You used to play a song a lot when I was younger. 'Dream a Little Dream of Me,' didn't you?"

"When you were a baby. It was a nap song my mother used to use to settle me with as well. Mama Cass's version is the best version. It seemed to work on you too. Why do you ask?" Evelyn blinked her eyelids.

"Oh, I just heard it, that's all."

"Mama Cass choked on a sandwich and died, you know," her father mused flicking his empty wine glass with his finger.

"No, it was a heart attack," Evelyn corrected him.

"Oh?"

Hope let them have the discussion and left the room.

∫

Showered, mostly cleansed from the mayhem of the day, an exhausted Hope hit the pillow with semi-dry hair. As her conscious mind waited for the inevitable fall into Sombre's clutches; lingering thoughts, drifted in her headspace like persistent ghosts.

Ether wasn't dead *or* gone *or* destroyed. She'd be a fool to think that. Could something like that even *be* killed? Ether was a force. A thing that could travel through her sleep into her waking world. It showed her that psychotic version of her mother from her rite of passage nightmare. Something that belonged and should have stayed in her unconscious mind. It had taken on her own form in that house; warned her of wasting her existence. Was she wasting her existence really? She thought fifteen was pretty young to making that call.

One thing she felt certain of – change was at hand. She wasn't scared of it. She should be, but she wasn't.

Hope fell asleep, defiant, ready to face her destiny.

∫

This was the end of the nightmare, it had to be, it simply couldn't go on any further.

Hope stood in a darkened room, the walls and floor were all dirt and earth. There didn't appear to be any sort of door to speak of. In the middle of the room stood a large, rectangular glass cabinet. Hands on her knees, she squatted down and peered through the glass. It was an ant farm, yet it wasn't an ant farm, just similar. It was a display, a showing of her unceremonious end. At the top of the display, she could see the empty cemetery, steamy mist filling the grounds, party of relatives long gone. A cold dark blanketed the paths and tombstones. Scanning the glass, she watched herself buried six feet down in a hole; door on a hap-hazard angle, compounded by dirt. Her head had slid down and sat atop her sloppy body bits, wedged between earth and burial door. Scanning closer she could see her head was actually slightly upside down. Her mouth was open, she had no nose left.

Drawing her eyes away from the form of her messy cadaver she peered up with dread. The roof of the room began to fall. Heavy bits of earth pounded down on her head and shoulders. She felt her neck break.

This was the end.

Hope Kelley, discarded, forgotten, buried and hidden away forever.

∫

Halliday had named her Gatherer's for the mission and they had come.

Drew Drucker The Speed Trucker drove his black and sleek eighteen-wheeler, 'The Devil Incarnate', in top gear, powering along the endless tarmac that was Loew Avion. Her dress clinging to her legs against the g-forces, hem flapping behind her, Halliday stood ready on the speed truck's shiny, flatbed trailer. Recalcitrance Bexley with token skinny cigarette in the crook of her mouth and a business-like Dave Biplane, busied themselves locking the heavy metal manacles on Halliday's wrists. Two ten-foot lengths of chain snaked along the trailer bed ending in slip hooks clasped to a wrought iron bar at the trailer's front.

Hamish the Mender had said the situation called for The Morphia. Halliday Knight's unfathomably violent and out-of-control monster, was a mere weapon, dangerous to herself and anyone within spitting distance of her. When it was time to engage her monster, it would have to be constrained.

Dave Biplane's Biplane sat parked at the back of the trailer, rotary engine running. Colonel Em Contusion stood next to it, hands on hips, staring at the Sopwith Camel's spinning propeller, as if willing it to fly – and quite dumbfounded as to why it wasn't.

"It's okay, Em," Halliday called over, "Poor thing, you do look very confused with all of this," she said to the Hell-Flyer as she shook her wrists, testing the weight of the manacles.

She thought Em had coped very well so far, but this was all probably far too much for her small mind to cope with; as above was a veritable plethora of all that the Hell-Flyer loved and existed for.

A Sombre-sonic roar from an endless convoy of aircraft.

Every species and style cluttered the skies of Loew Avion: oddly shaped blimps, air balloons, Zeppelins, old clunker bombers, helicopters, spitfire jets and hideously over-overstated airliners. All crammed against the other, all heading west toward a brilliantly setting sun; as if in a rush to some sort of aviator-invite-only convention at the end of the world.

Halliday admired Recalcitrance Bexley as she puffed on her skinny cigarette, looking all robust in her fitted leathers and spiky haired perfection.

Pocketing the key to the left manacle, the aviatrix gave a doubtful sideways glance to Em Contusion.

"Halliday, my most precious counterpart, I don't mean to be overly judgmental, but why in the world have we invited the Hell-Flyer along? I mean, she seems a bit of a wonky noodle."

She pulled round a chrome cigarette stubber on her belt and rubbed the used black filter across it. She flicked the butt away.

Halliday sighed, forcing a sympathetic smile Em's way,

"She is my burden I'm afraid. And she is quite a lot more than a wonky noodle, Recalcitrance - that would be putting it mildly. We can speak quite derisively of her and she won't have the slightest idea. If she wasn't here with me, she'd be bloody well crashing her plane and costing herself strokes. Really, I haven't got the time to explain it any more than that."

"Will she walk straight into my propeller?" Dave said with concern. "She's standing very close."

"She might just yet," Recalcitrance agreed.

"I wish she'd tie that hair back," Dave said.

"I'd doubt she'd know how," Recalcitrance observed.

"Yes ..." Halliday said trailing off in thought. She found it all very curious. The noise from the air was ferocious in volume, yet they could hear the other speak clearly. Had Sombre given them some sort of extra sensory ability for communication? She could even hear Drew Drucker's wildly out of tune and obnoxious singing as he drove his beastly truck.

Her next curiosity; the constant ticking sounding throughout Loew Avion, rising well above the aircraft thunder, it had been their calling here. This ticking she now knew belonged to Ether. And she was sure her Hope could hear it in the waking world as well.

"This ticking could give a girl a headache." Recalcitrance said as she rubbed her hands down her leather pants, "It is taking all of my patience not to go batty with it."

"I just want it gone," Dave said bitterly.

Halliday knew the monster had hurt him deeply, and it was more than just strokes on his Beating Clock, it had damaged the cut of his jib, his gall, his gullet. Dave had hardly cracked a joke or a smile since the mission had started.

"So, we are ready, Halliday. What is the plan? Loew Avion has no end, Drew Drucker can drive on and on until his bleedin' rig runs out of its fuels," Recalcitrance said with hands on hips. She raised her eyebrows, "I haven't even had the pleasure of meeting this 'Ether' miscreant. In fact, I'm only here because you wanted me here, Halliday. Risking my hide for you …"

"Ah yes, but let's not forget, for Hamish and The Menders as well," she said her voice breaking a little, she cleared her throat, "Hamish is convinced that my Morphia is the only thing that will stop Ether. Bullets will halt it, but not kill it. Ether can attack physically and mentally; it is quick with a blade. I have seen it enter a Nightmarer, take ownership and play with the body in the most savage fashion."

"You keep saying 'it', Halliday," Recalcitrance queried.

"It is an it!" Dave broke in, "It's no man. No man at all!"

"Steady on Biplane, you're spitting your words," the aviatrix said. "We know it maimed you."

Halliday grinned at the exchange. "Dave's right, Recalcitrance. But it needs to be one while it's in Sombre. And it's a very fast and lethal one. I'm going to catch it and destroy it! Well … The Morphia will. "Oh! Look!" Halliday pointed.

All eyes on the trailer suddenly went to the sky as a familiar balloon plummeted like a bag of trash, basket dangerously sideways, no fire, a distorted, 'PFFER' on its eggshell coloured nylon. With a heavy crash, the whole of Captain Andrew Pfeiffer's ride broke up all over the tarmac.

"Stop! Drew! Stop, man!" Halliday yelled rattling her chains. Drew Drucker obeyed the command and The Devil Incarnate slowed to a stop, around two hundred feet from the wreckage. With a 'phwssh', a door slammed, and Drew hopped down from the cab.

Dave was the first to speak. "Andrew will be finished. That thing dropped like a sky anchor."

"Yeah, he'll be rat-shit ... that's why I'll take wheels over wings any day," Drew said in his rough Australian, hands on his hips.

Recalcitrance used the opportunity to light up another skinny cigarette. She blew smoke sideways and said coolly, "No wings on an air balloon, Drew ... I'm stating the obvious there."

"You know what I mean ..." he said.

Halliday stared at Drew from her vantage point on the trailer. He was a bean pole of a man - she thought his look terribly odd; long thin legs that finished with heavy brown boots; so very short blue shorts and a faded blue singlet, red hair with an unfortunate cowlick at the back and a thick red moustache (the colour she supposed couldn't be helped) although the thickness could. She couldn't help but wonder, had anyone ever explained to Drew how to dress himself?"

"Another Gatherer down. Do we even bother checking on the man? The Menders will be along soon enough," Dave said turning toward them. "We should stay on track."

"That's quite callous of you Mr. Biplane," Halliday said letting her chains go limp. She was a little disappointed, but not at all surprised given what her Dave had been through.

"Oh, there you go! He walks!" Recalcitrance said. Everyone (barring Em, she was still far too perplexed by the grounded bi-plane) watched on in disbelief as Andrew Pfeiffer rose from the wreckage of his craft and came at them in a hunched and brisk walk. At twenty paces from the trailer, the airman lifted his head, his mouth was set in a sneer.

"Jesus, he has war in his eyes," Dave observed, "well and truly peeved."

"Captain Andrew! We have been looking for you! You have been missed," Halliday tried, her voice a little too high - like a whistle. Andrew seemed to register the greeting, yet his expression didn't change. She then realized how odd she must look. "Oh, I'm quite a sight aren't I, all bound up," she shook her chains. She suddenly had a need to relieve herself. "Bugger ... how does one use the toilet whilst in chains? Recalcitrance?"

The aviatrix didn't answer.

Dave yelled, "guns!"

The two jumped from the trailer.

Andrew Pfeiffer produced two Exaggerated pistols.

He opened fire.

Chapter 32
The Airborne Beast

Captain Andrew Pfeiffer's Exaggerated pistols dwarfed his hands, smoke poured from the chambers as he unloaded round after round.

Recalcitrance and Drew Drucker returned fire, using the trailer as cover.

"Oh, ha, ha, ha! Watch the chickety - chickens run! I've tried to run! But you see, you can't run! It won't let you! It needs! And it takes and takes!" Andrew yelled grinning darkly.

Halliday could see he was a man at the end of his tether. Fortunately, he was an incredibly bad shot, or he just didn't have the will or presence of mind to aim. A moving target, she ran all around the trailer bed, as much as her chains would allow her. Intermittent bullets pinged off The Devil Incarnates bullet proof cabin; filled the empty spaces of air above and around her counterparts on the ground. She pleaded to the unhinged aviator, "Andrew, we're here to take down Ether! Stop shooting at *us*! We're on your side!"

"Ha! You fool! You're all fools! There are no sides anymore! Don't you see? Aaaggghhh!" Andrew cried and staggered backward as a shot from the rifle of Drew Drucker hit him straight between the eyes. Andrew continued to shoot more stray bullets as he completely lost focus, swaying sideways, blood pouring down the bridge of his nose. "It's no use anymore ... Oh! We aren't any-body anymore ... w-what's a Gatherer in the f-face of thi-this!"

"Quit it, Andrew! This will only end with your bullet riddled corpse hitting the tarmac! You're just creating more work for us you dolt of a man!" Recalcitrance said as her own bullet punctured his shoulder. She ducked down under the trailer as Andrew aimed in the direction of her voice and unloaded more rounds.

Ceasing fire, Andrew steadied, wrenching his jacket open awkwardly with guns still in hand, he exposed a gaping hole in his chest. His Beating Clock had been cut out. Crying, spitting blood from his lips he spoke to his fellow balloonist, "Recalcccc ... iiitra ... see w-what it does, wha-what it can do ..."

Another bullet from Drew Drucker blew Andrew's throat open. Pistols falling from his limp fingers; like a hurt child, Captain Andrew Pfeiffer covered his face with his hands and collapsed.

Dave Bi-plane was first to the body. "Quickly, someone help get him up on the trailer!" Recalcitrance grabbed him by his boots and the two lifted the dead man up onto The Devil Incarnates' bed.

"Oh, good form, Dave!" Halliday cheered. She had noticed Dave hadn't shot at Andrew Pfeiffer at all. She could only guess he thought two against one was enough. She liked Dave Biplane - she admired everything about the man.

"He had no control over any of that - I *know* he didn't," Dave said grimacing.

"So, that's our first casualty," Drew Drucker said eyeing the corpse on his flatbed. "Seen 'im at the 'Spleen - talks like a bit of a loon actually," he chewed something in his front teeth and then spat it out, something brown. "Do I drive now?"

Halliday turned up her nose then just stared at Drew Drucker. Her opinion of him had taken quite a nosedive. She marveled at how different the two men present and still standing actually were. Other than the letter D, they had nothing in common - Drew Drucker, not even a speck of dirt on her Dave Bi-plane's boot heel.

256

"Somethings come over the man's balloon, look!" Recalcitrance said her voice reed thin. She pointed her burning skinny cigarette at Pfeiffer's wreckage.

Seemingly of its own accord, what was left of the balloon's basket and crumpled canvas envelope slid across the tarmac. As if by magic, a yellow gas flame ignited in the burner, the canvas caught fire and the Pfeiffer balloon shot up like a flaming turned-up umbrella.

"Well, that's just not something a balloon does, is it?" Recalcitrance mused.

The Pfeiffer balloon continued its ascent and re-entered the heavy air traffic of Loew Avion, vanishing between the strange pairing of a massive black airship and a white Cessna Skyhawk.

As if picking up a scent, Halliday's nostrils flared - she could feel her Morphia yearning to rise to the surface.

"Dave, that is Ether! Get me up there!"

Halliday felt the fast, heavy breathing, her jaw distorting, pain in the eye sockets, her face burned, tearing pain shot down her legs as every ligament pulled. The Morphia threw itself around, pulling on the chains. It growled, "UP! GET ME UP!"

$$\int$$

"Jesus! She's a hideous looking thing isn't she!"

Ignoring Drew Drucker's take on The Morphia, Recalcitrance turned to Dave. "One hook or two?"

"One - it'll be easier to shake her from the plane," Dave answered as they both ran up the tarmac on opposite sides of the trailer towards The Morphia.

"When you say *shake*, we haven't actually thought that part through exactly, have we?" Recalcitrance said as she hoisted herself up lithely, like a cat.

The bulkier, Dave, rolled onto the trailer and got to his feet in a more deliberate manner, he answered, "Attach the hook to a V strut on the wheel, and we'll release her from the air. You'll have to come along for the ride."

The speed truck started with a shake. Drew Drucker floored the accelerator and was soon racing through the gears.

"So, me on the wing, is that what you mean?" Recalcitrance said eyeing the biplane, already knowing the answer.

"Yes."

"Great."

"Colonel Em will have the other seat. Pretty sure she's already in it," Dave said and added, "No point trying to get her to move!"

"No point at all, who'd have the heart!" Recalcitrance agreed as she and Dave unclipped the heavy hooks. Instantly, The Morphia pulled them both toward the waiting plane with all the force of a junkyard Alsatian.

Dave planted his feet and stood firm, chain taut in his grip, he instructed the aviatrix, "You hook your side. I'll tackle the great beast."

Keeping well clear of the spinning propeller, Recalcitrance squatted and hooked the clamp at the left wheel. Jumping onto the wing she grabbed a strut, squatted down and readied herself. She greeted Colonel Em Contusion. "So, how's it all going, Hell-Flyer, you daft bugger?"

Em made a noise through her ghastly teeth that was meant to resemble a plane motor, then moved her mouth in a way that was meant to resemble a smile and pointed to the sky. Recalcitrance just shook her head then turned to watch Dave.

Dave approached Halliday's monster from behind, he eyed The Morphia's straw like hair, then her enlarged muscular back that threatened to burst and tear through Halliday's signature dress. The creature was grotesque. He slipped the key for the manacle from his pocket.

"Halliday, are you in there? You have to give me your wrist." Dave yanked on the chain.

With a sudden move that took him by surprise, The Morphia swung round and took his entire face in its hand and squeezed - *hard*. The pressure on his skull was unbearable, with his eyes covered, he fumbled for the lock, scratching the tip of the key across the face plate. Choking and spitting into The Morphia's hand he fought the urge to pass out. He found the keyhole. Letting out a jubilant and pained cry, he turned it, and the manacle fell open. The Morphia let his face go as it seemed to understand. Seizing his opportunity, he stumbled aboard his Sopwith Camel.

"You okay?" Recalcitrance queried, "that looked rather harsh."

"It was," he said rubbing his face gently, feeling for damage. "Just give me a moment ..."

With a deep breath and quick study of his gauges, he pulled the yoke. The motor sputtered and the plane rose straight up in its customary way. Giving it more throttle as the craft dipped and faltered with the extra drag from Halliday's Morphia, he made the necessary adjustments and the plane stabilized.

"CRASH AND BURN BABY!!!!" Colonel Em yelled with unbridled joy from the back as the nose lifted.

Recalcitrance stood steadfast on the lower right wing, holding on for dear life as the biplane pierced the air, targeting the hordes of Lowe Avion's traffic. Halliday's monster hung dead straight, clawing at the sky.

"TO HELL WITH US ALL, WOEFUL DOVE!" Em shrieked punching the heavens.

"What in all of Sombre is she on about?" Dave said peering over his shoulder at the Hell-Flyer.

"No idea! W-What is the plan again, Dave?" Recalcitrance yelled shakily as the roar of an implausible amount of Loew Avion engines stole the senses.

A Boeing 747 passed over like a bellowing air-whale and a gap was created in its wake. The little Sopwith' joined the stream of air traffic, nestled between a large black blimp and a putt-putt recreational helicopter. A grey old man with an impossibly pointy chin was at the controls of the copter, grinning.

"We'll have to fly above and drop The Morphia down somewhere, on something! After that, it's up to her!" Dave called out to the aviatrix. Holding his breath, he pushed the plane higher, dangerously high.

At his back, Em Contusion once again yelled like an excited commentator about how bravely they were to 'CRASH AND BURN' the plane as Dave straightened the craft.

He called out to Recalcitrance. "Signal me, when and where we let her go!"

Recalcitrance looked at the never-ending fleet of aircraft below her, all nose to tail; jet fighter to dirigible, bomber to balloon, hovercraft to parcel plane. Really, she couldn't have given too hoots where they dropped Halliday's friggin monster. She wanted off Dave's dodgy bird, and soon! She peered down at The Morphia's chain.

"Damn it to hell!"

The clip was hanging on the opposite axel. She had gotten on the wrong wing!

Holding the cabane struts, twin Vicker machine guns pushing into her gut, she climbed the hot engine bay, her leathers perilously close to the propeller. Gasping with exertion, she eased herself gently onto the other wing, took a quick glance at the big clip on the axel, and signaled to Dave, 'down!'.

The plane lowered. Like a daredevil, Recalcitrance crossed her ankles around the wing's wire bracing and hung her whole upper torso over into the undercarriage. With all her weight on the left wheel's V strut, she watched for a solid fuselage. After a dirty white balloon and a twin propellered army copter, a veritable colossus of an airliner passed beneath. With an almighty strain on her favored right bicep she lifted The Morphia up by its chain, unclipped the clasp with her left hand and let the creature drop.

The Morphia raised both arms defiantly as it fell.

Recalcitrance called down after it,

"See you Halliday! Go forth and conquer, my lovely monster girl! We'll have a drink at the Spleen' once you're free!"

∫

The Morphia landed on the airliner's great roof with a thud and clatter of heavy chainmail. With one wrist unrestricted, one manacled, poised on all fours like a primate, it sniffed the raging air and emitted a low growl. A lone form amidst a sky heaving with traffic.

Little more than a skerrick of Halliday Knight would have to guide The Morphia. As was always the case, she was completely overwhelmed by her affliction. Her knowing that Ether was the target would have to do. Everything else would have to be left to her monster's random thought patterns. The Morphia ran on scent and killer instinct. It saw a human body as flesh, blood and bone only. Something to bite and taste; dig its fingers into and tear apart.

It would be a pity for anyone who might get in the way.

Chain dragging behind, the monster took off into the rushing headwind, sprinting down the long fuselage. It sprung sideways from the airliner's nose and caught the basket of a fast travelling air balloon. Hooking its right arm, it hung on the basket's wall like a spider monkey and awaited another opportunity.

The pilot payed the intrusion no mind; busying himself with one hand working a brass control, the other opening the propane valve, a shot of gas flame filled the envelope and the balloon raced forward alongside a Cessna. The Morphia pushed off and scrambled onto the small plane's wing. Tipping right with the monsters weight, the Cessna's pilot corrected, and the plane accelerated. Halliday's monster crawled onto the roof of the cockpit.

"HUHHHHH!!!!!"

Suddenly overcome with the scent of outer sweat and inner flesh, The Morphia, hungry for the human inside, swung its chain down like a whip and cracked the pilot window.

The pilot's expression was comical; owner of a very small head and features, he wore overly large goggles and an open-faced helmet, looking for all the world like a shocked baby man. The Morphia rammed its strong jaw down, smashing the rest of the glass. It fished around for the man's face in the cockpit. The Cessna went into a momentary dive as the petrified pilot cowered and weaved away from the snapping, gnashing teeth.

Halliday fought to bring her monster under control. She had never engaged The Morphia Affliction for this amount of time, ever. She felt more of her own self coming to the foreground, her own intelligence seeping in. Her monster obeyed, screaming and spitting violent babble at the poor pilot as it begrudgingly pulled its head from the cabin.

The Cessna rose again, finding a place in formation with the rest of Loew Avion's air-throng.

A squadron of a dozen sleek and shining, silver P-47 Thunderbolts flew up on the right side of the Cessna; each front end emblazoned with loud and proud, second world war, flyboy regalia: lipstick smiling, leggy blondes and brunettes; Yankee red, white and blue patriotism and snarling air-sharks, all flying in perfect symmetry to the other, nose to tail.

The Morphia was suddenly overcome with the stench of Ether.

The temporary man was close.

Instincts taking charge, it bolted across the Cessna's wing and leaped like a cat for one of the Thunderbolts. It landed wrapping its fists around the plane's protruding aerial mast. Laying on its front laterally along the plane's round body, it took the ride.

The Thunderbolt squadron travelled fast, as if in its own slipstream of Loew Avion traffic, aircraft slipped left or right to make way for the speeding warplanes. The Morphia coughed and gasped, it's body shaking with bloodlust, feeling the enemy as it drew closer. Her Thunderbolt transport tipped right sharply as the whole squadron moved to avoid a massive obstruction - gargantuan, in fact.

"HHHHHEREEEEE!!!!!" It howled and got to its feet.

Balancing with one foot on the canopy, one on the Thunderbolt's body, The Morphia was dwarfed by the immense shadow of a Zeppelin airship.

The airship had a large torn hole in its silver-black wall.

"INNNNN!!!!!"

Halliday Knight's monster charged wildly across the wing of the Thunderbolt, spitting and snarling.

It leapt with clawed hands, tore through, and made another hole in the wall.

CHAPTER 33
It All Fell Down

The Morphia was in.

Clutching a girder support of the massive airship's round inner wall, it scanned the thin maintenance bridges, aerolite-beams and the perfectly segmented metal framework throughout the oblong structure. The ticking echoed throughout the ship, percussive and hollow in the vast surrounds.

"ETHER ..." it uttered.

The monster's nostrils flared as it focused; yellow eyes wild and alert - there was something more behind them now - Halliday Knight's intelligence. Creature and human slowly becoming one. An ultimate weapon. An intelligent weapon. It grinned and licked its lips.

Senses in overdrive, Halliday's monster listened to the whir of the motors, sucked the gassy air through its crooked teeth as it searched the passenger tiers, 90 feet below. Life and movement, it felt the gentle drum of Beating Clocks. The vessel was well inhabited.

Below, the bleeding had begun, it could smell it, taste it. A quick knife was cutting. It spoke the name again, this time very clearly,

"ETHER ..."

It estimated the drop to the passenger tier. A long way.

Something, or *someone*, was holding it back – Halliday Knight.

An Otherself spoke to The Morphia. *'You can make it, Halliday's monster! If you're to do any good at all on this bulbous balloon, you'll have to!'*

'The burden of letting so much of Hope's Halliday in, is that you will now have to listen to us. I agree with the Other, Other. You're a strong thing you are – jump!' said another Otherself.

'Indeed, jump!' said another Other.

The Morphia swung a tentative leg off the girder.

'Hopeless-Hope's-Halliday is the only thing holding you back at all! Doubting doleful that she is. You would have just gone and done it any other time. Listen to us! She is an unnecessary mental roadblock. Time to go, you!' said the original Otherself. *'Now!'*

The Morphia leapt, dropping like a bomb, crashing through the upper tier's roofing with heavy muscular legs. The whole of the airship shook with the impact. It landed on flat feet with folded knees, a deep dent in the floor. It peered up.

It had encroached on a dining and entertainment area. A pianist played against a wall in the corner - a tuxedo'd fellow with slicked black hair, his slow tango strangely falling into tempo with Ether's metronomic tick.

Showing complete indifference to the arrival of Halliday's beast, the passengers, richly dressed socialites from a bygone era, continued on in haughty party mode. The Morphia prowled the room, chain dragging, body coursing with adrenalin, it switched its glare from passenger to passenger. Men in top hats and suits, manicured nails, polished shoes and mustachioed faces – all laughed away, chins lifted in overly verbose amusement. Women with skin as smooth as porcelain, wore long flowing dresses of rich crepes and satins; shawls and cardigans were draped over shoulders to fend away the airship's draft. Champagne flutes were clinked. Cigar and cigarette smoke filled the air.

The Morphia was soon overwhelmed; the perfumes, the sweat, the saliva, the tobacco and liquor. Before Halliday could stop it, The Morphia's fist struck out and smashed a male's mouth – breaking straight through to the back of the skull. It wrenched the man in close and gnawed on the face, tasting flesh and bone; sucking an eyeball straight from the socket.

It stalled as it felt relent. It was being forced to stop.

"NO!!!!" it growled and unwillingly eased its mouth from the man's face. It flung the man's skull from its hand. The body slumped to the floor, dinner jacket flapping open revealing six strokes on his Beating Clock. Now he would have seven.

Halliday had regained control.

Ether's stink was below.

As was the bleeding.

The Morphia turned back to where it had crashed through the ceiling. It spotted a stairwell down. Charging with renewed urgency, Halliday's monster pushed through the crowd, knocking citizens to the floor in its haste. From a savage Morphia forearm to the chest, a man slid on his backside and hit the far wall, hard.

"Whoa!!!!" The whole room reacted with a few seconds of joint acclamation.

The Morphia left the room. The party went on.

At the foot of the third tier's stairwell, it surveyed the dimly lit hallway. One solitary light flickered above, illuminating the blood-spattered walls. Four uniformed bodies littered the floor, extracted Beating Clocks sat like gore trophies on chests just under the chin, sliced lips bled on open mouths.

Stepping over the bodies, The Morphia broke through a door off the hall into an officers mess. More of the airship's staff had been stilled at tables; stopped in motion like wax models. Unfinished coffee and half eaten meals; fingers were still hooked in mug handles, clutching knives and forks. Each had impossibly precise extraction holes cut from the front through the back. Beating Clocks were lying under chairs, Mender configured wires and entrails dangled, staining the linoleum floor.

Ether had struck fast.

The Morphia snorted its acknowledgement and left.

Upon re-entry into the hall, searing pain flashed across the beasts forehead, it stumbled sideways and slapped a hand against the wall of the narrow hall.

Its sensed another target.

It sensed two.

Someone or something, sharing the same makeup, embodying everything that was Ether.

The Morphia's yellow eyes were wide open but momentarily blinded as the head pain travelled. It could only stand and listen, face pressed against the wall. It heard the tinkling of the piano. The airship's whirring functionality, the propellered motors and hissing gas cells. It heard more blood being spilt below. Short gasps before choking noises – bodies and clocks hitting the soft air-lite floors.

It could now *hear* the second target as well.

It would have to destroy it the same way it would destroy Ether.

Ignoring the pain, The Morphia ran the length of the hall and took the airship's last stairwell, it jumped and landed on a narrow officers gangway, smashing through a closed door. Landing on all fours it looked up. A radio operator's podgy body had been cut in two, from the Beating Clock down. Headphones still adorned the man's head, wire dangling from the input in the control panel, his lower body bled out over handfuls of typed documents thrown across the linoleum.

Daylight shone through an open door.

∫

The light from windows to the outworld of Loew Avion momentarily stunned Halliday's monster. Like the most hideous child freshly awoken from a nap, it stood blinking its eyes as its vision adjusted from the comparative gloom of the rest of the ship.

The airships control car was decimated. Twisted, cut-up and gutted shipmen, from the captain and lieutenant down, lay all over. Running blood spread a spatter-canvas on the tin-plated floor.

Back hunched in a raincoat wet with blood, Ether stood beside the rudder wheel staring through the windshield at the endless sky traffic.

"You are here."

Raising his arms in the air, he turned to face The Morphia. He continued in a soft and measured tone, "I can try to outrun you, beast ... but I know I will only be prolonging my inevitable execution. You will have your way in the end."

He smirked as he lowered both arms and pulled his hair from his ashen face. He eyed the heavy chain on its wrist, "I need to speak with your other, Halliday Knight. Bring her to the fore."

Halliday licked the lips of The Morphia. For the very first time, she had almost complete control of her monster.

She was it. It was she.

The hunger was still there, the mindlessness wasn't. It was as Lucretia had said it would be - the ultimate. It was as how Hamish had explained it to her as well; her Morphia was so very much darker than she. Yet it was something to relish, not to be feared. The feeling of animalistic killer intertwined with her own remarkable self. She found it both painful and exhilarating.

But this was a pivotal moment in the mission. She couldn't show Ether intelligence.

"NO HALLIDAY ... ME."

'Oh, well played, Hope's Halliday! Make the miscreant move first,' said an Other-self with another well-intentioned, but unwelcome, invasion.

'*Speaking for all of us, we think we like you better as this version of The Morphia. A brainy yet ugly brute – never change!*' quipped another Other'.

Halliday's Morphia emitted a low growl.

Ether's glare was as sharp as the blade he produced from under his sleeve.

There was to be bloodshed.

Halliday gathered The Morphia's chain, breath quickening.

Another blast of pain jarred her beast's headspace as it sensed the second target again.

Eyes shifting left to right, her monster surveyed the room with frustration. Where was it?

"Very well," Ether said garnering The Morphia's attention. He sniffed and wiped his nose with the back of the hand that held the blade. "How fast are you beast, I wonder?"

With a knowing smile, he vanished.

The knife came quicker than his re-materialization.

The Morphia spun and whipped the chain just as the tip of the blade was at its back and digging. Metal opened Ether's face and The Morphia lunged, jaw wide and snapping. Ether's blade stabbed at its snarling maw and Halliday's monster caught it in its teeth, a third of the way in, biting down hard. Snarling, eyes wild, The Morphia wrenched its head sideways, ripping the blade from his grip, it spat it out letting it hit the floor. With a clawed swipe The Morphia went for the throat with the intention of removing his jugular. Ether was too fast. The temporary man vanished again. He reappeared briefly, slipping away like an illusionist, escaping through a hatch in the control cabins roof.

Howling with rage, The Morphia followed, launching itself up and through the opening, back into the airships vast inner. Catching the edge of maintenance bridging it swung itself up. On all fours, it canvassed the bridging and spotted the enemy. Ether crossed the structural inner as if catapulted along a fast-moving conveyer. With almost comical speed he scaled an adjoining ladder-well to a fourth-tier bridge, then crashed through the thin outer wall of the airship's ongoing dinner party.

The Morphia sprung and gave chase, boots banging like a snare drum on the hardened aluminum of the maintenance bridging. Halliday bristled just below her beasts surface. As it scaled the rungs, her head pounded. With the pain came an absolute clarity. She now knew every inch of her monster.

"HOPE!!!!!"

The Morphia blurted the name of Hope of the waking world, out into the atmosphere, her namesake, her version of Halliday. Everything was suddenly one. Her mind threatened to burst through her skull. With a wounded sounding growl, it swung onto the bridging and burst through the broken wall.

Skidding to a stop on the linoleum, The Morphia arrived at a party being quickly decimated. Ether working as a blur. The smartly dressed and smarmy passengers it had ran into upon entry were dropping to the floor, bodies folding like ribbons; unfinished cigars and cigarettes rolled around the room. Small fires were gaining momentum fast.

The Morphia stood in the rooms centre, tense and ready to lunge, watching one murder then another and another.

It searched for two, it still felt *two* – yet it only saw one. His dark hair and raincoat appearing as shadow-motion at each victim's back, just seconds before they were felled.

The mission was almost over, the target, Ether, was tantalizingly close.

Halliday held The Morphia back. Her smarts telling her that Ether would have to be closer for her monster to have its best chance. "Patience, monster," she spoke out loud for the first time, with her intelligence - yet in The Morphia's tone, a low and evil command.

Another violent stab of agony tore through The Morphia's head, from one temple to the other. Bracing its skull with both hands, shutting its eyes, it howled with pain. Valuable seconds passed.

Ether taunted, his waspish voice enveloping the room. "So close! You need to stop this, monster! But can you stop this? I am Sombre's future! I am plague! I am this world's forever!"

The Morphia opened its eyes.

And Halliday saw it.

The presence she had been feeling all along flashed into view, in the corner of the room. The figure of a girl. Peering down. It flickered and then vanished like bad transmission.

"UHHHH!" Confused, The Morphia gasped. Halliday switched the beast's focus from the real target, then back to where the girl had stood. Power coursed through her body, a violence so pure, boiled and craved release.

Something still told Halliday to hold her monster back, just a few seconds more.

"Act, beast!" Ether slung another male victim to one side and then threw the fellows Beating Clock, the timepiece hitting her square in the mouth.

The Morphia growled, chest heaving, spit spraying from its open grimace.

'Oh, I agree with the smelly wet fellow! Finish the bastard!' said an Otherself, *'You have control of your Morphia, Hope's Halliday. Something none of us had ever achieved! Do it now!'*

'I was close! Let's not forget that!' said another Other', indignant. '

'No, you weren't, you liar!' the first Otherself countered with a laugh.

'I was!!!'

'No, you ruddy well weren't!'

The ill-timed exchange went on, eventually fading to the background.

Halliday still held The Morphia back. Smoke now engulfed the room. She blinked away tears from its weeping eyes.

A mere shadow in the fiery grey dark, now just a foot away from The Morphia, Ether screamed with frustration, "What is wrong with you monster? Act!!!!"

Like a fast-moving smoky apparition, the girl, came running back into the room. The time was now.

"ACT!!!!" The Morphia mimicked and lunged. Mouth snapping, it ripped into Ether's upper cheek as its full body hit the temporary man, with a vicious slam into the floor. "Kill me beast! This is what you do!" Ether laughed madly, wrapping his long thin arms around Halliday's monster. "Show her your potential! Your potency! Through your pitiless dark comes clarity for all! This road you are on is incalculable! Could it even be infinite? So full of opportunity! Show herrrrrrr!!!!!!" Ether slurred and fell into silence as he was gored. Hands ripping into his torso; pulling out fistful after fistful of flesh and organ. The Morphia's teeth cracked then crunched cheekbone, mauling Ether's eye sockets - its tongue spat out the temporary man's jellied eyes as if they were rotten food. The Morphia ripped Ether into two pieces, then four, then six. It all took seconds.

Finished, it picked up the monster's long-haired skull. Prying the jaw wide open, The Morphia ran its chain through the mouth, rammed it through the back of the cranium, and let it hang. This time Ether hadn't been hollow – he was solid, human, man.

The mission was complete.

Halliday transformed; her jaw shrinking, mouth easing into a loose smile, before grimacing once her nostrils copped the full brunt of the smoke.

Her fingers felt stiff and sore as she wiped them down the front of her dress. Everything was aching, everything felt heavy.

"Oh, this is all sorts of trouble," she understated with a throat as dry as stale bay leaf. "Time to go."

A cracking explosion shook the area as she spun in a tired pirouette and made back toward her entry; flames at her boot heels, flames at her back, licking at the hem of her dress.

Ahead, she saw the hazy shape of Ether's accomplice, bolting through the smoke.

"A-ha! *-Cough! -* Wait! You'll be wanted by the Menders, you devil's left-hander, you! *-Cough! -Cough! -*" She tried again, "you there! Girl! Stop ...!"

Halliday threw herself out through the smashed entrance wall as another explosion followed her onto the maintenance bridging. Landing on all fours, she peered up as the girl climbed the ladder-well, fast, higher and higher toward the top of the airship's massive envelope. Halliday started her own climb up, right as the airship was showing the first real, horrifying signs of faltering. The fourth-tier fire had quickly ignited the bottom of the envelope, its gas filled gut exploding. A sea of whirring and folding flames ripped through the ship's framework. The craft only had seconds left in the air.

Eyes only for her target, Halliday now had a better view of Ether's accomplice; as out-of-place on this airship as a barking cat in a dog kennel; she wore trainers and jeans, a white, short sleeved t-shirt. Was there something familiar about this brown-haired girl? Not that she could see the transitive's face at all, she'd not looked down once.

The girl crossed a girder to a torn opening and climbed out.

"Goodness! Like a whippet!" Halliday marveled at her pluck.

That was the last she saw of her.

Halliday scaled the ladder faster as a swirling pool of gas flame whirred and fizzed, an airborne hell-pit at her boot heels. Deciding that her best chance of any sort of survival was as The Morphia, Halliday engaged once again.

Without hesitation, The Morphia jumped. Its master crossed her fingers and hoped she didn't have to lose another stroke.

Like one massive, burning, skeletal tea bag, the airship's walls quickly disappeared as more explosions filled the air of Loew Avion. Spreading the destruction, flames caught every surrounding wing and fuselage, rotor and balloon – greedy in its impending demise, the airship was to take plenty of unwilling participants with it on the plummet down to the tarmac.

It all fell down.

CHAPTER 34
Take out at The Kelley's

Friday evening, Evelyn Kelley had invited Hope's new friend around for a meal. On the menu: takeout taco's and enchiladas, cokes and ice cream. The typical Health and Co. inspired fair had been vetoed for a showing of parental coolness.

An unusually bubbly Kate Kelley approved of both Parker and the food, she wiped salsa from her mouth. "If we start eating like this, I might invite my friends over more often. This is yum!"

Not really sharing the same love of the meal, Devan Kelley cleared his throat and pressed a napkin to his mouth. "So, Parker. Hope's relatively new to Centurion High, what do *you* think of the school? How long have you lived in Pento?" He took a big skull of his water and smiled warmly.

Using her napkin, Parker wiped her mouth. "Mum moved me and my brother here when I was five. And I have to tell you, Mr. Kelley, it's been a pleasure ever since ..." she smiled raising her eyebrows, not quite able to take a break from the Parker Wright brand of sarcasm.

Hope glanced over at her mother; Evelyn Kelley chewed her food slowly and studied her daughters new friend. She had worn a weak smile ever since Parker stepped through the door.

Parker continued, "Actually, Pento's quite nice really. Even in the part where we live. The bins get emptied before they get kicked over; they have a go at removing the graffiti here and there. We've got pretty much everything." She gazed down at the rest of her meal and picked up her fork. "Centurion's alright as well. Has your usual teenage cliques and dramas I suppose. The football team's only so-so; I know, I used to cheer' for them." She broke off more burrito with her fork. "They won the regional championship a few years back."

"I can't wait to go," Kate said.

Hope slowly shook her head at her sister. "My god you lie, Kate! You called it a hole the other morning."

"Every school's a hole ..." Kate shrugged, "... we just gotta go."

"Ha! Well said!" Parker giggled as she sipped her Coke.

Evelyn Kelley rolled her eyes. "Don't encourage her, Parker. She's a semi-solid B student at the moment. I'd rather she didn't slip any further upon entry into high school."

"Thanks, mother!" Kate said and blushed.

"You make your bed, Kate, you lay in it."

She swung the subject back to the antics of the previous day, "So, skipping school you two. I'm not a fan. Not a fan of getting calls. Not much of a fan of any of that sort of thing, really."

Thankfully, Parker came in with a save before Hope could.

"Oh, no, Mrs. Kelley, you don't need to worry, that's was just a oncer'! Seriously, Jerry's just an extended family friend who's ran in to some trouble – mixing with a bad crowd. I've been watching out for him since the first time he got beat up and crashed into Hope. Actually, that was sort of how Hope and I met." Parker finished, tying the bow up tight on the lie.

Nails tapping on her glass of water, Evelyn gave them both a knowing smile, a slow nod of the head. "Okay, just don't want your grades to slip. That boy sounds like trouble you don't need."

The two girls gave each other a look and got up from their seats. Parker nodded to both parents.

"Thank you for the meal. It was nice."

Wiping her mouth, Kate got up with them, "Hope, can I hang out?"

"No," was Hope's curt reply as she pushed her glasses up on her nose and left the dining room. She knew Kate just wanted to witness her weird big sister hanging with the new cool older girl.

"So, do you reckon I passed the 'folks' test?" Parker said keeping her tone low as she glanced around the living room on the way to the front door. "I like your house - looks brand new."

"Thanks." Hope said giving the room an offhanded once over. She burped and rubbed her stomach; the semi ingested Mexican sat like a cheesy brick in her insides. "Geez, I think a walk will be a good idea ..."

She pulled open the front door and let Parker step out first. The night was warm, a gentle breeze relaxed the senses, that sometimes special - twilit time as the day slipped away lazily to a close. Hope breathed in deep and exhaled as they hit the sidewalk. She answered Parker's original question.

"I think they're both just happy I have a real friend – the well's been fairly dry for a while there. But we wouldn't want to be skipping school too often," Hope said gazing down at the ground, "Sorry about my mother, with the sermon about us skipping school and the rest. She got a bit carried away. Not like her."

Parker shrugged, "Your folks are a little tightly wound, but at least they care Hope. My gem of a mother didn't even mention it. Too busy pouring wine down her throat. She'd had a hard day, yesterday. She has a few too many hard days, really ..." she sighed and shrugged, "Anyway, to change the subject - do we think Ether is actually gone now? Now Halliday has done the business in Sombre."

Hope pulled her hair out of its ponytail and gave it half a tussle. "I wouldn't have a clue. I think Halliday thought it was finished at the time. Her Morphia monster thing certainly made a mess of him. He was very dismembered."

Looking straight ahead down the quiet road, Parker raised her eyebrows and grinned savagely. "Cool as fuck."

"Colonel Em Contusion played her part as well," Hope added.

"Oh, good god! That's all sorts of bullshit, Hope! Don't make me laugh! I don't need you to extend me some sort of dream charity! Ha! You know, when your monster was swinging on the axle of that bi-plane, and that spikey haired aviatrix woman was climbing all over the wings in mid-air?"

"Yeh."

"Well, I'm sure my Em Contusion was just sitting in the back seat actually making plane noises with her mouth! You know, like 'bbbbrrrrrruuuuuuuummmmmm!!!!!' She's just a fucking skull full of marbles, isn't she!"

The two girls burst into laughter.

"Em's a little endearing though, you have to admit," Hope said.

"I suppose so. I'm still just a little stunned at who I got lumped with. Maybe she'll sharpen up sooner or later."

"She might," Hope agreed as the two girls reached the end of the street and turned down another.

Hope gazed up at a lazy looking, orange sun as it hovered over a pitched landscape of suburban rooftops - a day in Pento drawing to a close. At this moment, she was about as relaxed and contented as she could ever remember being. The food in her belly seemed to be finally digesting, the hour had just passed eight pm on a Friday night, and she wasn't already indoors in her pajamas. Indeed, she was walking the streets with a cool Parker Wright. She felt like some sort femme-warrior post battle; having just vanquished a dream demon of the highest order, both here on earth and as Halliday in Sombre. The only thing left undone was her book report on 'To Kill a Mockingbird.'

She would finish it tonight.

278

Parker, who had been scrolling on her phone, continued to do so as she shared some news, "Huh! Shit, eh? Guess what?"

"What?" Hope watched a small gang of what looked like twelve-year-old boys about a hundred feet up the road. They were flipping skateboards and trying to land back on, to varying degrees of success.

"Just got a message through the social-pipeline. Jerry Cowle has been admitted to a psyche ward upstate for treatment," Parker said without even a hint of humour.

Hope stopped in the middle of the path. She had to catch her breath. Jerry. Mental hospital. Upstate. That was what she heard.

"Parker, what does that mean?"

The older girl shrugged, "It means he's ridin' the barking bus, I guess."

"He probably still thinks he's Captain Andrew Pfeiffer," Hope said in horrified wonder.

"I'd say the poor thing has gone full-blown Andrew, actually. At least he's alive. I thought he was dead." Parker said not taking her eyes from her phone.

Sombre had actually sent someone mad. The cold reality of their situation suddenly dawned on Hope. The setting sun now seemed ominous, reminding her of the orange orb from the day before. The orange orb that had guided them to the bizarre house that was shaped like her. The house full of her past and warnings about her future. Ether telling her to wake up or she would die a thousand deaths. That it was all for her and she had to wake up. Wake up to what?

She considered Parker as she watched her new friend read something else and furrow her brow. Sombre was the only reason they were together at all. Through Sombre, was she unwittingly dragging Parker toward their shared death? Suddenly on edge, she pulled at her fingers one by one.

"Parker, this could kill us. You know that don't you."

The two set off again.

"Yeah, I know," the older girl frowned. "But you know, so what? What the hell can we do about it? We can't stop sleeping, we can't stop dreaming. We can either be chickenshit and lose our minds like Jerry, or we can just strap ourselves in and take the ride – ride it like a couple of hellhounds." She gave Hope a wink, "at least we'll be doing it together."

Hope gushed. Then she grinned, baring full teeth. Parker recoiled comically at the sight of it. "Jesus, that was a bit mad to look at, Hope! Not used to seeing you smile like that. Got quite the full set of choppers there, haven't ya!"

"Yes ..." was all Hope could say as she shut her mouth like a trap door. She pressed a finger to her lips.

Parker laughed, "It's alright, Hope! It's a compliment! Julia Roberts has big teeth and a big mouth. She's the Pretty Woman, Hope! She smiles away like the Joker! She's beautiful!"

"Hmm ... Julia Roberts, right." She rolled her eyes.

"Believe it, Hope Kelley. You are much prettier than you think, that's why I told you to dump the specs ..."

Parker's phone pinged, she read the message, "Right, Josh is on his way. We'd better start heading back toward yours'. Make sure you thank your parents for me. I would like to say I'll be returning the favor sometime soon, but don't hold your breath. Mum couldn't organise a fire in a matchstick factory."

As the two girls entered Hope's street, Josh Wright's noisy ride turned the corner, exhaust grumbling, obligatory death metal roaring through open windows.

"Turn that shit down, Josh!" Parker ran across the nature strip and yelled through the passenger window. The electric windows were rolled up and the music continued to pulverize the drivers senses.

"God he's a dickhead," Parker said as she returned to say her goodbyes. She smiled and took Hope in an embrace.

"I cuddle no one, Hope. But I will cuddle you. Thank you, my geeky badass friend. Have a goodnight. Sleep well."

CHAPTER 35
THE WONDER OF IT ALL

'To Kill a Mockingbird'.

After Parker had left, Hope showered and read the final ten chapters with one eye open, determined to finish it. She only had the weekend left to write her paper. After a solid two hours of sluggish reading, the hardcover dropped from the bed to the floor with a heavy *'thlunk'*.

Hope fell asleep, satisfied and exhausted.

∫

A new rite of passage.

Hope saw herself standing on a familiar street corner. Not a corner in Pento. This was Sacramento. She read the signpost, Thistle Grove – the street where she used to live. She gazed down the adjoining Billiton Avenue. The streets were empty. It was late afternoon and hot - what her father called a 'soft-tar day,' or 'daytime in hell', depending on his mood. She could almost see the road cooking through her foggy lenses. Dressed in cargo shorts and a white singlet, her feet felt glued into the white sandals Kate had picked out for her on a mall run a few weeks back. She appeared to be the only one dumb enough to be out in the heat. Her skin was burning like a bitch. There was only the one excuse for such behavior.

She was waiting for someone.

She pulled at her fingers.

The sound of the shot-to-hell motor was unforgettable, as was the rattling muffler. The 89' dark green Buick Century turned into Billiton Avenue and moved toward her.

She could just make out the driver and passenger. She smiled.

∫

"Oh, my nag, can I just say how impressive a performance it was by me. Now I'm not one to boast unless it is warranted, you know this ... needless to say, Hamish is *very* satisfied," Halliday chortled to Wilder as she parked the machanihorse at the foot of The Unexplained Mountain. She peered up at The Ruptured Spleen longingly. "Mmm, some liquor is most called for."

She hopped down and patted the mare on the rump. Wilder turned her head away, she stood rigid, seething, she knew what was to come later - a drunken master with heavy breath and slurry commands. Holstering her Remington, Halliday left her horse to her own devices and headed toward the elevators.

The unmistakable rev and rumble of Lucretia St Aimes' motorcycle entered the parking area. Halliday turned and watched the leather clad, raven haired figure kill the engine and load off her bombastic transport. Wilder had already bolted.

"Hold the lift, woman." With a tousle of her hair, Lucretia swaggered toward Halliday. "I'll be having a drink with you tonight, Halliday. We have things to discuss."

"Do we?" Halliday said curious to what the woman could be on about. Halliday pressed the up button and the two ascended the inner of the mountain. Within the flaps of her open leather, she noticed the Death-Witch's Beating Clock - she'd lost another stroke.

Lucretia caught her gaze and gave her a bemused look. "It was at Travesty Isle," her eyes darkened. "Rode my bike straight over one of those vanishing cliffs. Piece of shit of a place ..." She put her hands behind her back and pushed back on the elevator wall. "So, I hear you've been busy doing some specialist type of work for Sombre."

"Of a kind, yes, I have," Halliday said not entirely sure of how much she should divulge to this woman.

The elevator 'pinged' and the doors opened to the small, familiar foyer of The Ruptured Spleen. The two stepped out; the muffled din of boisterous laughter and clinking glass beyond the twin oak doors promised a large showing of Gatherer's. Halliday needed her drink rather badly. Orty would want to be on song tonight, she thought to herself. She was confident she wouldn't be stuck with Lucretia for long, there'd be plenty of chances to wander off and latch onto just about anybody else. She pushed on the door's lock rails with Lucretia stuck to her shoulder and entered. The Ruptured Spleen was alive and overflowing; smoke filled the air, the musty aroma of bodies, brewed hops and a myriad of distilled tonics bombed the senses.

Lucretia grabbed her forearm with force.

"Hey!" Halliday shook it off.

She grabbed it again and actually pinched her skin.

"Stop it, you festering, backside-boil of a woman!" Halliday tried pulling her arm away again and regretted it. Lucretia's thumb and index finger pulled the skin taught in a pincer-like grip. "Ow!" she cried out loud to a few glances from patrons.

The Death-Witch smiled. "You're not joining your usual crop of Sombre-sheep until we talk. I'll have my usual - Orty knows."

Halliday wondered what in all of Sombre could be so ruddy important! Ruing the vile woman's presence on this night, she turned and leant on the bar. She felt Lucretia's eyes drilling into her back. Rubbing her smarting arm, she ordered. "Orty, my Scotch please, and *her* usual as well, whatever demonic substance that is."

The little bald man nodded and went to work. He rarely spoke did Orty or wore an expression. He was a very efficient bartender though. Drinks were delivered, Halliday skulled her own before she gave Lucretia hers. She slammed the empty tumbler down.

"Another please Orty."

284

"Here," she turned and gave Lucretia her Black Russian, thinking it did actually look like it would be worth trying.

"Many cheers to you Halliday. You are a Gatherer among Gatherer's. A sublime beauty," Lucretia sipped her drink and licked her tattooed black lips.

Halliday reached behind for her second drink. "So, what is all this about Lucretia? Why is it so crucial we talk?"

The Death-Witch's face went ridged. "I know what happened at Loew Avion, Halliday. I know you what you did to Guiles."

Halliday pressed her glass to her lips. "Who is Guiles."

"The chosen Ether."

"What do you mean, the chosen Ether?"

"Guiles' was a waking agent. A figure plucked from the waking world. He was chosen."

Halliday shook her head. "No one in Sombre can exist without a Beating Clock, Lucretia. Everyone is reconfigured, you know this!"

Lucretia gave her a mock expression of shock. "Oh my god! Halliday! I forgot about that! You *are* such a wise thing, aren't you?"

"Don't laugh at me or there will be fisticuffs - you'll be on the floor, and I will walk," Halliday threatened.

Lucretia didn't bite back, instead she continued with a grin. "Best you know this, beauty. You didn't kill Ether, you killed Guiles. Shock! Horror! Ether still exists! The mighty Halliday Knight failed! Ha!" She scoffed then added, "Although you must have done some wonderful work with that Morphia of yours. It would have been a sight to behold. I helped you out there didn't I. Did you even cost yourself a stroke?"

Halliday was still amazed at how she had survived the plummet from the flaming skies of Loew Avion - the control she now had over her Morphia was an amazing and wondrous thing. She recalled how her monster had burst through the flaming wreck of the airship and touched down on the tarmac. It was so light-footed, almost cat-like - first the left foot, then the right hand, then right foot to left hand - scampering away from the exploding blanket of falling aircraft like a criminal on the run.

"No, I didn't," she answered.

"Good for you," she raised her brow and smiled. "So, Halliday, here's something you may as well know. Ether also has clock' wearing agents all over Sombre. And guess who is one of them?"

"Traitor. I hope you swim in The River soon," Halliday said.

"I'm the only *Gatherer*, mind you. The very first. The second didn't quite work out ..."

"Andrew Pfeiffer!"

"Was a frighteningly wonky choice. He was meant to be an easy grab. He floats in The River, I hear?" she said stirring the bottom of her glass with a straw. "But there'll be more of us taken, mark my words."

Halliday drained the balance of her scotch and slammed it down on the bar. "Orty, another of mine, another of hers as well, please. You're doing well, man. Keep my mix the same! You can spit in hers for all I care!"

She turned to Lucretia and grinned mischievously, her head starting to get that nice warm feeling. "This is all very interesting. So, in a very round way, what you are saying is that Ether is planning some sort of takeover of Sombre?" she scoffed, "Not bloody likely is it?" She handed Lucretia another Black Russian.

"I think you'll find its more likely than you think. Ether is all sorts of persistence and cunning. And it is learning more as time passes. Tell me Halliday, have you ever stopped to think about what all of this means? This nightmare world we exist in. Where it all comes from? Its source?"

286

Halliday stifled a gingery burp. "Sombre is Sombre. Sombre is everything, Sombre is everybody and everyone. We live by the strokes on our Beating Clock. When we finish, we float."

Lucretia shook her head and lowered her eyes. "That, my pretty thing, is far too simplistic. That is what Hamish will tell you over and over; as he hitches your dress, straightens your pretty face and stitches your gut up. Ether knows of the source of all of this. Ether is a megalomaniac, as much as Sombre is its own megalomaniac. Ether is about change, and it can't be stopped. We are all tiny little parts in the path of a much bigger process."

Halliday began feeling a little sick. She hated this. She needed to move on from this discussion. With a forced snort, she tried to show the woman nonchalance. "Why do I need to know this, Lucretia? If you are just trying to ruin my evening, you are well on your way, witch!"

She gave Halliday a straight look. "Ether wants you aboard. I don't know why. It has a use for you."

Halliday had heard more than enough. "I work for Sombre. How Sombre is allowing you to function with this split allegiance is beyond my thinking, but I've heard enough! You disgust me! This discussion is over – get your own drinks, wretch!"

Halliday left the bar with the last half of her drink. She pushed passed the very amused Death-Witch and began searching the rest of The Ruptured Spleen. Lucretia called out to her from the bar,

"That's what I thought you'd say. Small minded fool that you are. It won't be stopped!"

Second-hand tobacco smoke invading her nostrils making her feel even queasier, she spotted Recalcitrance Bexley, skinny cigarette in her fingers. The aviatrix exhaled her own flange of smoke. "Halliday Knight, my warrior! Good to see you! Dave's here, just in the toilet ... oh, you look like my dead mother's ghost!"

"The balcony. Let's have some air," Halliday said grabbing her by the arm.

"Oh, okay. But please don't vomit. It's such a blight on an evening," Recalcitrance followed her out. "Busy out here as well," she said looking at the full tables and benches.

Halliday leant over the balcony and shut her eyes. "I hate Lucretia."

"We all do, my lovely. She is the devils armpit hair," Recalcitrance rubbed her back with a firm hand. "Dave and myself did notice you speaking with her, and we wondered why? Whatever she said to you to get you into this state, will be the utmost rubbish."

Halliday swallowed hard and finished her scotch and dry. "I would like to believe you, Recalcitrance, but I don't think it was. I wish it was. But I am sure she was speaking the truth."

She turned and faced her friend. She spotted Dave inside as he made his way back from the toilet. She was feeling a little better. "I think I need another drink."

"Oh, I'm sure you do," Recalcitrance said and added, "your colour is coming back, let's see if we still can't get you all happy, red faced and boot-filled, eh!"

Dave stepped through the door.

"David Bi-Plane, this woman needs her Scotch and Dry, and I need another of mine as well," Recalcitrance said brightly.

Dave looked Halliday up and down with concern. "Okay, just for you two though, nothing for me. I've just been given a mission. You okay, Halliday?"

Halliday gave him a sad and drunken smile, "getting there, Dave. Getting there ... Lucretia St Aimes."

"Oh, say no more," he said. "Back in a minute."

"He's good, is Dave," Halliday whispered.

288

Recalcitrance raised her eyes, "You might want to let him know it sooner or later, Halliday. It would do you both well to clear that air," Recalcitrance said.

"I, uh ..." Halliday wanted to say something about this, to agree with her good and clever friend, but she was suddenly lost for words.

She was being watched. The girl stood just inside the bay window of The Ruptured Spleen. It was the brown-haired girl from the airship – Ether's accomplice. Hair tied in a ponytail, she wore the same jeans and trainers. Looking so out of place it was uncanny. She pulled at her fingers.

She was so familiar!

Was she really there at all?

Her eyes drilled into Halliday's through a thick lensed pair of glasses.

∫

Hope woke with a jolt. She sat bolt upright. Blinking fast. She peered around her room. Everything appeared illuminated.

It was.

She realized her sight was clear.

Her sight was clear?

Her sight was clear!

"Oh wow! Oh shit!"

Rubbing her temples, she checked to see if she'd slept with her glasses on. She had, but they weren't on now. She looked down. The heavy set lay next to her on her sheets, they'd fallen off her face in the night.

"Jesus ..." she uttered, tentatively swinging her legs over onto the floor. She stood, shut her eyes and opened them again. Breathing in deeply and exhaling, a smile slowly formed on her lips. Her vision was brilliant, crystal clear. She had been given a gift. She was truly seeing for the first time.

She peered over at her closed bedroom door. There was something else. A dark circular shadow had formed on the white paint.

"What in the hell?"

She walked toward it. It was a ghostly stencil of a clock.

A single hand pointed to the three.

"Sombre ..." she whispered.

She let the word hang in the air.

COMING IN 2021...

SOMBRE

2

THE VENTURIST

9 780099 427283